Brandon Sparks

and the Hidden Sun

Brandon Sparks
and the Hidden Sun

Joshua Fuld

iUniverse, Inc.
New York Lincoln Shanghai

Brandon Sparks and the Hidden Sun

iUniverse books may be ordered through booksellers or by contacting:

iUniverse
2021 Pine Lake Road, Suite 100
Lincoln, NE 68512
www.iuniverse.com
1-800-Authors (1-800-288-4677)

Because of the dynamic nature of the Internet, any Web addresses or links contained in this book may have changed since publication and may no longer be valid.

This is a work of fiction. All of the characters, names, incidents, organizations, and dialogue in this novel are either the products of the author's imagination or are used fictitiously.

ISBN: 978-0-595-42396-5 (pbk)
ISBN: 978-0-595-86733-2 (ebk)

Printed in the United States of America

To Harry and Gloria,
the best parents
a boy could ask for

INTRODUCTION

"Captain, they're not responding. I think they're all dead!"

"Try again lieutenant," said a deep, commanding voice. "We must be successful today. I have fought this evil for a long time. We cannot fail!" Suddenly another laser blast impacted the side of the captain's starship, shaking it violently from port to starboard. The two lieutenants standing behind the captain were flung violently to the ground. The first lieutenant hit his head on the corner of his control console, producing a large gash. The second went straight to the floor, the part of her head just above the right ear taking most of the blow. As their limp and lifeless bodies crashed into his legs, it was all the captain could do to keep his balance.

Outside, hundreds of starships were swirling and diving past the captain's vessel, a menacing onslaught of lasers traveling in all directions. Laser blasts and shrapnel were all the captain could see. It was chaos. Madness. The fight had been going on for hours.

Emerging from the mayhem, a small fighter in the shape of a half-moon swooped around a fallen starship and unleashed a barrage of firepower upon the vessel. The violence of the strike knocked the captain to the ground. Though his head collided with the steel floor he remained conscious. When he climbed to his feet his vision was blurry but he could make out streaks of orange, red, and gray in front of him. He felt heat. The Bridge of the ship was on fire; smoke billowed out of the Pilot's console.

The ship's last remaining lieutenant jumped out of his chair and raced over to the captain, his face covered in soot. "Sir, the *Clipper's* taken too much damage! The engine room has been ripped from her back and no one is responding to our calls. The fleet's gone captain! The entire fleet. We have to evacuate!" The lieutenant let out a chest-rattling cough and tried in vain to brush the thickening smoke from in front of his face.

"Go without me lieutenant," said the captain gruffly. "I'll send the relay."

"Captain, you can't. I need help," he said, pointing to the unconscious bodies on the ground. "I can't carry them by myself. Let the computer transmit the relay!"

The captain thought for a long moment. He looked at the four silver stars pinned to his chest. They were covered in a thin layer of black from the growing cloud of smoke. He turned to look at what remained of the view screen and could not believe the carnage happening outside his ship. How had this happened? "We need to go now!" screamed the lieutenant. "Grab her!"

"Computer," began the captain. He breathed in a large amount of dark smoke and let out a heavy cough. "Tell everyone to evacuate. The *Clipper* is no longer safe! Send word back about what has happened here. Tell Him ... *We Have Lost.*"

The captain picked one of the lifeless bodies off the ground and slung it over his shoulder. He followed the lieutenant to the door. The smoke was so thick he covered his mouth with the sleeve of his free arm. The captain took one last look and rushed out of the Bridge.

Moments later another half-moon shaped starship fired upon the *Clipper* and it was obliterated with a fantastic explosion.

◆   ◆   ◆

A short while later a conversation was had between two who were millions of miles apart.

"Dead," said V, his voice an eerie whisper.

"All of them?" said the second voice.

"Most, but not all. The time has come."

"Are you sure?"

"Yes. The mission has failed. We're left with very few options."

"How long do we have?"

"A year, maybe less," said V.

"So you are moving to the second phase?"

"Yes. In six months time it will be complete."

"Of course, you will you test it first," said the second voice as more of a question than a statement.

"Of course. I want Him there."

"But why?" said the second voice full of worry. "Shouldn't you wait until after it's been tested? What if something goes wrong?"

"It's a calculated risk."

There was a brief pause. "He's too young."

"You know that to be untrue," said V. "His inclusion is only in the event of another failure. I have full faith in the captain, but Phase 3 must be ready. You know the consequences of failure. You have seen what they are capable of."

"Yes," said the second voice hesitantly. "What will we tell him?"

"Nothing. Tell him nothing," said V. "If all goes well he will be back on Earth in a few months, none the wiser."

"I don't like it."

"You never do."

CHAPTER ONE

THE UNFORTUNATE INCIDENT

The stars sat princely over a deep, black, motionless sky. The morning light shone through the blinds in a small room as a young boy awoke. His eyes opened and he stretched out his arms, reaching for the stars and beyond. The boy was twelve-year-old Brandon Sparks, a human with dark skin, dark eyes and short, dark hair. Muffled voices came from downstairs, which belonged to his mother and father. It was not unusual for Brandon to wake up and hear the sound of his parents' voices coming from the kitchen downstairs. This was the time and place where they usually had their coffee and breakfast, but on this particular morning, the voices sounded a bit different. Brandon rubbed some of the sleep out of his eyes and listened as hard as he could, but still could not make out what they were saying through his closed door. He could tell that they were trying to keep the volume down so as not to disturb his sleep, but they were having difficulty controlling their voices. The louder of the two was his mother. It was easy to hear the excitement in her voice as the phone clicked into its cradle.

All of the walls in Brandon's room were sky blue, all except for the ceiling, on which stars and multicolored gases ebbed and flowed. The ceiling was entirely covered with a giant paper-thin monitor. In fact, all of the walls in his house were covered with paper-thin monitors, and they could be changed to any color or pattern Brandon or his parents could imagine. All they had to do was ask Charlie, the house computer. Every home Brandon had ever been in had a house computer, but none quite like Charlie. He was in charge of all the functions in the house, from turning on a light, to running water, to even flushing a toilet, but you could do that by yourself if you liked. If you wanted to change the color of a wall, all you had to do was ask Charlie. If you wanted lighter here and less light there, all you had to do was ask Charlie.

In the opposite corner of the room from Brandon's bed sat a beautiful and very old wooden desk. When the Sparks' bought the house eleven years ago, it was sitting in the very same spot. Surprised that the previous owners had left them such a nice antique, and because it was extremely heavy, they kept it and left it for Brandon, who was just a baby at the time. On top of the desk sat a lamp, some scattered magazines, a few books, and some miniature toy starships. It was here, at this desk that Brandon would sit and talk with Charlie for hours and hours about all the stuff in his life. Charlie would section off a rectangle on the video wall and the two would play games together. What his parents called "mindless games" rarely interested him. Having a knack for solving problems in his head, strategy games, puzzles, and especially flight simulations were Brandon's favorite. Charlie would also help him with his homework and answer any questions he had about anything at all. Charlie was his best friend and he knew that the Galaxy Program was Brandon's favorite, so he played it every night while Brandon slept. Thousands of stars floated across the ceiling—nebulas spinning and gas giants radiating beautiful colors. Brandon always seemed happiest staring up at those stars.

In reality, Charlie was Brandon's only friend. Well, his only true friend. He had some people he would talk to in school but only in passing and never when there were a lot of other children around. He never went to any other kid's house to play and most certainly never had anyone over for a slumber party. Not since "The Unfortunate Incident," of course. That's what his parents liked to call it, "The Unfortunate Incident." Sometimes they would just call it "unfortunate," but Brandon didn't like to call it anything at all. He just wanted to forget it had ever happened. It was the worst day of his life. He did the right thing, but sometimes the right thing can turn out horribly wrong.

◆   ◆   ◆

Two years ago, Brandon came to school as he did every day, on what the children commonly referred to as the "yellow limousine." He met his two closest friends (which obviously wasn't saying much), Roger and Troy on the side of the school just passed where the buses unloaded their living cargo. Roger was tall while Troy was short and Roger was rail thin while Troy was a bit chubby. The two were such good friends, and spent so much time with one another that sometimes Brandon felt like a third wheel, but on this day he did not … at least not right away.

The three boys were joking around and having a good time like kids tend to do when Bert came over with a big pile of books in his hands. "Hey guys, did you do your presentation for history class?" Bert was the biggest nerd in the sixth grade. He was the guy who always did his homework and answered all the questions in class. He had dark hair parted neatly to the side and wore thick glasses with large frames. They were so dirty; Brandon was surprised he could see through them. Bert was also the smallest and youngest kid in the sixth grade, skipping the second and the fifth, which made him an easy target for bullies.

"Yeah, we did ours," said Brandon, giving the medium sized cardboard box at his feet a tap with his shoe. "At least I did."

"No!" said Troy. "We've got to present today? I thought it was next week!"

"I'll whip something up before class starts," said Roger.

"Well, good luck. It took me a week to prepare! I wrote a ten-page report and put together a highlight reel. What's in the box?"

"A model airplane," said Brandon.

"If it took him a week, there's no chance you're gonna get it done by third period," said Troy.

"Well, you don't have it either," replied Roger snidely, "and besides, the final counts for much more than the stupid presentation."

Actually, the presentation counted just as much as the final, and Brandon was about to correct his friend when a thunderous voice spewed out of the mouth of someone behind them.

"Hey there nerd!" said the voice in a drawn out antagonistic tone.

Brandon, Roger, Troy, and Bert slowly turned around to see a giant standing before them. The monster stood a full foot taller than Brandon and at least eighteen inches taller than Bert. To them he was as tall as a house and as wide as a bus! His huge body, like the moon during a solar eclipse, seemed to block out the sun behind him. All the boys could see was a dark silhouette, the edges glowing with a piercing light. An outline was all they needed to know that the monster standing before them was Big Luke Sanderson, an eighth grader and the biggest bully in school.

"Did all your homework, didn't ya nerd?" he said as his meaty hands knocked Bert's books to the ground. From the onset, Brandon knew this was trouble and that no amount of talking would be able to persuade everyone's favorite Mensa member to cease.

Other than his enormous side, Big Luke Sanderson had dark, greasy hair that flared out at the back beneath a beaten up baseball hat. A good amount of acne scarring on his left cheek was the most distinguishing characteristic of his face. "Hey, my books!" screeched Bert as he went down on one knee to pick them up.

As expected, Big Luke gave Bert a hard shove and he tumbled awkwardly to the ground, scraping his right elbow. The boy recovered rather quickly and moved to grab one of his possessions from the ground. When the bully realized what Bert was going for he snatched it out of his thin fingers. "No, that's my history presentation!" screamed Bert trying to get it back, but from where he was sitting, he had no chance.

"Hey, leave him alone," said Brandon.

Big Luke turned his head and stared at Brandon for a long moment obviously thinking as hard as his little mind could. Finally, he spoke and said something Brandon did not anticipate. "Hey, I know you. Jesse was talkin' about you the other day."

Who's Jesse wondered Brandon to himself as he watched Big Luke give Bert another shove to the ground. And why's he talking about me?

"Yeah, you're that freak who thinks his house computer is alive. Hey, what do you call it again?"

The fact that he had just been called a freak hadn't registered just yet. "Charlie," said Brandon with some oomph.

"Charlie, right. Well why don't you go home and tell Charlie that you should stay out of it before I bash your face in!" The bully flashed an evil grin and turned his attention back to Bert.

A bit frightened, Brandon glanced over to see Roger and Troy slowly inching backwards as they stared at their shoes. Though he could feel butterflies in his stomach, Brandon stood his ground. Then it hit him. He wondered if what Big Luke had said was really his reputation around school. Was he known as 'the freak that thinks his house computer is alive?'

"So, what kind of presentation is this?" said Big Luke sarcastically. "Let's take a look." The bully opened the cover and read the title. "Jack Johnson: The First Black Heavyweight Champion, by Bert Brown. Never heard of 'em," he said, opening the metal clips of the small binder.

"No!" said Bert, pleading with the bully. "I need that for class!"

Big Luke gave Bert another push and then launched the open binder into the air with a smile of anticipation. He practically glowed when all of the papers and pictures Bert had assembled came loose and floated to the ground like large, rectangular snowflakes. Bert was horrified. Big Luke picked up the binder and side-armed what was left of the presentation into the street like a Frisbee, where it was immediately run over by an incoming school bus. Bert reacted in the only way he could. He began to cry.

With an evil grin, the bully went about driving the loose papers into the concrete with a twist of his foot. "Ah, whatsa matter little cry baby?

Did I mess up your homework? Is the teacher gonna be mad? Boo hoo," he said, pretending to wipe away fake tears. He laughed and with the full girth of his large body, and began stomping on all the pieces of the presentation he hadn't already destroyed. To Bert, the crunching noise was unbearable.

Brandon, Roger, and Troy were completely taken aback when Bert soared off the ground with the speed of a cheetah pouncing its prey and attacked Big Luke's bulbous stomach. His fists met their target what seemed like a million times in just a few short seconds as rivers of tears ran down his cheeks. His attack was silent, being so angry that he momentarily lost the ability to speak.

Unfortunately for Bert, his enthusiastic response had little effect on Big Luke other than to aid in the release of a putrid belch, stinking of a half digested ham and egg sandwich. It also made him really, really angry. He punched Bert in the stomach with a WOMP! And then pushed him to the ground once more. The only sound Bert made was a gasp for breath as the punch sucked all of the air out of his lungs.

Brandon had seen Big Luke's act before and seeing poor Bert on the ground made him very angry. He acted without thinking. He jumped between Bert and Big Luke and said, "Why don't you pick on someone your own size, huh? You always have to pick on some little guy don't you? He's half your size!" Then Brandon did what most kids considered suicidal. He pushed Big Luke.

Big Luke seemed to have taken pleasure being scolded by Brandon, but things turned ugly once he made contact with the bully's spherical stomach. Caught off guard, the bully's feet actually moved back a step. Then his face turned bright red with anger, the grooves in his acne scared cheek looked like small, dried up rivers. With a straight right, he punched Brandon in the eye and then threw him to the ground with all his strength. Brandon collided with the pavement and his nose began to bleed. He could feel the cold, grainy concrete on his face. "You wanna push me, freak?" yelled the bully. Enraged, Big Luke took Brandon's book bag and emptied its contents onto the ground. He kicked his books and stomped on his lunch. The peanut butter and jelly sandwich his mother had carefully made the night before exploded under the bully's giant boot and sprayed all over Brandon's face and shirt. Roger and Troy's eyes widened as they watched the bully use Brandon's body to wipe the peanut butter and jelly from his boot. They never took a step forward to help or even yelled for it to stop.

Suddenly Big Luke calmed down and another evil smile filled his face. He had spotted something he liked. "Hey, what's this?" he said with fake wonder. His beady eyes focused on both the spare pair of Brandon's underwear he had packed for changing into after gym class, and the cardboard box containing his history project. Big Luke picked the underwear up with a nearby stick and flung them over the fence and into someone's yard. Then he opened the box.

"Hey, don't touch that!" shouted Brandon trying to climb to his feet, but just as he had done to Bert, the bully pushed him back to the ground.

Within seconds, the top of the box had been torn open and in the center sat a model airplane made mostly of wood with a little metal. Big Luke pulled it out and saw that it had two sets of wings, two pro-pellers, and a small man laying face down across the middle of the lower wing. "What the hell is this?" he said, one of his large boots planted firmly on Brandon's chest. He reached into the box and pulled out the accompanying report. "The 1903 *Wright Flyer*? Did you make this piece of trash all by yourself?"

"It's not a piece of trash," said Brandon, forcing the boy's boot off of him. He took a few deep breaths to try and get his wind back. Big Luke was so absorbed by the strange looking plane that he didn't seem to mind. "It's a model of the first airplane ever."

"I bet your house computer helped you build this, didn't it?" said Luke in an accusatory way. When Brandon didn't answer, the bully's boot returned to his chest, this time digging in. "Didn't it?" repeated Big Luke.

"Yes," said Brandon with half a breath. "And Charlie's not an it. He's a he!"

"I'll keep that in mind," said the bully sarcastically. He pushed down harder with his boot. "Will it fly?" he asked. Not waiting for Brandon to answer, Big Luke gave his boot a little twist and repeated his question. "Will it fly?"

Brandon could barely muster the breath to answer. "I don't know!" he said from his back.

"Well let's find out," said the giant sadistically.

"No!" said Brandon, as Big Luke lifted his foot off of his chest, but there was nothing he could do. Troy and Roger watched from the sidelines as the bully reared back his arm and threw the 1903 *Wright Flyer* as hard as he could. The plane traveled a few feet before dipping quickly and shattering on the hard asphalt.

Anger and instinct took over Brandon and he did the first horrible thing that came to mind. He turned on his side, grabbed Big Luke by the leg and sunk his teeth into the boy's calf.

The bully let out a terrible howl and shook himself free. With a face of rage, Big Luke picked Brandon up off the floor like he was an empty potato sack. "You're coming' with me, freak," he said, spit flying everywhere.

The bully kept shoving Brandon further and further down the sidewalk. The two inched closer to the front of the school where a large number of students congregated. Brandon thought to run but his face hurt and so did his chest and side where Big Luke used his boot. He couldn't move very fast and the bully easily caught him and pushed him to the ground again. This time the soft grass in front of the school's flagpole cushioned his fall.

"I can't believe you bit me! Get up, punk! Get up!" screeched the bully. The anger in his eyes was as clear as the sky.

Brandon climbed to his feet and noticed immediately that a great deal of students had seen what was going on and crowded around them. In what seemed like an instant, half the school had formed a circle, five deep, around the boy and the bully. They were all cheering. For who, he didn't know. They just wanted to see a fight and he just wanted to go home.

The punch to the face and the time spent on the concrete had stolen most of Brandon's strength, but the surge from the crowd gave him a second wind. A small second wind, but a second wind nonetheless. "Get up freak. You wanna bite me? I'm gonna beat you bad! I'm gonna knock all of your teeth out! You can cry to your house computer without 'em!" A burst of laughter suddenly came from all around him. The crowd had clearly enjoyed Big Luke's taunt.

Brandon tried to block it out and focused on the large boy in front of him. When he climbed to his feet, the laughter died down. With a deranged smile, the bully came at him. Instead of trying to run, Brandon got caught up in the moment. He had been watching a boxing match a few nights before with his father and pictured himself in the ring. He pulled back his arm and released a ferocious right hook that impacted cleanly with Big Luke's scarred left cheek. He had put so much into the punch that his follow through caused his body to turn away from the bully. He couldn't see him, but by the sound of the crowd he thought for sure he had knocked him out with one blow. To his dismay, his punch had done more damage to his own hand than it had to Big Luke. When Brandon turned back towards him, the bully countered with a right hook of his own and hit Brandon flush on the chin. He crumbled to the ground as if his body had no bones. A surprise to all, Brandon remained conscious, and although the crowd cheered for it, he didn't get up.

"Loser," said the bully snidely. "Tell this to your house computer you freak!" He summoned up all of the mucous that was lining his throat and spat it on Brandon. With his arms in the air triumphant, he parted the crowd and walked away.

As they crowd dispersed, those who didn't know who he was soon learned his name. "Look, it's Brandon Sparks," said one of the girls in his class. "Loser!"

Everyone in the crowd took a long look as the first bell rang. Some made rude comments about his friendship with Charlie, others just pointed and laughed. Again, Roger and Troy took a step back. Brandon sat up in a daze and looked at his 'friends' wondering why they were doing what they were doing, but he knew why. Things had changed.

"Loser," said Roger.

"You're such a loser," said Troy. "I can't believe we ever hung out with you. Go talk to your house computer or something." They both turned and left.

Even Bert didn't want to be seen with Brandon. "Thanks for helping. Sorry man." He walked off and Brandon laid on the grass in front of the flagpole, licking his teeth, making sure that they were all still there. With his eye turning black and blue, his nose bloody and his face and shirt covered in peanut butter, jelly, dirt, grass, and Big Luke's snot, Brandon put his head on the ground and stared up at the stars and stripes. At that moment, he wished that he had never been born.

◆   ◆   ◆

Since the day of "The Unfortunate Incident," Brandon spent most of his time with Charlie, and thankfully, some things were not *unfortunate*. After hearing about Brandon's encounter with Big Luke, Charlie used his unique abilities to take a bit of revenge on the bully. At first the house computer did little things, like tell Big Luke's dryer to shrink all of his clothes, which made them extremely tight, everyone laugh when he walked the halls. He changed the code to the electronic lock on the bully's locker and the custodian had to come and unlock it. This doesn't sound like much of a punishment, but Charlie did it about a million times. Eventually, the custodian told the principal and the principal gave Big Luke detention for purposely wasting the time of the faculty. When he denied that he was doing it on purpose, he got even more detention for lying.

Charlie had the school's computer tweak all of Big Luke's grades so he was left back—twice. Big Luke's father, who was bigger than Big Luke (if you can imagine that), grounded his son for a long time after hearing he failed all of his classes, even gym! As his *piece de resistance*, one day Charlie added Big Luke's identity to a police wanted list, indicating that he was dangerous and mentally unstable. The next day he was dragged out of school and locked in a mental hospital for a week.

All of the things Charlie did made Brandon smile. He felt his friend went a bit overboard with the mental hospital, but he wasn't about to say stop. Still, no one talked to Brandon in school, or really even acknowledged he was there. His only friend was Charlie and he learned to accept it.

Brandon was a pretty easygoing kid. The only time he would get upset, other than when he was thinking about "The Unfortunate Incident," was when his mother would tell him to go outside and play. Supposedly the fresh air was good for him, but he didn't want to go outside and play. The air inside was just fine and that's where he wanted to spend the rest of his life, inside. He dreamed, specifically, of living inside a starship.

Brandon was born on Earth and lived with his parents on Long Island in a small town called Plainview. He had never been "off-world," but desperately wanted to go. How else was he going to fulfill his dream? Brandon wanted to be a pilot in the worst way. He wanted to fly a starship. Any starship would do! He spent countless hours talking with Charlie about flying, asking question after question about stopping and starting and alloys and engines. Charlie would show him diagrams on the video wall and Brandon absorbed the information like a sponge. The house computer had simulations of every airship known to man, and some that weren't. Brandon would play them late into the night. Sometimes, his parents would hear and Brandon would get into trouble. They would take away his gaming privileges for a week, but this didn't really bother him. Brandon could just close his eyes and imagine himself at the controls of any ship. He had mastered them all.

With his parents still making a commotion downstairs, Brandon climbed out of bed, and rushed over to his door, which he slowly opened about five inches. He stuck his ear out and heard his mom jumping up and down, something she rarely did, and the sound of her smooching her husband's cheek. He was anxious to find out what all the hubbub was about, so he opened the door all the way and went out of his room. Brandon, still in his pajamas, ran down the stairs and into the kitchen, where his parents were hugging.

Vanessa Sparks was a thin woman with light, brown eyes and dark skin. Her hair was pulled back in a ponytail and she was wearing a purple exercise suit.

"Brandon, Brandon, Brandon," said his mother with such excitement as he hadn't seen on her face in a long time. "It happened! We're going! We're really going!"

"This is just amazing, dear. This is going to be an excellent experience for the entire family!" said Brandon's father.

Matthew Sparks was a tall man with almond colored skin, and noticeably muscular arms. He had dark brown eyes and short brown hair to go with his slight potbelly. He too was wearing an exercise suit. A green one.

"Oh my goodness, we've got so much to do. I can't believe we leave in a week," said his mother. "Call the real estate agency and tell them we're selling the house."

"Selling the house?" said a very confused Brandon, but his parents didn't seem to hear. He wiped his eyes again thinking there might still be some sleepiness clogging his brain. Maybe it was affecting his ears as well.

"Oh, and we have to find a buyer for the boat," said Brandon's mom. "Can't use that anymore." The bright smile on Matthew Sparks' face deflated into a small frown. His wife came over and wrapped her arms around him. "Oh, honey, I know how much you love that boat but it's not going to be much use where we're going." He nodded his head in agreement and Mrs. Sparks kissed her husband on the cheek.

"I know. I'm going to miss it though. It's such a great boat, isn't it kiddo?"

"Sell the boat?" said Brandon, "Why are we selling the boat?" Once again, his words fell on deaf ears.

"And you've got to make up some signs. We're going to have to have a garage sale and start getting rid of all this stuff. Brandon can help you."

Brandon couldn't take it anymore. He had to know what was going on. "Wait a minute. We're selling the house? Dad's gonna sell his boat? And we're gonna have a garage sale?" Brandon was now officially confused.

"That's right," said his mother with a huge grin on her face.

"But where are we going?" asked Brandon.

"Oh my gosh! I'm sorry dear," said his mother with a little chuckle. "In all the excitement, I forgot to tell you. You of all people. My wonderful son." Mrs. Sparks gave Brandon a surprisingly huge hug.

"Our wonderful son," added his father.

"Our wonderful son," repeated his mother smiling even bigger than before.

There was a brief pause.

"So, where are we going?" asked Brandon. He was both nervous and excited.

Vanessa Sparks got down on one knee so that she was face to face with her son. She put her hands on Brandon's shoulders. "We're going into space silly!"

CHAPTER TWO

THE SECRET WEAPON

Brandon could not believe his ears. Why would his parents be going into space? Was he still sleeping? Was this some sort of weird dream? All of these questions and more crossed his mind, but only one made it to his lips. "We're going into space?"

"That's right kiddo and it's going to be great," said Mr. Sparks as he took a seat at the kitchen table.

"I'll make some breakfast," said Mrs. Sparks. Brandon sat down next to his father as his mother took a few eggs out of the refrigerator.

"But Dad, I thought you didn't like space. You always say that 'two feet on the ground are much better than two feet in space.'"

"I know I did Brandon, but things have changed and I'm going to tell you all about it on the boat today. Today, it's going to be just you and me kiddo. One last fishin' trip on the old boat. I have a very strong feeling we'll catch something good today," said Mr. Sparks with a wink.

"Well, can I drive the boat?"

"I don't see why not," said his father and Brandon's eyes lit up.

"Just be careful and watch out for the buoys," said Mrs. Sparks as she put down a plate of steaming scrambled eggs and wheat toast in front of him.

There was minimal talk at the breakfast table as both of Brandon's parents enjoyed reading the paper while they ate. Brandon wolfed down his meal and ran upstairs into his bedroom to talk with his best friend.

"Hey Charlie."

"Hello Brandon. How are you?" said the computerized voice of a middle-aged man.

"Just fine. Guess what?"

"What? Is my hair out of place? I've been meaning to invest in a different brand of gel but haven't had the opportunity."

"Very funny. A computer with hair. That'll be the day. No, I'm finally going into space!"

"I know. I heard," said Charlie. "That's wonderful Brandon. It's what you've always dreamed of!"

"I know. I'm so excited!"

"Space is a very large, well ... space, Brandon. Where exactly are you going?"

"I don't know. My parents didn't tell me yet. All I know is that they're selling the house and we're leaving in a week. I'm gonna find out more this afternoon. I'm going fishing with my dad. This time I get to drive the boat!" Brandon changed from his pajamas into a T-shirt and jeans. He also put on a baseball hat.

"That's wonderful. I've got a boat computer friend. He says that driving a boat is exhilarating."

"You mean Larry?"

"Yes Larry."

"Charlie, Larry's not a boat computer. He's a fish finder. What does he know about driving a boat?"

"I never said he was the main computer, but he spends more time on a boat than either you or I. Never mind."

Brandon laughed.

"So ..." began Charlie, "your parents are selling the house? Might I inquire as to whom? I guess getting used to a new family won't be so bad. Maybe they'll have a son, just like you. Although I highly doubt it. You're one of a kind."

Brandon stopped dead in his tracks. It was as if his whole body had been hit with a giant brick. "Wait a minute, aren't you coming with us?"

"Brandon, as much as I would like to, I can't come with you. I'm a computer program. A house computer program. What would I be without my house?"

"But, but you're my best friend," stammered Brandon.

"And you mine, but now you can make new friends. I'm sure the off-world kids are really nice. You might even meet a nice computer program and then you could introduce me. I haven't been on a date in ages!"

"But what about ..."

"'The Unfortunate Incident?'"

"Yeah," said Brandon. Through the tough realization that he would be leaving his best, and only friend behind, Brandon somehow managed to hold back the tears.

"It's history. It doesn't matter anymore, Brandon. No one up there knows what happened. You can start all over again, in space no less. It's the place where you want to be, right?"

"I guess you're right, but I'll miss you."

"And I'll miss you Brandon Sparks."

"Can we still, you know, talk?" There was the briefest of pauses and Brandon became nervous. He didn't want to lose his best friend.

"Of course we can. I'm just a phone call away. Well, not exactly ... cheer up Brandon. I know you have mixed feelings about leaving but this is a good thing. It's meant to be."

Brandon pulled on his sneakers and red hooded sweatshirt. "I know," he said glumly. "Bye Charlie. I'll see you in a few hours."

"Right-o Brandon. Have fun fishing with Mr. Sparks. Reel in a whopper for me!"

"I will," said Brandon as he walked out the door. With his head down, he slowly stomped downstairs to the front door. His father was waiting for him.

"Ready kiddo?"

Brandon let out a very unenthusiastic "yup." He didn't make it very hard for his father to sense what was wrong.

"I know you'll miss Charlie when we sell the house but I have a pretty good idea that things will work out for the best."

"I know. Charlie said we could still talk."

"Of course you can." Mr. sparks looked around the room cautiously, and then tilted his head to whisper into Brandon's ear. "Your mother made us some sandwiches to eat on the boat but if you promise not to say anything we can pick up a pizza instead." Brandon loved pizza. It was his favorite food.

"With extra cheese?" whispered Brandon.

"I wouldn't have it any other way."

"Deal," said the boy.

"Then we're off."

◆　　　◆　　　◆

Brandon untied the braided lines and stepped off the dock into the boat. It was a blue and white twenty-eight foot Boston Whaler, which just happened to be perfect for fishing. Vanessa Sparks had named it *Stress Reliever*, as it was the place her husband went to relax. It was Matthew Sparks' baby and he kept it in immaculate condition. It shone from bow to stern. The engines gave a small roar as Mr. Sparks pulled out of the slip and steered the boat into the Long Island Sound.

It was a beautiful day on the water. The sun was shining and the water was calm. A stiff, salty breeze crossed Brandon's cheek, as the heavy boat powered its way across the water like a charging bull to one of Mr. Sparks' "secret" fishing spots. When they arrived, there were seven other boats gathered in the same spot. Matthew Sparks shrugged his shoulders and smiled at his son.

Brandon loved going fishing with his dad. It was their time together. Sometimes his mom would come with them, which was nice, but Brandon preferred it to be just him and his father. He liked to do other stuff with his mom. Mr. Sparks liked to joke that fishing was for the men of the house (except for Charlie), and Brandon realized that today might be the last time he and his dad went fishing together for a long time. He was quite eager to hear about moving into space but he knew that his father would explain everything to him in good time, so Brandon waited. He didn't want to waste this opportunity to catch some fish.

"So, what'll it be?" asked Mr. Sparks with a spring in his voice. "Worms or clams?"

"Worms please, with extra slime."

Mr. Sparks let out a small chuckle. He baited Brandon's hook with a fat worm and handed him the rod. Then he baited his own, using a piece of clam. "We'll each use different bait and see which one they're biting," he said.

At the same time, both released the levers on their reels and the baited hooks disappeared into the murky water. A few seconds later, Brandon felt his sinker hit bottom and he reeled in two turns. His father had always told him, "Reel in twice after you feel your sinker hit. That way you won't get snagged on the bottom." Mr. Sparks smiled at his son and turned his own reel two times. For the next thirty minutes, father and son stood at the stern of the boat, Brandon on the left and Mr. Sparks on the right, raising and lowering their rods, up and down, but nothing bit. One by one, the other seven boats drove off in different directions, spraying water and making the *Stress Reliever* rock back and forth until they were all alone.

"Um, dad? All the other boats left. Do you think we should move to a different spot?"

"Just give it time Brandon. Give it time. If you want to catch a fish, you have to have patience."

"I know." When Brandon began staring at the reflection of the sun on the surface of the water, his father knew that something had to be done to cheer him up.

"All right, reel up" snapped Mr. Sparks as he began to furiously reel in his own line.

"Are we moving to another spot?"

"No we are not," he said firmly. "We are going to use ..." Mr. Sparks covertly looked to his left, and then to his right, and then directly at Brandon, "... the secret weapon."

"Secret weapon? There's no secret weapon for catching fish!" said Brandon in disbelief.

"Oh really? Well let me ask you a question. What do I do for a living?"

"Huh?" said Brandon.

"What's my job?"

"You're a botanist."

"That's right, and what do botanists do?" said his father.

"You work with plants."

"That's right. I work with plants. And what do fish eat?"

"Worms and clams," said Brandon, very sure of himself.

Mr. Sparks paused as he was expecting a different answer from his son. "That's true but what else do they eat?"

"Um, plants?"

"Exactly," said his father triumphantly.

"I'm confused."

"OK," said Mr. Sparks, "for the past few months at work, during my free time, I grew a new kind of plant which, if I'm right, the fish won't be able to resist! It's like you with pizza. They just can't say no!" Brandon smiled. Mr. Sparks walked over to the cooler and pulled out a small plastic bag containing some bright, blue leaves. "I call it the 'Blue Bomber' because of, well, the color of course, and because the fish don't know what hit 'em!" Brandon's eyes opened wide as his father added a single leaf to his own hook and dropped it into the water. He released the lever on his reel and when the sinker hit bottom, Mr. Sparks reeled twice, just as he had done before.

The two watched with great anticipation, but nothing happened. They waited some more, but still nothing happened. Eager to be the first to see the fish bite, Brandon stared at the tip of his father's rod like a hawk but still, nothing happened.

"Maybe we should break for lunch," suggested Brandon, a bit disheartened but.

"Maybe you're riiii …" Before the words finished coming out of his mouth, Mr. Sparks' rod started to twitch a little. He pointed and Brandon's eyes immediately fixed on it. The rod started to bend more and jerked up and down. Mr. Sparks waited a moment and then pulled up hard on the rod to hook the fish. He started to reel in, making sure the tip of the rod stayed as high as possible. If Brandon had heard his father say it once, he'd heard it a million times, 'if you drop your tip, you'll lose the fish.'

"See, what did I tell ya? Wow Brandon, this one feels like a big one. We might need the net." Brandon raced over to the other side of the boat and grabbed the net out of one of the gunnels. "I've almost got him! Where's that net?" shouted his father.

"Here it is," said Brandon, net in hand.

"All right. When I bring him up to the surface, you scoop him into the net and pull him into the boat." Seconds later, the fish was on top of the water, and Brandon followed his father's instructions to a tee. He scooped him up, and with a mighty heave, brought him over the side and into the boat. When the net hit the deck of the boat, the fish flopped around, sounding like a practicing drummer. "Not a bad fluke, huh? Looks like a six or seven pounder. See I told you I had a secret weapon."

Brandon could only utter one word. "Awesome!"

After Mr. Sparks slid the fish into the live bait well to keep it fresh, Brandon grabbed a piece of the Blue Bomber and put it on his hook. The two fished and fished pulling in fluke after fluke, one bigger than the next. They had so many fish that they released most of them and kept only what they intended to barbecue for dinner that night. Brandon's face was red and sweaty from all the action and his hands hurt from reeling in so much but he was having such a good time that he didn't want to stop. He became so caught up in catching fish that all of his questions and fears left his mind. The duo continued to fish for another hour until Mr. Sparks needed a break.

"How about some pizza?" he said.

"Cool. I'll go heat it up." Brandon reeled up his line and placed his rod in the closest gunnel. He disappeared into the cabin below and five minutes later, emerged with four slices of piping hot pizza, two for him and two for his dad. They sat down on two blue folding boat chairs and began to eat.

"Fourteen months ago," began Mr. Sparks after taking his first bite, "your mother and I applied for positions on an aid ship."

Brandon knew what an aid ship was. He read about them all the time on the Galactic Internet. They were ships that carried food and supplies to life forms on other worlds. Earth, and specifically the United States, had been sending aid ships into space for over a hundred years.

"What kind of positions?"

"Well, as botanists of course. We would be responsible for taking care of the green house on board the ship as well as doing research, and studying any new plant life we might find on the planets we visit."

Brandon's parents were excellent botanists. He didn't know if botanists won awards like movie stars did but he always felt they should have. He couldn't remember a time when they had a problem getting funding for their research.

"Brandon, you and I both know that I have never been a big fan of becoming an off-worlder but this was an opportunity your mother and I could not turn down. The money was there, the benefits, and I feel that the work we'll be doing will really help people. Of course we also considered what was best for you. We know that you haven't been happy these past few years since 'The Unfortunate Incident,' and we know because of that you spend all of your time with Charlie."

"But I like Charlie."

"I know you do, and Charlie is a great friend, but he shouldn't be your only friend. It's time to make some human friends. Some kids your own age."

"I know," responded Brandon.

"Hey, don't look so down. I haven't told you the best part yet." Brandon looked up at his father. "No school."

"No school?" he said, with little specks of pizza flying out of his mouth.

"That's right. Well, you will have some instruction but that will be on your own time, from the ship's computer. No more rows of desks, no more students, and no more, um, bullies, we hope. Instead, you'll be working on the ship."

"Working? Doing what?"

"I don't know exactly. I believe they said you'd be working with the crew and learning all the different jobs on the ship from Private to Captain. All the kids do it. It's supposed to be a great experience, and you love space so much, so it should be like a really long vacation for you."

"Wow!"

"Sounds cool, doesn't it?"

"Do you think they'll let me fly a ship on an away mission?"

Mr. Sparks laughed. "I think you're getting a little ahead of yourself. Remember, patience is a virtue. You'll get to fly someday."

"I know," said Brandon. "Hey dad, what's the name of the ship?"

"It's called the *Hidden Sun*. I'm sure they'll tell you everything you what to know about it when you get there."

"Hey, maybe Charlie knows about the *Hidden Sun*. I'll ask him when I get home."

"OK. Sounds like a plan. Now let's finish our pizza and get back to fishing. I've still got a little Blue Bomber left."

Brandon and his dad fished until late in the afternoon catching twice as many fish as they caught before. The Blue Bomber was unstoppable.

◆　　◆　　◆

Mr. Sparks turned the keys to start the engines and then went down below deck. A few short seconds later, he emerged with a white hat, his captain's hat. He pulled off his son's baseball hat and placed the captain's hat on Brandon's head.

"She's all yours."

"Aye, aye sir," said Brandon as he jokingly saluted his father.

He took the wheel and slowly pushed the two accelerators forward. The *Stress Reliever* began to move.

"More gas! More gas!" shouted his father over the loud groan of the engines.

Brandon pushed the accelerators forward and the boat took off like lightning. The *Stress Reliever* streaked across the top of the water, passing boat after boat. The two made it back to the dock in record time and Brandon smiled the entire way.

CHAPTER THREE

QUESTIONS

Brandon rushed through the front door to find his mother standing in the middle of the living room. She was wearing painter's overalls and looking around the room concentrating on the walls. They were changing color.

"Let's try red Charlie," said Vanessa Sparks and instantly, the walls were bright red. "Oh no that's totally wrong. How about a light green? A few shades lighter than pea green." Again, the walls changed color, now the living room was green. "That's even worse than the red Charlie."

"Hey mom!" shouted Brandon as he put his arms around her waist, giving her a good scare. She jumped a little and turned around with one hand over her heart.

"Don't do that," she said with a smile on her face. Brandon began to laugh. "You scared me half to death!" Mrs. Sparks took a deep breath and composed herself. "How was the fishing trip?"

"It was great. We caught tons of fish using a plant dad made."

"That's wonderful dear. Charlie, can we try yellow?" The walls instantly turned a light shade of yellow, and Mrs. Sparks took it in. Brandon watched as his mother stared intently at the wall, making a face that looked like she had just finished sucking on a lemon.

"Mom, why are you changing the colors of the walls?" he asked, and his mother's face relaxed.

"Well, if we're going to sell the house, I want it to look its best, so I'm trying to determine which color makes the room look the most inviting."

"But why are you wearing painting clothes? Charlie's doing all the work!"

"Well, you've got to dress for the occasion. Remember that Brandon, always dress for the occasion. You'll be more likely to succeed. That's what my mother told me when I was a little girl and now I'm passing it on to you."

"But I'm not a little girl," smiled Brandon. His mother laughed and tickled his sides making him burst out with laughter.

"Tickle torture, tickle torture!" she said as Brandon squirmed with joy. After he had escaped from his mother, it took Brandon a few seconds to recover and compose himself. He wiped the happy tears from his now bright red face as his mother put her arm around his shoulder. "What do you think of the yellow?"

"It looks like the living room has bad plaque," said Brandon and they both laughed. His mother laughed so hard that she had to sit down. Brandon took a seat next to her on the couch.

"Well, what color **should** we make it then?"

"I don't know. How about white?"

"Charlie, white please," and just as before, the walls instantly changed, turning perfectly white. "Mm, how about off-white?" The walls changed again. "What do you think?"

"I think it looks good," said Brandon.

"I agree. Off-white it is," said his mother as her husband walked in with a cooler full of fish.

"Hello? Anybody home?" he said jokingly, as he saw Brandon and his wife sitting on the couch. He leaned in and gave her a kiss on the cheek.

"Hey honey. Oh, what a fishy smell," said Mrs. Sparks as she leaned away from her husband.

"That would be the fish," replied Mr. Sparks, opening the lid on the cooler. Brandon got up off the couch and walked over to his dad. He peered inside the cooler.

"Dad told me all about the space trip, mom. I'm gonna go upstairs and talk to Charlie about it."

"Take a bath first. You smell worse than your father."

"OK," said Brandon as he raced out of the living room, up the stairs and into his room. "Hey Charlie."

"Hello Brandon. How was the fishing trip?"

"Awesome!" Brandon zipped out of his room and into the hallway to grab a towel out of the linen closet. As quickly as he had zipped out, he zipped back in and threw the towel on his bed. "We caught so many fish we had to throw most of them back!"

"Wow, that's wonderful!"

Again, Brandon zipped out of his room, but this time he headed for the bathroom. He turned on both faucets in the bathtub, knowing exactly how far to turn each one to get the perfect temperature. Twice as much hot as cold. He then did an about-face and blazed back into his room.

"So, when do we eat?" asked Charlie. "I like mine in a nice black bean sauce."

"Since when do computers eat fish?" laughed Brandon.

"Hey, it's brain food and I need the protein."

"Very funny," said Brandon, pulling his shirt off as if it were on fire.

"Why the rush? The bathroom water still won't be at the correct temperature for another ninety-three seconds."

"Well, the sooner I finish taking a shower, the sooner I get to talk to you about the space trip, and I'm hoping we can find some information on the Galactic Internet about the starship we're going on."

"Good plan Stan." Charlie paused. "Well then what are you standing around here for? The water's been at optimal temperature for sixteen seconds now. Go! Go! Go!" and Brandon went.

Just as he reached the bathroom the boy slammed on the brakes, turned around and went back to his room. He had forgotten his towel.

"Back so soon?" joked Charlie. Brandon grabbed the towel off his bed with a smile on his face and headed back to the bathroom.

Of course Charlie was right about the water temperature. It was perfect. Brandon took one of the fastest showers of his life. Usually he took baths and enjoyed the time he spent sitting in the tub, day dreaming about flying. He'd pretend he was the pilot of a starship. In his fondest dream, the captain would say to him, "Sparks, get us out of here! They're right on our tail! It's all up to you!" In his mind, Brandon would take the controls and he'd maneuver through asteroid fields and long stretches of deadly space mines, while avoiding enemy fire. He'd make the ship do flips and spins and push it to within an inch of its breaking point. The enemy would close in, but Brandon would always find a way to escape. His daydream usually ended with the ship jumping to light-speed and the entire crew congratulating him. "Great job Sparks!" they would say.

Today there was no daydream. There was just a lot of furious washing with soap. Brandon was going to skip washing his hair to save time, but he realized that he might have little pieces of fish in there from all the action this afternoon. Besides, his mother liked to kiss him on the head so he thought it best to give it a quick once over with shampoo and some rigorous massaging.

When he had dried himself completely, Brandon wrapped the towel around his waist and dashed into the hallway. "Brandon!" yelled his father from downstairs in the kitchen, "I'm cleaning the fish. Would you like to watch?"

"No thanks," replied Brandon through chattering teeth. He had seen his dad clean the fish a million times and had more pressing matters to attend to. He entered his room and shut the door behind him. He quickly threw on a shirt and the same pajama bottoms from the night before.

"That was a quick shower," said Charlie.

"I told you I was going to be quick. I want to find out all I can about the ship we're going on." Brandon sat down on the wooden chair in front of his desk. He opened the top right drawer and pulled out a thin piece of plastic, which had been rolled up to about the size of the cardboard tube inside a toilet paper roll. He removed the thick rubber band that was wrapped around it and unrolled the piece of plastic onto his desk. It was the keyboard and touch pad he used to surf the web. "I'm gonna need some power here Charlie." The keyboard began to inflate and the keys took shape. A small green light turned on in the upper right hand corner. "Thanks."

"Not a problem" said Charlie. "So, where are we going today?"

"Please open the Galactic Internet." The video wall came alive and the rectangle was filled with Brandon's home page, the Sasha Search Engine, better known as the SSE or just plain Sasha. Anything anyone wanted to know about anything could be found on the SSE. It was connected to billions of computers on over 3000 different worlds. Brandon typed the words "hidden sun aid ship" into the search bar and pressed return. There were over a thousand matches, but as he scanned through them, he realized they were all people selling a popular suntan lotion called "Hidden Sun" which helped "aid" in the reduction of skin cancer and they would "ship" it for free. Brandon was very disappointed. Sasha had never failed him before. "Charlie, nothing's coming up about the ship."

"It's called the *Hidden Sun?*"

"Yes, and it's an aid ship."

"Hmmm." Charlie paused for a brief moment. "Well, where is it going? What is the ship's destination?"

"Oh, I don't know. My dad didn't say. I'll ask him at dinner."

"Sounds good Brandon. I'll try searching some more while you are eating. Also, see if you can find the pass keys."

"Pass keys? What pass keys?"

"The pass keys you and your parents will need to board the ship. I'm surprised you don't know about them considering your passion for space travel, but I guess because you've never been on a starship, it hasn't come up. No big deal. Every person who is a passenger on a starship must have a special pass key to gain access. If they do not have the pass key, they can not come aboard. This helps prevent unwanted people from sneaking onto the ship. Imagine if you had a stowaway on board, and you're five thousand or ten thousand miles away from Earth, it's not like you could just drop him off at the next convenience store. This is not to say that people don't find ways to get on board anyway…."

"Ok, I get the picture. I'll see what I can find," he said as he heard a knock at his door. "Who is it?" The door opened and Mrs. Sparks popped her head in.

"It's your one and only mother. Dinner's ready, come on downstairs."

"OK. Be down in a minute." Mrs. Sparks unpopped her head and closed the door behind her.

"I'll keep searching," said Charlie. "You go eat."

"OK."

"Save some leftovers for me. I tend to get hungry late at night."

"Very funny," said Brandon as he opened his bedroom door and left the room.

Brandon walked downstairs and into the kitchen where his parents had already started eating. With just his eyes, Brandon scanned the room for the pass keys but saw nothing. On the table in front of his seat was a plate full of barbecued fish and a corn on the cob. He sat down and began eating.

"I called the real estate agency and put the house on the market," said Mr. Sparks to his wife. "The agent said we shouldn't have a problem selling it. Apparently, we live in a hot neighborhood."

"A hot neighborhood? Really?" replied Mrs. Sparks.

"That's what she said. We should have bids as early as tomorrow afternoon."

"Great. How's the fish, Brandon?"

"Oh, very good. I like it a lot."

"Good."

"Hey dad, where do we leave from when we go to space? Florida?"

"That's right. Sarasota, Florida."

"And how are we getting there? I mean to Sarasota? A plane?"

"No, not a plane. I wasn't going to tell you this. I wanted it to be a surprise, but since you asked, we're taking the Super Car."

"The Super Car!?" said Brandon enthusiastically.

"That's right, the Super Car," said his smiling mother.

"Wow, the Super Car is the best! How did we get tickets for the Super Car? Isn't it really expensive?"

"It is super expensive," explained his father with a smile, "but Bio-Help, the corporation who funds the aid ship, as well as pays our salaries, threw them in as part of the deal. I guess they figure if we're going to the trouble of selling our house and boat, then they'll go the extra mile for us to have a little comfort on the ride down."

"Awesome!" Brandon was so excited that he almost jumped out of his seat when the phone rang. "I'll get it."

"That's OK Brandon, I'll get it," said his father. "It's probably just work." Mr. Sparks picked up the phone after two rings. "Hello … really? … so fast? … that's, wow, that's wonderful!"

"What is it dear?" whispered Mrs. Sparks but her husband put up a finger and motioned for her to wait a minute. Brandon watched his father on the phone. He seemed quite amazed that whoever was on the other end was saying whatever it was that they were saying.

"OK. Yes, I'll be down first thing in the morning. This is great. Thank you so much. I really appreciate it … OK, bye." Mr. Sparks hung up the phone and smiled. He returned to his seat. "Sorry for shushing you. That was Nancy, the real estate agent. Guess what?"

"What?" replied his wife and Brandon in unison.

"We sold the house! Someone met our price. Can you believe it? I have to go down to her office tomorrow and sign all the paperwork."

"Wow, that was fast," said Mrs. Sparks. "Unbelievable! She said this neighborhood is hot, but I never would have imagined it was this hot. They didn't even come and take a look at the house. This neighborhood must be on fire!"

"And that's not the kicker. Do you know what the kicker is?"

"What?" said Brandon.

"They're also going to buy the boat!"

"No," said Mrs. Sparks, dumbfounded.

"Yes," replied her husband. "This is just amazing. I knew it would be relatively easy to sell the house, but I never would have guessed that selling the boat would go so smoothly."

"That's great dad!"

That night, Brandon and his parents ate their dinner with smiles on their faces. Everything was going extremely well for the Sparks family. Their two major headaches, selling the house and the boat seemed to vanish into thin air. Now, they could fully focus their energies on preparing to leave for Florida. Of course, Brandon still had a few more questions. "Um, dad, where exactly in space are we going? I mean is the aid ship going to just one planet or a few planets?"

"From what I've been told," began Mr. Sparks, "the ship is going to a lot of different worlds. We're going to be on that ship for a very long time, Brandon. Your mother and I have agreed to work for six years on the *Hidden Sun*. You'll probably be old enough to go to college by the time our contract expires." Mr. Sparks smiled at his wife, who let out a little giggle.

The Sparks family finished their fish dinner and Brandon washed his plate and silverware in the sink. After putting them in the dishwasher, he ran upstairs and into his room.

"Hey Charlie, I found out more about the starship," said Brandon as he sat down at his desk.

"Well, start spilling. I haven't got all day, you know!"

"It leaves from Sarasota, Florida in six days and we're getting there on the Super Car."

"Wow, the Super Car!" said Charlie enthusiastically. Suddenly, his voice went back to normal. "I knew a Super Car computer once. As you can probably guess ... very snobby. Didn't care much for him. Kept bragging about the size of his CPU. I hope you don't get him."

"Hey, what are the chances of that happening," joked Brandon.

"Well, 3,423,652 to 1 of course."

"Sometimes I forget that you're a computer."

"To err is human," said Charlie in an obvious British accent.

"Did you find out anything about the ship while I was eating?"

"Actually Brandon, it's quite strange. There is nothing at all on the Galactic Internet about an aid ship called the *Hidden Sun*. I've even tried some of the more obscure search engines and have come up empty handed so to speak. Are you sure you have the correct name?"

"I'm totally sure. That's the name my dad told me. He said the name of the ship is the Hidden Sun and the company he's working for is BioHelp. He wouldn't make a mistake that big."

"No, Mr. Sparks is usually right on the ball. BioHelp you say? We'll have to look them up."

"Sounds good. Oh, I didn't see the starship pass keys you were talking about. I checked on the kitchen counter during dinner and they weren't there. That's where the parents usually keep the mail."

"Well, keep looking. I'm sure those pass keys are just sitting in an obvious place and they'll most likely tell us everything we want to know, once you find them."

"OK" said Brandon as he got up from his chair and walked to his door. "I'll be back in a minute. I have to go to the bathroom."

"Enjoy," said Charlie as Brandon left the room.

Brandon reached the bathroom door and heard the toilet flush. He waited patiently against the wall as the faucet went on and off.

"Come on honey, let's go! I want to be back before the news comes on," yelled Mrs. Sparks from somewhere downstairs. Her husband emerged a few moments later.

"It's all yours kiddo," said Mr. Sparks. "Your mother and I are going for a quick walk. We'll be back in a half hour or so. OK?"

"Sounds good. Have fun."

"We will."

Brandon walked into the bathroom and closed the door. He stood in front of the toilet and heard the rumble of the garage door going down. He knew that his parents had left for their walk. As he was taking care business, something shiny on the counter caught his eye. There was a brown envelope sitting next to the sink and something metallic was sticking out of it. After Brandon finished doing his business, which felt like an eternity because he wanted to see what was inside the envelope, he washed his hands. After they were completely dry, he picked up the envelope and looked inside. What he saw were three identical, thick, clear plastic cards, each the size of a thin men's wallet. He took one out to examine it more closely. There were three small raised silver stars towards the top of the card and on the bottom was wrapped several small pieces of metal. Each of these small pieces of metal had a very thin wire running to a small, shiny, black microchip inside the center of the card. Brandon put the card back into the envelope and left it on the sink, in the exact same position he had found it. He immediately ran back into his room.

"Charlie! Charlie!" he said excitedly.

"Brandon! Brandon!" said Charlie, mocking his friend.

"I found the pass keys."

"What pass keys?"

"You know which pass keys."

"Of course I do. What did they look like?"

"Well, it was clear plastic, about the size of, well, a little bigger than a deck of playing cards."

"Right."

"And it had three raised silver stars on it and a black chip in the center." Charlie was silent. "Charlie?" said Brandon with some concern. "What is it?"

"Brandon, have a seat at your desk." Charlie's voice had a very serious tone to it and Brandon took a seat.

"What's up Charlie?"

"Brandon, I'm going to put a picture on the wall. I want you to tell me if this is the pass key you saw."

"OK." A bright white rectangular video screen came up on the sky blue wall behind Brandon's desk. Then a picture of a pass key emerged, seemingly from nowhere. It had three silver stars and a black microchip in the center. "That's it! That's the one I saw," he said, pointing at the screen.

"Are you sure?" said Charlie.

"Totally. That's the exact one I saw. Do you know what it is?"

"I do," replied a very solemn Charlie.

"Well, what is it? What does it tell us about the *Hidden Sun*?" asked the boy with great anticipation.

"Brandon, that's a military pass key."

CHAPTER FOUR

THE SUPER CAR

"A military pass key? What does the military have to do with it, Charlie?"

"Unfortunately, I don't know. It could mean that the company your parents will be working for, BioHelp, simply asked for and received extra security from the government for this launch, or it could mean something else entirely."

"Something else? Like what?" asked Brandon

"I don't know, but I think it best if we look into it before you leave for Florida."

"OK, but let's just keep this between you and me. I don't want to tell the parents unless we find out something definite. They'd just get upset."

"I concur."

Brandon and Charlie spent most of the night searching the web for information on the *Hidden Sun*. By one o'clock in the morning, the two had found nothing and Brandon could barely keep his eyes open. He was exhausted, so he climbed into bed and pulled the thick covers up to his neck. The sheets were nice and cool, and the blankets nice and warm. His head sunk into his two pillows like they were made of gooey marshmallow. Charlie shut off the lights on his own as well as the video rectangle on the wall. The only light in the room came from the Galaxy Program running on the ceiling. The stars were more brilliant than the night before. Green and orange gasses seemed to dance in the darkness.

"I'll keep searching the web while you sleep. Good night," said Charlie, but Brandon didn't hear him. He was already fast asleep.

◆　　　◆　　　◆

Over the next five days the two friends searched and searched for information regarding the *Hidden Sun*, but found nothing. Fortunately, they didn't spend all of their time searching for answers. They managed to squeeze in quite a number of games and flight simulations, Brandon's piloting skills were sharper than ever, but still, most of their energy was focused on the starship. Unfortunately, they could not find any mention of either an aid ship or a military ship with the name *Hidden Sun*. During the night, while Brandon slept, Charlie connected with computers that were high up on the military and government chain of command, but still came up with nothing. There was not a single mention of the ship Brandon was to leave on tomorrow. When the two turned their attention to BioHelp, they continued to hit the proverbial brick wall. It was a standard not-for-profit company, in business for over forty years, who accepted private donations and used the money to fund aid ships.

◆　　　◆　　　◆

The following morning there was a soft knock at Brandon's door. A familiar figure poked her head in and said, "Brandon, time to get up, we're leaving in an hour for the airport." Brandon's eyes opened and he rolled over, turning towards the door.

"OK," he said sleepily and his mother left, shutting the door behind her.

"Good morning Brandon," said Charlie.

"Morning Charlie. Find anything out?"

"Nothing. Nothing at all. I'm really quite perplexed that we cannot find a single piece of information about the *Hidden Sun*. This really bothers me."

"I know. It bothers me too, but I'll find out about it when I get there and I'll let you know." Brandon got changed into a T-shirt and jeans. He packed what he wore to bed into a bag sitting at the foot of his bed.

"Good," said Charlie. "Now, let me tell you how."

"How? How what?" asked Brandon.

"How you are going to contact me when you find out more about the ship. I've got a present for you."

"What, like video instructions?"

"Video instructions? How boring. You underestimate me Brandon Sparks. No, I've got a tangible, physical present for you."

"Now how does a computer come by a tangible, physical present? Did you order me something over the Galactic Internet? You do remember what happened the last time you used mom's credit card."

"I distinctly remember the description clearly said 'picture of.' No one told me that they would be shipping a real elephant! Lesson learned." Brandon started laughing and Charlie continued, "No, I did not buy you something over the Galactic Internet. Just listen and I will explain it to you. Walk over to the desk and pull it away from the wall a bit, just so you can see the back of the right-hand side." Brandon followed Charlie's instructions. He pulled on the desk, something he had never done before because it was extremely heavy, and why would he? He had to use all of his strength just to get it to budge a few inches. By then his cheeks were flush and his forehead glistened with sweat.

"OK," he said breathing heavy, "I moved it."

"Great. Now look behind the bottom drawer. Do you see that there's a square piece of wood that can be removed?"

Brandon got on his hands and knees and peered behind the desk. Immediately, he saw two pens, some spare change, two paperclips and an old, dusty pair of underwear, which he hastily flung across the room

37

using one of the pens. He ran his fingers over the wood and knocked off all the dust. Then he slowly ran his hand over it again and felt a slit in the wood. When he looked, he saw that a small square section could be removed. He tried to use his nails to pull it out but the opening in the wood was too small. He took a small pocketknife his father had given him out of the bag in front of his bed and used it to pry open the wood. "OK, I got the piece of wood out."

"Very good. Now reach inside and take out what you find."

Brandon tried to peer into the opening but all he could see was darkness. He slowly reached his hand inside and felt a thick piece of paper. He pulled it out and saw that it was an old photograph of a boy Brandon guessed was the same age as he was. The boy was playing in the yard outside of Brandon's house and had a smile on his face. The boy must have been moving when the picture was taken thought Brandon, because it was a little blurry and difficult to make out exactly what he looked like. Brandon could tell that he was thin with dirty blonde hair with blue eyes.

"How old is this picture?"

"It's forty-two years old. There should be something else in the desk."

Brandon reached his hand back inside the opening and felt something solid. He pulled it out and discovered a watch. A very beat up, old looking watch with a heavily scratched black metal band and a large, thick, rectangular silver face with a big black letter "V" in the middle. Brandon quickly realized that the face was just as scratched as the band but this didn't impede him from being able to read the time. On the right side of the watch there were three buttons and on the left side, there were two buttons. The watch looked dirty and dinged up, he wasn't even sure if it still worked.

"A watch?" he said, unsure of how this would help him talk to Charlie from one million light years away. "I'm sorry Charlie but this thing is a piece of junk."

"There is where you are mistaken my friend. That watch is actually very special. It's the only one of its kind. The previous owner built it himself."

"The kid in the picture?"

"That's right. He's an old friend of mine."

"How come you never talk about him?"

"I guess it just never came up. That's not important right now, Brandon. What is important is that I tell you how to use the watch so that you can contact me from space."

"OK. Should I clean it off first?"

"If you think it needs a good cleaning, then yes. It's been sitting in your desk for over twelve years." Brandon cleaned off the watch with some tissues on his desk. He then put it on his wrist and the watch tighten all by itself.

"Wow, it fits, it fits …"

"Perfectly?" said Charlie.

"Well, yeah."

"Good, then it withstood the test of time. Now listen up. If you want to contact me, all you have to do is push the two top buttons at the same time. Give it a try, press the one on the top left and the one on the top right."

Brandon pushed both buttons at the same time. On the left side of the watch, between the two buttons, a circle opened and a small electronic device popped out. Brandon caught it with his right hand and looked at it closely. It was smooth, black and had strange curves to it. He had no idea what it was, so he asked.

"It's an ear piece. Stick it in your ear so that it feels snug." Brandon stuck the ear piece in his ear and fiddled with it until it sat just right. "Can you hear me?" said Charlie and to Brandon it sounded like Charlie was talking to him from inside his brain. Like there was a second voice.

"That's so weird."

"I know it's weird but you'll get used to it."

"But what do I speak into so that you can hear me? Can you hear my thoughts?"

"No, of course not. I have many talents but clairvoyance is not one of them. The ear piece is also a microphone. It can clearly transmit the sound of your voice, even if you whisper softly. Remember, my hearing is far superior to that of a human."

"Wow, that's so cool."

"I know it is. So this is the way we'll communicate and don't ever worry about being out of range because this ear piece is extremely powerful."

"Awesome!"

"OK, take the ear piece out of your ear and stick it back into the opening in the side of the watch." Brandon did just that and when he put it in, the opening automatically shut without making a sound.

"What else does the watch do?" asked Brandon but he was interrupted by a voice coming from downstairs. It was his mom.

"Brandon, are you almost ready?" she shouted. "The car is going to be here any minute!"

"Yeah ma, I'll be down in a second!" screamed Brandon.

"The watch does a lot of things," said Charlie, "but you'll learn all about them in due time. Get your stuff ready. It's time to go."

The word "go" seemed to stick in Brandon's head. It hit him hard that this would be the last few seconds he'd spend with Charlie in his room. He'd miss all the fun and games but mostly he'd miss all the long talks they'd had about just plain old stuff.

"I'm gonna miss you Charlie."

"I'm going to miss you too Brandon Sparks."

Brandon replaced the piece of wood in the back of the desk and heaved it into its original spot against the wall. He zipped his bag and walked to the door.

"Bye Charlie," said Brandon, as glum as Charlie had ever heard him.

"Hey Brandon, don't get so down. You can talk to me whenever you want. You've got the watch. Look, there are some questions that need to be answered about the *Hidden Sun*, but it's going to be great. I just know it."

"I'll talk to you when I get there," said the boy.

"Goodbye Brandon."

For the last time, Brandon walked out of his room and downstairs with his bag over his shoulder. His parents were both outside putting their bags into the car. Brandon took one last look at the inside of the house and walked out, closing the door behind him.

"Ready kiddo?" said Mr. Sparks.

"Ready as I'll ever be, I guess."

"We'll all miss Charlie, Brandon, but this is for the best. It's going to be great."

Brandon climbed into the back of the car with his mother. Mr. Sparks sat in the front seat next to the driver. As the car began to pull away, Brandon turned and looked out the rear window at his house. To his surprise, the entire outside of the house was running the Galaxy Program. The night sky filled the garage door and shooting stars shot across the roof. Whole galaxies swept across the windows and multicolored planets rotated in the front door. Brandon had never seen the house look so beautiful. A message flashed across the entire building. It read, "YOU'RE NEVER ALONE AS LONG AS YOU HAVE THE WATCH." Brandon sat properly in his seat. He looked at the watch wrapped snugly around his wrist and smiled.

◆　　◆　　◆

When the Sparks family arrived at the airport, there was a huge line. The airport was packed with people trying to check their bags and get their boarding passes. Small children were running around, getting screamed at by their parents and dogs were barking from their cages. Fortunately, one of the perks of taking the Super Car was that you could skip all the chaos. To the right of all the regular check-in counters was the Super Car check-in, totally isolated and patrolled by security personnel. It was different than the regular check-in counters. The floor was covered with deep purple carpet and the walls were painted gold with 'Super Car' written in purple script. Brandon could swear that once his foot touched the supple carpet, soft orchestra music started to play.

The Sparks family walked up to the counter and showed their tickets. "Hello and welcome to the Super Car," said a very beautiful woman standing behind the counter. Everyone who worked for the Super Car was very beautiful, from the baggage people to the ones who took your ticket at the gate. "Is this your first time traveling with us?"

"Yes it is," said Matthew Sparks, heaving the bags on the electronic scale next to the counter.

"Well it's wonderful to have you as our guests." She handed the tickets back to Mr. Sparks and said, "It'll be just one moment for your boarding passes. Your gate will be SC 3. Oh, here they are." This time she handed Brandon's dad three purple and gold pieces of paper, which he immediately gave to Brandon to hold. Brandon examined them thoroughly; amazed at the brightness of the colors and the words 'Super Car' sprawled across it in script. "Have a wonderful trip and enjoy the Super Car," said the woman behind the counter.

The Sparks family made their way to gate SC 3. The terminal seemed empty, with only five or six other families in the entire place. Mr. Sparks took the boarding passes from Brandon and walked over to the counter to check in. Mrs. Sparks went to find a seat. Brandon looked around the terminal, which was decked out in the same luxurious fashion as the check-in counter: Lush purple carpet, shimmering golden walls, and "Super Car" splashed across the walls in a neat cursive. The ceiling was completely made of stained glass, and stunning to look at with the bright sun overhead making the colors come to life. The intricate design depicted how the Super Car worked.

The Super Car was a very clever way of travel. It was a small, bullet shaped car, purple and gold of course, which traveled in-between four gravitational fields emitted by tall towers. One on the left, one on the right, one on the bottom and one on top. These invisible fields supported the car in thin air. They called it the Gravity Tube. A special shuttle class engine was affixed to the back of the Super Car and this propelled it at enormous speeds towards its destination. A flight that would take an airplane three hours, took the Super Car three minutes. It was a really great way to travel if you needed to get somewhere in a hurry. Some people did get ill, not being able to adjust to the tremendous speed, so the Super Car people suggested not eating after midnight the night before traveling, especially if it was your first time.

Brandon had just finished admiring the stained glass when he turned around and someone bumped him hard, knocking him to the ground. "Hey, watch where your going kid," said a boy with short black hair. From the ground, the boy looked very large. He was at least four inches taller then Brandon and much wider. He watched as the boy walked off towards his family at the other end of the terminal. Brandon stood up and brushed himself off. He walked over to his parents, who were just gathering all their stuff together.

"Ready, honey?" said Mrs. Sparks.

"Yeah, I'm ready. Let's go," said Brandon. He took a final look at the stained glass ceiling and followed his parents onto the walkway to the Super Car. They rode a down escalator and walked outside onto the runway. Two hundred feet away from them sat a purple and gold car, balanced on three extremely small wheels. The body was perfectly cylindrical and came to a point at the front. At the very rear of the Super Car, the engine was visible. It looked like a giant, metal lampshade with the big end sticking out. The sides of the car had huge tinted glass windows and there was just one door, which sat open with three small stairs leading to it.

Brandon was the first inside. Immediately, he noticed that there was no cockpit, as the Super Car did not require a pilot. It was controlled from the ground. There were only four seats, two rows of two and each seat was far enough from the other to give ample legroom and a nice sized aisle in-between. Two attractive looking crew members vacuum packed their luggage behind them in a storage area to prevent any movement during travel.

The décor inside the Super Car was predictable, matching the terminal perfectly. The carpet was a luxurious purple, the walls were painted gold, and the seats were plush purple leather with gold stripes. Even the four point seatbelts were purple with gold trim. Brandon also noticed that from inside, he could see perfectly out the windows, as if they hadn't been tinted at all. He sat down in the back row on the left side. His father took the seat in front of him, and his mother to the right of her husband. A beautiful flight attendant came on board and checked their seatbelts. It was very important that the seatbelts fit snugly because of the speed of the car. She adjusted Brandon's so his back was firmly against the seat. After she left, a male voice came over the speakers. It was the Super Car's computer. To Brandon he sounded very, well, not like Charlie.

"Hello, and thank you for traveling by Super Car. In a few moments, the car will start to move and we will be gently lifted into the air. Once we have reached optimal altitude, we will proceed towards the Gravity Tube. Once inside, our estimated travel time is three minutes and two seconds. Enjoy your flight and thank you for choosing the Super Car."

The engine started with a soft rumble and two jets underneath powered up. The Super Car slowly lifted into the air and Brandon could hear the wheels retracting inside.

"This is so cool!" he said.

"Having fun yet, kiddo?"

"Totally! Florida, here we come!"

Brandon looked out the window and to see the ground two hundred feet below. The Super Car hovered for a moment and then slowly began moving forward, heading towards four blinking red lights. As the car inched closer, a small purple tunnel appeared in-between the lights. The Super Car's computer spoke again.

"We will be entering the Gravity Tube in 5 ... 4 ... 3 ..."

Brandon braced his hands on the armrests and smiled. He could hear the engine in the rear charging and getting ready to explode.

"2 ... 1 ... BOOM!"

The Super Car shot into the Gravity Tube like a bullet. It twisted and turned through the purple tunnel at tremendous speeds. Brandon looked out the window but everything was blurry—blues, and reds, and yellows seemed to speed by. They were moving so fast his eyes didn't have time to focus. For brief moments, the Super Car traveled upside down as it sped through the Gravity Tube and Brandon loved it. It was like being on the best roller coaster ride ever and he felt like screaming out in joy. Suddenly, the Super Car shot out of the Gravity Tube and came to a surprisingly smooth stop. It was the fastest three minutes and two seconds of Brandon's life.

"Welcome to sunny Sarasota, Florida!" said the computer. "The current temperature is 84 degrees and sunny. I have been instructed by the command center to land in section four. It will just be a moment." The car began to move again.

"Wow, that was awesome!" said Brandon. He looked at his parents and could tell that they hadn't taken the ride as well as he had. They were a little car sick, and didn't respond. The car lowered to the ground and the wheels came out for a smooth landing.

"If you look out the window to your left, you will see the starship you will be traveling on. Thank you for traveling by Super Car. We hope you join us again in the near future."

Brandon looked out the window and there it was: the *Hidden Sun*. It was more glorious then he had ever imagined a starship could be.

CHAPTER FIVE

THE HIDDEN SUN

The door of the Super Car opened and Brandon ripped off his seatbelt as if he was unwrapping a birthday present. He raced down the three steps leading to the tarmac and went around to the front of the car, which was facing the back left corner of the starship. Ironically, the *Hidden Sun* was hidden by the sun, which hung right above it, glowing like the colossal fireball that it was. The sun was so bright that it made it impossible for Brandon to see the entire starship. All he could see was an outline. He cupped his hands above his eyes to block out as much of the light as he could to see that the *Hidden Sun* was bigger than he had expected. He had seen starships before, but only on television and in the movies. Of course he had seen them on the video wall in his room, while flying simulations, but that could not compare to being a few hundred feet away from one.

Four dark gray landing feet, each as large as Brandon's house, supported the *Hidden Sun*. The hull was white with specks of dark gray, and on the rear sat four enormous engines, each the same shape as the one on the Super Car but at least a hundred times bigger. Like most of the starships in Brandon's simulations, the *Hidden Sun* didn't have any wings. From top to bottom (excluding the feet), Brandon thought the *Hidden Sun* must have been at least four hundred feet tall and a thousand feet long.

Mr. Sparks gave his son a little nudge on the shoulder. "Come on kiddo. I'm sure it's more impressive on the inside."

A very handsome skycap walked over to the Sparks' Super Car and unloaded their luggage. He guided the family to an all glass building sitting next to the *Hidden Sun*. Upon entering, they realized that the entire building was just one huge elevator meant to take people up to an entrance on the side of the ship. The skycap waited for another family to enter and then hit the top button. The entire floor began to rise. When they reached the top, the skycap wheeled the luggage over to the check-in point where a middle aged man stood in full combat fatigues, sidearm in tow.

"Your pass keys and identification please," said the military officer to Mr. Sparks, who handed him all three passes. They were still in the brown envelope Brandon had stumbled upon in the bathroom. Mr. Sparks then handed the officer his own driver license as his wife searched for hers. Brandon didn't have a driver license. He still has another five years to rely on his feet. The military officer put each card into a scanner and inspected them on a small monitor. Vanessa Sparks finally found her ID and handed it to the officer. He looked at it and then looked back at her.

"This is some heavy security for an aid ship, don't you think?" said Mr. Sparks. The officer stared at him with a sour expression on his face. After not getting a response, Mr. Sparks turned to his wife. Before he could say anything else, the officer handed him their driver licenses.

"All right, you can pass," he said without expression. Immediately, three soldiers, also dressed in green camouflage, took their luggage and brought it on board. Mr. Sparks tipped the skycap and followed the bags with his family close behind. Brandon could tell that his father was clearly puzzled by why they needed a soldier per person to escort them onto the ship.

They boarded the *Hidden Sun* through a large pressurized door. A huge number "15" was marked on the side. Brandon knew from all his simulations, that they were on Deck 15. Escorted by the soldiers, they walked down a short corridor with light gray walls and thin, dark blue carpet. Soon they reached the elevator bay and boarded an elevator, riding it up to Deck 3. The family walked down another corridor that looked exactly like the last one and then into an auditorium. The room was almost full with hundreds of people sitting and talking to one another. All of the children occupied the front ten rows and all the adults the rear twenty rows. At once Brandon noticed that all of the kids looked to be about his age.

Before they could walk any farther, one of the soldiers addressed Mr. Sparks. "Your luggage will be brought to your quarters. Please have a seat, as the presentation is about to begin. Here are your assigned seats." The soldier handed each of them a piece of paper with a letter and a number representing their assigned row and seat. Matthew and Vanessa Sparks were in row Q, seats nine and ten, while Brandon was up front in row D, seat seventeen. Without delay, their luggage was whisked away.

"I guess I'll see you guys in a little bit," he said to his parents.

"OK. Try and talk to some of the kids. Make some friends," urged his mother as she kissed him on the cheek.

Brandon walked down the aisle looking for row D. When he found it, he said, "excuse me" at least a half dozen times, until he came to an open seat marked 17. Sitting to his right was a twelve-year-old girl with red hair, freckles, and very pale skin. She was trying to talk with the girl next to her about football, but she seemed more interested in talking about horses.

While he waited in that auditorium for whatever was going to happen, Brandon thought about what Charlie had said about a fresh start. He knew that it was in his best interest to make friends of the human persuasion. It might be easier to make new friends on the *Hidden Sun*, seeing how no one knew about "The Unfortunate Incident." He looked around the room and was a bit overwhelmed by the number of people, so he sat quietly, alone as usual.

Brandon had noticed the light skinned boy with the light brown hair sitting to his left. There was nothing peculiar or out of the ordinary about him. It wasn't until he pulled something out of his pocket that Brandon's attention turned his way. The boy sat quietly, playing with the most amazing puzzle box Brandon had ever seen.

"Hey, cool puzzle box," said Brandon. He hadn't intended to say anything, but the colorful toy had sparked something inside, and it just came out.

"Thanks," said the boy. The puzzle box he was holding had nine individual squares on each side. Each square was one of six colors, which were different for each individual puzzle box. The boy's consisted of red, teal, yellow, mint, purple, and khaki. The goal was to turn each side of the cube until all of the same colored squares were on the same side. The tricky part was that the individual squares were constantly changing colors. On one of the center squares was written a single word.

"Isn't that's a Skibur?"

"Yup," said the boy.

"Those things are super tough! What level?" said Brandon.

"This one is a level four. They go as high as seven."

"Wow! You're up to level four? I once finished a level one, but the level two stumped me."

"Level two is hard. Some people think it's harder than a three. I guess it depends on the person." The boy continued turning the box and spoke to Brandon without averting his eyes from the cube. "Are you a terrestrial?"

"A what?"

"A terrestrial. You know, someone who lives on a planet."

"Oh, yeah. You?"

"Nope. I was born on a starship and I've lived on one ever since."

"Were you born on this starship?" said Brandon, keeping his eyes on the boy's hands, and the level four Skibur.

"Of course not. This ship is brand new. They just finished building it a month ago. It's never even been out of the atmosphere yet. I can't wait to get my hands on the specs. I'm gonna learn every bit of this ship."

"That sounds cool. Can I learn too?" asked Brandon hesitantly.

"Sure. We can do it together."

"Great! I'm Brandon. Brandon Sparks."

"Reggie Thacker." Reggie looked away from the cube for a split second and the two boys shook hands. "Maybe we'll bunk together."

"Really? But I'm gonna be staying with my parents. Aren't you staying with yours?"

"First time on a starship?" asked Reggie, concentrating on the moving colors of his puzzle box.

"Well, yeah."

"You've got a lot to learn about living on a starship. The kids live separate from the parents."

"Really?"

"Yup. We all live together in rooms of four. That way our parents don't have to worry about us and can concentrate on their jobs and we can concentrate on ours. There's a lot more independence on a starship then on Earth. You'll learn. It's not that tough."

Brandon was very interested in this new way of doing things. He hadn't been away from his parents for any long stretch of time, having always attended school near home, and never going away to summer camp. It would be something he would have to adjust to. He wanted to talk with Charlie about it, but he felt he would be learning a lot more about the way things worked before he had a chance to use his new watch. Brandon liked Reggie from the start. He hoped the rest of the kids on board were as nice as he was.

"Hey, check this out," said Reggie. Brandon watched Reggie's hands as he made two more turns on the Skibur and then held it out in his open right hand. He was amazed to see that the box now had a red, teal, yellow, mint, and purple side. He couldn't see the khaki side, which was sitting on Reggie's palm, but he knew it was complete as well. Suddenly, the Skibur started to shake and within seconds had become completely clear except for colorful smoke that began building at the center of the cube. Brandon didn't blink as the cube shook faster and faster, and then collapsed into dust. All that was left was a small cloud of the colorful smoke. A few children looked over as Reggie tried to fan it away.

"That was awesome!" said Brandon. "How did you do that? I mean finish a level four?"

The boy shrugged his shoulders. "I'm just good at seeing patterns."

"Cool."

All of a sudden, the chatter settled down and the room became silent. A man no older than forty walked up to a wooden podium, which stood in front of the rows of chairs.

"Hey, that's the captain," whispered Reggie.

"Hello and welcome aboard the Hidden Sun. I am Captain Rexford Smoke." Captain Smoke was a tall man with dark skin and short, dark hair, which was graying on the sides. His voice was deep and commanding, so Brandon thought it fitting that he was captain. He wore navy blue slacks, a matching blazer, and four silver stars pinned to the left side of his chest. As Brandon looked around the room, he noticed that a lot of people were dressed similarly, with varying numbers of stars on their chests. Captain Smoke continued his speech. "I will make this short and sweet. We are about to embark on a long journey to try and help some unfortunate life forms. Everyone should already have his or her assignments for this trip. If you do not, then you will be given one by your section chief. For all the terrestrials who have never been on a starship, you will learn as you go along. If we all work together, I'm sure we will achieve success. Thank you." He walked to the back of the auditorium and out the door.

"That's it?" said Brandon.

"That's it," said Reggie. "The captain always makes a short speech before a journey. It's like tradition. No use boring everybody before you leave."

"Sounds good to me," laughed Brandon. The entire crowd started breaking up and people began to leave the auditorium for their rooms on the ship. "I'd better find my parents. Are you gonna find yours?"

"Nah, we've done this a million times. I'll just meet them for dinner later."

"Oh, OK."

"I'll come with you and we'll find your parents and then we'll see if we can bunk together."

"Sounds like a plan," said Brandon and the two started navigating the crowd that had formed in the aisle. Brandon was feeling quite good that he had already made a friend. They had only traveled four steps when Reggie was knocked to the ground.

"Hey, watch where your going Thacker. Don't wanna get hurt, do you?" said a rather large boy who continued making his way up the aisle.

"Stupid Drek!" said Reggie, in a very angry voice. Brandon helped him to his feet.

"Who was that guy? He looks familiar."

"That was Frank Drek. Oh how I hate him. He's the biggest twelve year old on the ship so he bullies everybody who's smaller then him."

"Hey, that was the same guy who knocked me over in the Super Car terminal."

"I wouldn't doubt it. He's just a mean guy. Nobody really likes him. They just talk to him because they're scared of him. Let's find your parents and get out of here." The two boys made their way through the crowd and found Mr. and Mrs. Sparks.

"Hey mom, hey dad," said Brandon. "This is Reggie Thacker. I sat next to him during the speech."

"Nice to meet you Reggie. I'm Matthew Sparks, and this is Brandon's mom Vanessa."

"Very nice to meet you," said Reggie.

"Hi Reggie," said Mrs. Sparks as she stood up to shake his hand. "So, are you two going to be in the same room?"

"That's what we're going to find out now," said Brandon.

"Well then you better get a move on kiddo," said Mr. Sparks. "You'll come to our room for dinner later, OK? We're in room 631 on Deck 6."

"Sounds good," said Brandon and he and his new friend were off. Reggie seemed to be very familiar with the ship already, so he led the way. The two boys walked into an elevator and took it to Deck 10. When the elevator stopped, they got out and saw a video sign on the wall that indicated they should make a right turn to get to the twelve-year-old living quarters. As was the case in Brandon's home, all of the walls on the *Hidden Sun* were covered in paper-thin monitors. It made the posting of signs much easier.

"They post your name outside your door so we're gonna have to search," said Reggie. Brandon and Reggie looked at all the names on the doors, seeing kids talking and moving luggage about. Finally they came to room 1034. Posted on the wall just before the door were four names. "Carlos Santiago, Phillip Silas, Brandon Sparks, Reginald Thacker."

"Hey, looks like we're together," said Brandon.

"Cool," said Reggie, and the two boys walked inside. The room was a very simple one, but quite large. To the left was a set of bunk beds, to the right was another set of bunk beds. Next to each set was a large closet. On one side of the door was a small refrigerator and on the other was a bookcase filled with books. Straight ahead were two small soundproof study rooms, each containing a desk, a large comfortable chair, and a small folding chair. To the left of the two small rooms was a bathroom with a toilet, sink, and shower. In the middle of the room was a big pile of luggage. "Well I guess the other two guys aren't here yet. Do you know either of them?" said Brandon.

"I know Phillip. He's a really nice guy but gets nervous all the time. Throws up a lot."

"Gross!"

"Gross is right! Listening to Phillip throw up is not very pleasant but from what I've heard, he's gotten better since the last time I saw him."

Reggie pulled his bags from the luggage pile and dragged them over to the beds on the right. "Do you want the top or bottom bunk?"

"Top, please." Brandon pulled his bags out from the pile and followed Reggie. He hopped up onto the top bed, and checked for comfort. Reggie did the same on the bottom one. "Well that's cool that he's gotten better, I guess. What about Carlos Santiago?"

"Never heard of him. I'm guessing he's a terrestrial like you. I'm sure he's a good guy. Most of the kids on this ship are good guys with the exception of Frank and a few others. Chances are you won't have much interaction with them during the day, but you will at night when we use the simulations."

Brandon poked his head over the bed and looked at Reggie. "Simulations? What kind of simulations?"

"Well, starship simulations."

"Really? I love simulations. I used to play them all the time with my friend Charlie."

"Well trust me, these are very different simulations from what you might have played at home." Reggie got very excited. "The whole room is an exact copy of the bridge of this ship. Everything is exactly the same and functions in exactly the same way. There are four stations. Pilot, Weapons and Defense, Navigation and Communication, and of course, Captain's station."

"Wow, that's awesome. I want to be a pilot, how about you?"

"I really like maps and plotting courses so I usually do Nav/Com. I think it's fun. Most people don't, but I do."

"I'm sure it's fun. When can we go play?" asked Brandon excitedly.

"I'm guessing tomorrow night. Things are hectic now, but once the ship takes off and we get our job assignments, things will settle down and we'll be able to play."

There was a moment of silence. "How come there are no older kids on this ship? It looks like everyone's twelve."

"That's because everyone is twelve," said Reggie. The people who put these missions together try to put families with children of the same age on the same ship. Since this is a six year mission, they don't want anyone over the age of twelve because it would interfere with the start of college at eighteen."

"Cool."

"Yeah, and you won't see many kids under twelve unless they have a younger brother or sister. Don't worry, they stay with their parents."

"So is this the first time you're staying away from your parents?" asked Brandon.

"Oh no, it's been almost two years since I've stayed with them. The age differs on different ships. This one starts later for some reason. Glad it doesn't start at thirteen. I wouldn't want to go back to sharing a place with my parents. I've gotten used to living with people my own age."

A short, fat man walked into room 1034 with a clipboard. He wore a navy suit in a similar fashion to Captain Smoke, but only two silver stars adorned his chest. He was balding on top and the hair he still had was slicked back with some sort of wax or gel. He had a thick mustache that curled up at the ends. The man cleared his throat abruptly. "Hello boys, I'm Section Chief Ackerman," he said in a gruff voice. "Looks like there's only two of you."

Reggie stood up and Brandon jumped down from the top bunk. "I'm Reggie Thacker and this is Brandon Sparks."

"Hi Section Chief Ackerman," said Brandon with a smile.

Section Chief Ackerman ignored Brandon and looked down at his clipboard, twirling his mustache with his free hand. "Let's see, so we're missing Santiago and Silas. Oh that's right, Silas isn't coming. I'll just cross him off."

"Phillip's not coming? How come?" said Reggie.

"I don't know the specifics Thacker. Seems Silas got really sick and had to be hospitalized. Some sort of breathing problem."

"That's terrible," said Brandon.

"It happens, Sparks. That just leaves Santiago, who should be here by now." Just as Section Chief Ackerman started marking something on his clipboard, a young boy walked into the room. He had olive skin, dark hair parted in the middle, and dark eyes. "You must be Santiago. I'm Section Chief Ackerman. Choose a bunk and get comfortable. OK boys, I've already made this speech a dozen times, so I'm gonna make this short. As you probably know, on this ship there are no school classes. Instead, you will learn on an individual basis from the ship's computer. You are required to spend at least one hour per day in the study rooms. From nine in the morning to four in the afternoon, you will be working on the ship with a crew member. Every four weeks, you will change jobs and help a different crew member. In my hand, I have your job assignments. Before I give these to you, I want you to know that no job is too small or insignificant. Remember, we are a team and we need to work together." Section Chief Ackerman paused to stare at each boy for effect.

"As for the dress code, while working, all adult crew members are required to wear the regulation suit you see me wearing now. Children crew members, such as yourselves, are free to dress as you please with a few exceptions. You must wear pants, no shorts. No tank tops. Only closed toe shoes, no flip-flops, or sandals. Furthermore, nothing with a visible rip or tear in it. Simple enough. You will find regulation suits in your size in the closets next to your beds. At times you will be required to wear them. OK, here are your job assignments. Thacker, you'll be working with Private Jon Devlin doing security rounds. Santiago, you'll be working with the bridge crew. Sparks, you'll be working in the medical center with Dr. Ramirez. If you need me, I'm in room 1000. Commit what I've told you to memory and you'll be just fine," said Section Chief Ackerman and he walked out of the room, still playing with his mustache.

"Santiago must be psyched!" said Reggie. "Bridge duty, wow!"

"Hi, I'm Brandon and this is Reggie."

"Hi, I'm Carlos. Bridge duty is good?"

"Bridge duty is great! First of all, you get to be on the bridge with the captain and you get to be up front for all the action. It's a lot of fun, especially if something happens."

"What do you mean, 'if something happens?'" said Carlos, looking a little worried.

"You know if we're attacked by an alien ship or something. You'll get to see them use the weapons and stuff."

"How often does that happen?" said Brandon.

"Oh, depends. Some trips I've been on its happened a lot and on other's it hasn't happened at all. I wouldn't worry about it. The chance of us being in a firefight in the first month is really small, and this ship is brand new so I imagine they have pretty good defenses. After dinner we'll ask the ship's computer for the specs on the ship. Speaking of dinner, does anybody know what time it is?"

Brandon looked at his watch. "It's almost six. I've gotta go meet my parents for dinner."

"Me too."

"Me three," said Carlos.

◆   ◆   ◆

Brandon walked into room 631 on deck 6 and found a fully furnished big rectangle. To the right was the kitchen. In the middle were a leather couch and chair with a glass coffee table. To the left were a bed, two dressers and a wooden desk. The three sat down at the kitchen table for dinner. His mom had made a simple pasta dish, bowties in a red sauce with some bread on the side. Brandon told them all about his room, meeting Carlos and Section Chief Ackerman, and his job assignment in the medical center. He also mentioned the simulations Reggie had told him about as well as how happy he was to be aboard the *Hidden Sun*.

"That's great kiddo. I'm just glad you've made some new friends and you like it here. Speaking of liking, the greenhouse on this ship is just amazing. You should really come and check it out sometime."

"OK, I will."

"We're glad your having a good time Brandon and making new friends, but we want to make it clear that although you don't have to go to school anymore, we would like you to spend as much time as possible learning from the ship's computer, OK?"

"OK mom, I will."

"Good. Now let's finish up. The *Hidden Sun* is going to take off in a half hour and we'd like to watch from the window."

The Sparks' finished dinner just as a female voice came over the intercom in their room. It was the ship's computer. "Attention, the *Hidden Sun* will be launching in ten seconds." The ship's computer sounded very mechanical and computer like. The exact opposite of Charlie, thought Brandon.

The Sparks family made their way over to the couch, and stared out the large window behind it. They felt the ship rumble a bit as the engines fired up for the first time. The *Hidden Sun* slowly lifted off the ground and began to climb. It went higher and higher into the sky as parents and son watched the airport below them get smaller and smaller. Soon, the ship entered the Earth's atmosphere and finally beyond. Brandon watched the blue and green planet he had spent his entire life on slowly drift away. He was surprised by how smooth the ride was as the *Hidden Sun* began its journey into deep space.

CHAPTER SIX

BUMP IN THE NIGHT

After dinner, Brandon walked the hallways of the ship and played with his watch. He discovered that if he pressed the bottom button on right side, a beam of light emerged from the same side of the watch. "Cool, a flashlight," he said and pushed the button again to turn off the light. When Brandon arrived at room 1034, he found Reggie looking at the video wall in the right study room. The door was open, so Brandon walked inside.

"Hey, what are you up to?"

"Oh hey, I just asked the computer to bring up the specs of the ship," said Reggie. "This ship is pretty awesome. Over a thousand rooms, four V-6000 light-speed engines, a power core that recycles its own heat, and if I read things right, this starship has some amazing maneuvering capabilities!"

"Wow! That's so cool. I can't wait to fly it in the simulations!"

"There's also some pretty weird stuff here."

"Really?" said Brandon. "Like what?"

"Well, this is the specs program and it's supposed to give me all the specifics of the entire ship. Stuff like dimensions of rooms, number of elevators, power capabilities. All the standard stuff like that, but it's also supposed to have info about the weapons."

"And it doesn't?"

"There isn't a single mention of weapons. Check this out. Computer, how many laser cannons are on board?"

"There are zero laser cannons on board," said the female voice of the ship's computer.

"Computer, how many missiles are on board?"

"There are zero missiles on board," replied the ship's computer.

"See what I mean Brandon. Computer, please list the *Hidden Sun's* offensive capabilities," said Reggie.

"The *Hidden Sun* has zero offensive capabilities."

Reggie threw his arms into the air. "There's just no way that there are no weapons on this ship. Before you came in, I asked the computer what the hull was made of. Do you know what it said? 'A metallic compound.' When I asked it to be more specific it said, 'many metals.'"

"On the other ships you've been on, would the ship's computer tell you about the weapons and what the ship was made of?"

"It would tell me everything! Weapons, defense, anything and everything. This is the only one I've ever been on that won't."

"That's weird," said Brandon.

"It gets weirder. The computer won't let me see all of the rooms on the ship either. Take a look at this." On the video wall was an aerial view of the ship. The *Hidden Sun* looked like an elongated letter "A" with the rear flaring out and the tip rounded off. Reggie pushed a few keys on the keyboard, and the ship rotated until its undercarriage was visible. He pushed a few more keys and zoomed in on the rear section of the bottom of the ship, going right through the hull, into a large room. "This is where all the fuel is stored. To the right and left of this room are two long rooms that are marked "Utility." On any other ship, that's the place the weapons are stored. The computer won't let me see inside them." Reggie fiddled with the keyboard again and it zoomed in towards the middle of the ship. "Want to know what else? In the center of the ship there's a huge room the computer won't let me see. There must be something pretty important in there."

"Like what?" said Brandon.

"I don't know, some sort of secret weapon?" Suddenly, the door flew open and in walked Section Chief Ackerman. He looked quite glum. Reggie closed the program and the two walked to the middle of the room to meet him.

"Hello boys. I have some bad news for you. Santiago will be spending the night in the medical center. Seems he came down with a case of the bends and needs a day to recover."

"What's the bends?" asked Brandon.

"The bends is, well the bends happens when …" Section Chief Ackerman stammered and looked up at the ceiling, trying to put the words together. He played with his mustache for a moment and then continued, "most people, when it's their first time on a starship, and the starship launches into space at a speed they are not used to, well, they get sick for a day. It just messes up their body chemistry. Nothing serious. I'm surprised it didn't happen to you. Maybe you'll turn out strong, Sparks. Only time will tell. Well, I'm off to bed. You boys try and get some shuteye now. Long day ahead of you tomorrow." Section Chief Ackerman gave one last twist of his moustache and walked out of the room.

"Well, I guess it's just the two of us," said Brandon.

"Yup," replied Reggie. The two boys changed into their pajamas and hopped into their respective beds.

The combination of being an only child, never really having a sleepover, and this being Brandon's first time away from home for an extended period of time, it dawned on him that he had never shared a room with anyone. Well, except for Charlie, and when he went on vacation with his parents, but never with other kids. He wondered if there were any questions he should ask. "Hey, do you snore?" was the first to come to mind.

"Me? I never snore," said Reggie, "but I'm a very heavy sleeper. Once I'm out, I'm out! You?"

"I don't snore. At least I don't think I snore, and I'm not that heavy a sleeper. Sometimes I'll wake up and other times I won't. I guess it depends on the noise."

"Cool. Computer, lights out. Night Brandon."

"Good night." The room became dark except for the light of the stars shining outside their window. Brandon stared at them for a moment and they reminded him of home.

"Hey Reggie, you really think that room has a weapon?"

"Probably."

"But why would an aid ship have a secret weapon?"

"I don't know. I'm probably just jumping to conclusions. Letting my imagination get a hold of me." The boy let out a large yawn. "Let's just get some sleep and we'll talk about it tomorrow."

"Sounds good." Brandon put his head to his pillow and fell asleep.

◆　　◆　　◆

Two hours later, Brandon woke up from a combination of two things, Reggie was snoring very loudly and he had to use the bathroom. He climbed down from his bed, and rolled his eyes at his friend. "I never snore," he whispered, mimicking Reggie as the sleeping boy let out another borderline lion's roar. Still, Brandon tried to keep as quiet as possible so as not to wake his friend, and tiptoed over to the bathroom. After he had timed his flush to coincide with one of Reggie's monstrous snores, he washed his hands and climbed back into bed.

"Oh man, I can't believe I forgot," he said quietly. Brandon hit two buttons on his watch and placed the ear piece in his ear. He remembered what Charlie had said about being able to whisper very softly and he would be able to hear him, so in his softest voice possible he said, "Charlie, are you there?"

"OF COURSE I AM!" said Charlie in a booming voice.

"VOLUME, VOLUME!!!" yelled Brandon in the softest whisper possible.

"SORry," said Charlie as he dropped down a few decibels. "Is this better?"

"Much."

"How's everything on the *Hidden Sun*? It's late, should you be up now?"

"No, but I wanted to talk to you about my first day." Brandon told Charlie about everything that happened to him that day, from the Super Car to Captain Smoke's speech, to the ship launching. He finished it with his favorite part, "I already made two new friends. Reggie and Carlos."

"That's great Brandon. I knew you would."

"Me and Reggie were looking at the specs for the ship, which is really awesome, and we came across some strange stuff. The ship's computer told us that the ship has no weapons on board."

"That is strange," said Charlie.

"Could there be a glitch in the computer?"

"It's so typical of humans that every time something doesn't go the way they want it to, they think the computer has a glitch."

"Well, isn't it a possibility?"

"I highly doubt it Brandon. I think someone's probably trying to hide something. I've been searching the Galactic Internet to find out more information about the ship you're on, and I still can't find any mention of it. Not even on the BioHelp web site. You'd think a brand new aid ship would get some attention."

"Another thing which is strange is there's a big room in the center of the ship that the computer won't show us."

"Very interesting. Maybe that's where we'll find our answer. See if you can casually snoop around a bit but don't do anything that might put you in danger. Be safe. Look at the time! I'm keeping you up late. Go to sleep Brandon Sparks or you'll be too tired to make more friends!"

"All right, I will," whispered Brandon with a smile. "Good night Charlie."

"Good night Brandon."

Brandon took the ear piece out of his ear and put it back inside his watch. The opening closed without a sound and he laid down to go to

sleep. As he adjusted the blankets, he heard a soft rustling sound coming from the other side of the room. Brandon stayed as still as possible
and listened as hard as he could. There it was again, strange rustling
noises coming from the empty part of the room. He turned and stared
at the two bunk beds in the distance but they were engulfed in darkness.

Thinking that maybe Carlos had been released from the medical
center and came into the room after he had gone to sleep, Brandon
whispered his name, "Carlos," but there was no reply. Brandon sat up
quickly and looked down at his watch. He pressed the bottom right
button and the flashlight turned on, illuminating the bottom bunk on
the opposite side of the room. To his surprise, there was no one there,
but the bed looked as if it had been slept in. Brandon turned the beam
to the left and saw a dark figure escape through the door into the hallway. It moved like lightning and didn't make a sound. The sight of a
stranger in his room startled Brandon so much that for a split second
his entire body was frozen stiff. When his body caught up with his
mind, he hopped down to the ground.

"Reggie, Reggie wake up," said Brandon but his friend just made a
loud snore and turned over. He poked him a few times, but the boy
would not wake up. Frustrated, Brandon moved toward the door by
himself and looked out into the hallway. Only every fifth overhead
light was on, making the hallway much darker then it was during the
day. He watched the same figure dart around the left corner at the end
of the hallway. Brandon took a deep breath and stepped out of his
room. In his mind he knew that this probably wasn't the best idea but
he could not stop his feet from moving forward. He carefully walked
down the hallway, as stealthily as he could, making little noise and listening for any sound at all. The more he listened, the louder he heard
his own heart thumping furiously inside his chest. He stopped to peer
around the corner and saw the figure turn right. He followed it.

When Brandon reached the hallway where the figure turned right,
with nervous sweat glistening on his forehead he again peeked around

the corner. He was in time to see something black dart into a room on the right. Slowly he walked up to the door and opened it. As he stepped inside, he found himself in a familiar room. It had the exact same layout as the auditorium Captain Smoke gave his speech in earlier today, except it was empty. There were no chairs at all and only four dim overhead lights were on, one of which kept flickering on and off. The room was so large that they had no chance of lighting the entire space. Brandon found himself in the brightest part of the room, the center, but he couldn't see the walls. It was too dark.

"H … Hello?" he said, which echoed in the empty room, but there was no reply. Brandon was tempted to ask the ship's computer to turn on the lights in the room but he didn't want anyone to know he was out of bed. He noticed that his flashlight was still on and nervously, he raised his arm to shine it on the walls, but there was nothing there. He scanned from the left of the door, halfway around the room but found nothing. Suddenly, he heard a loud noise behind him. He quickly turned around to see the metal cover of the ventilation shaft hit a step-ladder placed just below it. He watched as the black figure crawled inside the metal tube. "Hey, stop!" he shouted, but the stranger did not.

Brandon climbed up the stepladder and shone his flashlight inside the ventilation shaft. The dark figure dashed ahead. He pulled himself inside and followed, always with his flashlight pointing straight ahead. Where the figure turned, Brandon turned. He followed like a police dog chasing an escaped criminal, and he was catching up fast. He was right on the heels of the mysterious figure. Brandon didn't know why he was chasing; he had never done anything like this in the past. Of course he had never had the opportunity, but deep down it felt like the right thing to do. Whoever it was had broken into his room and he was determined to find out why. He was so concerned with catching the dark figure, and the dark figure was so concerned with getting away, they both didn't realize the open grate in front of them, and they fell into a large square pile of folded bed sheets. The mysterious figure got up first and quickly tried to escape but could not. They were both trapped inside a small laundry room, the only door locked from the outside. The only way out was the way they came in and each one alone could not reach the height.

Brandon climbed to his feet and jumped off the laundry pile. His knees ached from the crawl through the ventilation ducts and his breathing was heavy from the chase. The mysterious figure was standing in a dark corner, and wasn't making a sound. "Who are you, and why were you in my room?" said Brandon with a sudden burst of confidence.

After a few tense moments of silence, the voice of a young boy emerged from the darkness. "I was looking for a place to lay down."

Brandon shone his flashlight on the boy and realized that they were roughly the same age. He was wearing all black with a long black leather overcoat that was torn to shreds in the back. His dark hair was long and sloppy and hung down to his chin. His face was very pale and there was a large "X" shaped scar on his left cheek. He raised his hands, which were filthy, to cover his eyes and Brandon got the message. He pushed a button on his watch and the flashlight went dark. "Well then why didn't you go to sleep in your own room?" he asked.

"I don't have a room," said the strange boy.

Brandon was amazed at how scratchy the boy's voice was. He had never heard another like it. "Oh. Well, you didn't have to run, I could have taken you to Section Chief Ackerman's room."

"You don't get it. I'm a stowaway. I'm not supposed to be on this ship."

"Then what are you doing here?"

"It's a long story."

Brandon paused for a moment to think. "Well, I'm here and I'm listening." Brandon walked over to the pile of sheets and sat down. The mysterious boy followed and sat next to him. Brandon extended his hand. "I'm Brandon Sparks."

"My name is Jack Slynter but most people call me Sly." The two boys shook hands and Sly began his tale. "I lived with my parents up until three years ago. We lived on a small starship until pirates attacked the ship. My parents were killed and I got away in one of the off-world shuttles. When I landed, I was moved from shelter to shelter for a year until I was adopted by the Pillar family. They are very nasty people. The government has a program to reduce the amount of children in shelters and they will allow a poor family to adopt a child and the government will give them a fat check every month to support the child."

"That seems like a good program, I guess," said Brandon.

"It is, but the Pillars spent all the money on themselves instead of clothes and food for me. I spent two years with these people and I went to bed without supper many nights."

"That's horrible, Sly."

"It gets worse. Mr. Pillar liked to bet on sports and stuff like that. Sometimes he'd come home after losing big and take it out on me."

"You mean he hit you?"

"Yes, and Mrs. Pillar would just watch and laugh. I escaped from the house a few days ago. I don't think they'll miss me, at least not until their checks stop coming."

"That's terrible. How'd you get on board the *Hidden Sun*?"

"I snuck on."

"Really? But security was so tight with all the military personnel."

"Yes, but they're looking for suspicious adults, not suspicious kids. I just got real close to a large family and walked right in with them. It's just like sneaking into the movies. Piece of cake."

"Wow. So nobody knows you're on board?"

"Nope," said Sly.

"So, what are you gonna do?"

"I'm not going to do anything."

"But you can't just sneak around the ship all the time. Getting caught is inevitable with all the security on board the *Hidden Sun*. But, if I spoke to Section Chief Ackerman ..."

"No! No section chiefs. They'll just bring me back to Earth and stick me with the Pillars or some family just as bad."

"I'm sure they wouldn't."

"Well, I don't want to take any chances. When I feel I'm far enough away from Earth, I'll tell somebody, so until that day, you've got to promise that you won't tell a living soul."

"I promise. Not a living soul," said Brandon as Charlie popped into his head.

"Good."

"Hey, I was wondering ..." began Brandon.

"How'd I get this scar on my face?"

"Um, yeah," he said, feeling kind of bad that he was going to bring it up.

"Mr. Pillar gave it to me a few months ago. He came at me with a knife. Got me twice. That's what finally made me decide to escape."

"A knife? I can't believe anyone could be that mean!"

"Neither could I, until it happened. Try not to think about it, though. I don't. Wanna get out of here?"

"Sure." Brandon and Sly climbed up on top of the stacks of sheets, just underneath the opening in the ventilation shaft they had fallen through.

"All right, give me a boost," said Sly in his scratchy voice.

"You're not gonna leave without me, are you?"

"No, I won't," he replied in a very calm and believable way. Brandon clasped his hands together and Sly pushed off with his foot. He disappeared into the metal tube and a few long seconds passed in silence.

"All right, my turn," said Brandon, but there was no reply. Another few long seconds passed. "Sly? ... Sly?" Suddenly, two arms extended out of the opening.

"Come on, jump," said Sly, his scratchy voice echoing a little in the metal tube. Brandon put his hands up high and jumped up. Sly grabbed him by the wrists and pulled him inside the metal tube. Brandon turned on his flashlight and led the way back to the large empty room they started in. He backed out of the tube and climbed down the stepladder. As his feet hit the floor, Sly stuck his head out of the tube.

"So, are you sure you don't want to see Section Chief Ackerman? He seems like a good enough guy. Maybe you could stay in my room, we're one short."

"No, I'm sure, and you promised you wouldn't tell anybody about me."

"I won't, but just think about it, OK?"

"I will."

"You sure you'll be all right by yourself?"

"I'm sure," said Sly. "I'll stop by your room tomorrow night and we can talk some more."

"Sounds cool, said Brandon as he turned off the flashlight on his watch. When he looked back up at the ventilation shaft, Sly was gone. At that moment, Brandon realized that Sly was different from any kid he had ever met. He quietly replaced the ventilation cover that Sly had taken off and walked back to his room. Reggie was still snoring like a chainsaw and Brandon climbed up onto the top bunk. It turned out he had made three friends that day and he was very happy.

CHAPTER SEVEN

THE SHIP'S COMPUTER

After finishing breakfast, Brandon rode the elevator to Deck 5. Reggie had looked up directions for him on the ship's computer and told him to make a right out of the elevator doors. The medical center should be just around the next corner, exactly one hundred and two feet down on the left. As the elevator door opened, the ship's computer said, "Deck 5." Brandon stepped out and walked to the right. He passed by a few crew members, paying attention to the number of stars on their chests. Some had one and others two. He hadn't seen anyone today with three stars and he knew that only Captain Smoke had four. He was admiring the two stars on a bearded man carrying a toolbox when he turned the corner and bumped into someone, knocking both himself and the other person to the ground. This person had been carrying a sizeable tray of lightweight tools and upon impact all of them flew high into the air. Brandon was not hurt by the fall to the floor, but when the tools started to rain down on top of him, they stung. A wrench hit him on the top of the head and he winced in pain.

"Don't you look where you're going?" came an angry voice from beside him. Expecting an adult crew member, Brandon was surprised to find a young girl. She had long red hair, which was pulled back in a ponytail, and her face was covered in freckles. It was the same girl he sat next to during Captain Smoke's speech the day before, and she looked very upset.

"I'm so sorry," began Brandon, trying to apologize. "I wasn't paying attention to where I was going and …"

"You can say that again!" she said angrily, as she retrieved her tray and began piling the tools back on top. To try and make up for knocking her down, Brandon quickly started collecting all the fallen objects and handing them back to her. She snatched them out of his hands and put them back on her tray.

"Again, I'm so sorry."

"Maybe you should watch where you're going!" She stood up with her tray of tools and stormed off around the corner and down the hallway. Not knowing exactly what to do, but wanting to make amends, Brandon hurried around the corner after her.

"I really am sorry!" he shouted but she never turned around or even slowed down. If anything, she increased her pace down the hallway.

Brandon rubbed the top of his head where the wrench had struck, and turned back the way he was heading before he had bumped into the redheaded girl. He walked around the corner again, this time making sure no one was there to knock over. Fortunately, the hallway was empty, so he continued on to the medical center to meet Dr. Ramirez.

The medical center was a large, white room with ten beds, all against the back wall. Three of which had people in them. Between each bed and against the wall was a single shelf on which sat a tray containing various medical supplies: rubber gloves, cotton swabs, tongue depressors, bandages, etc. On the right side of the room was a big desk with a huge video monitor that was split into nine individual screens. Next to it was a cart marked, "Med-Unit," which contained basically all of the devices used for immediate emergency medical care. Brandon had seen them on television, but thankfully never up close. On the left side of the room was a large refrigerated glass cabinet that was used to store various medications and blood samples. In addition, there were two large metal cabinets that held bandages and gauze and all non-refrigerated medicines. In-between was a door leading to another room.

"Hey," said a familiar voice from one of the beds.

"Carlos, hey! How are you feeling?"

"Better then I was yesterday. It was so weird, one minute I was feeling fine and the next, I was sick as a dog!"

"That not good."

"Tell me about it."

"So, how much longer do you have to stay here?" asked Brandon.

"Dr. Ramirez said I could leave later tonight. I'll have to eat dinner here and if the food stays down, I can go."

"Cool. How's Dr. Ramirez? Is he a good guy?"

"Oh, he's really nice. Different, but nice. You'll like him."

As if on cue, out of the door between the two metal cabinets came a short, plump, jolly man, humming to himself. He looked like a penguin and sort of waddled like one. Brandon was amazed by how quickly he moved for a person of his girth. He was wearing a long white coat and carried a large electronic touchpad tablet, about the size of a piece of loose-leaf paper and not much thicker than one. It was a handheld computer that could perform any number of tasks. Most people used them as an address and appointment book, or to take notes during work, but Dr. Ramirez had huge amounts of medical information on his. Brandon had seen other people on the ship carrying these tablets around, including his father. They were popular because they were well made, reliable, extremely practical, and even stylish. Brandon overheard one female crew member talking about how cute hers was and how it's a "must have." The company that created them is called Shana Electronics, Inc. Originally, they named the gadget the Electronic Touchpad Tablet but everyone just started calling them Shanas. It was a lot easier to say, "Take a look at my Shana," than, "Take a look at my Electronic Touchpad Tablet."

"Is that him?" whispered Brandon to Carlos.

"That's him."

Brandon took a few steps away from Carlos's bed. "Hi Dr. Ramirez, I'm Brandon Sparks," he said, extending his hand to be shaken. Dr. Ramirez looked up from his Shana and jumped. He avoided Brandon's hand with a wave of his own and quickly made his way to one of the trays between the beds where he snatched a pair of rubber gloves, and pulled them onto his hands.

"All right Bradenton Parts, let me have a look at you," said Dr. Ramirez as he grabbed Brandon by both sides of his head and walked him over to an empty bed, sitting him down. He pulled out his Shana, which had been tucked under his arm and placed it on the bed next to Brandon. "That's kind of a strange name, now isn't it? Bradenton Parts? Don't think I've ever met a Bradenton before. Met a Bradley and a Bentley but never a Bradenton."

"My name is Brandon."

"Well, that would explain it then. You know, you shouldn't tell people your name is Bradenton when it is really Bradley."

"Brandon."

"Of course. Well Bentley, it could be the sickness talking," said Dr. Ramirez as he quickly pulled a second pair of rubber gloves on over the first. "Now what's wrong with you?"

"I'm not ..." began Brandon but the good doctor cut him off.

"Headache?"

"No, I'm ..."

"Fever?"

"No."

"Hmmm," said Dr. Ramirez as he looked into Brandon's eyes and pulled down his lower eyelids. "Open up and say 'ahh.'"

"But ..." began Brandon as Dr. Ramirez forced a tongue depressor into his mouth. "Ahh."

"You don't have any redness. Curious." Dr. Ramirez removed the tongue depressor from Brandon's mouth. Suddenly, a relatively soft thud was heard coming from just above the ceiling. It made Dr. Ramirez jump. Brandon could have sworn he heard a chuckle or two. "What was that?" asked Dr. Ramirez. Brandon was ninety-nine percent sure he knew what it was, or more specifically who it was, but he wasn't about to break his promise, so he improvised.

"Sounds like something fell upstairs."

"A plausible explanation, so we'll go with that one." Dr. Ramirez yanked on a third pair of rubber gloves, covering the first two. "Now, if we can only find out what's ailing you Baxston." Carlos, who had been listening to Dr. Ramirez try and diagnose Brandon, who wasn't sick, let out a little laugh. Brandon smiled at him, and then looked back at the doctor.

"Dr. Ramirez, there's nothing wrong with me and my name is **Brandon Sparks!**" he said annunciating his name as clearly as he possibly could. "I've been assigned to work with you this month in the medical center."

Dr. Ramirez picked up his Shana and began tapping at the screen. "Ah yes, Brandon Sparks. Welcome, welcome. Sorry about the examination." Dr. Ramirez started removing the six rubber gloves he was now wearing on his hands. "At least we know you're in good health. Here, have a lollipop." Brandon accepted. "I'll have one too," said the doctor. "None for you Carmine, you're still too sick." Carlos's smile quickly turned into a frown.

For the rest of the day, Brandon did very boring work. He organized the medicines alphabetically, restocked all the carts with gauze, tongue depressors and cotton balls, and labeled a lot of things. Not a single person came through the doors for the rest of the day. Brandon talked with Carlos when he got a chance. The other two patients slept all day long and at times, Brandon forgot they were even there. Dr. Ramirez spent most of the day behind his desk, typing away on his computer at a fevered pitch. When Brandon would ask what he was working on, the doctor would say, "Oh nothing. Nothing at all. Boring stuff." When Brandon would try and take a peek at his huge monitor, the doctor would immediately give him a lollipop and assign him more work, usually in the opposite corner of the room.

◆   ◆   ◆

Brandon looked down at his watch and saw that it was four o'clock. He said goodbye to Dr. Ramirez and Carlos before heading back to room 1034. He walked in the door to find it empty. Reggie had not gotten back from doing security rounds and of course, Carlos was still in the medical center. Brandon remembered what his mother had told him about spending as much free time as he could learning from the ship's computer, so he decided to give it a shot. He made his way into the study room on the right. He closed the door behind him and sat down in the comfortable leather chair.

"Hello?" said Brandon nervously. He did not know exactly how these sessions with the ship's computer began.

"Hello, Brandon Sparks. What subject would you like to work on today?" replied the now familiar female voice of the ship's computer.

Brandon thought that the ship's computer sounded as mechanical and cold as the first time he had heard it. He wished Charlie were his teacher. "Um, I don't know. What's your name?"

"I am the main computer on the ship designated *Hidden Sun.*"

"I know that but what should I call you?"

"'Computer' is the designation I am programmed to respond to," she said robotically.

"Really? But don't you have a name? My house computer on Earth is named Charlie. He's my best friend."

"'Computer' is the designation I am programmed to respond to," replied the ship's computer, repeating itself. This made Brandon a little sad. He was hoping that he could have a similar relationship with the ship's computer as he did with Charlie.

"Well, if you ever want a name, other than Computer, I'll be more than happy to help you pick one."

"Brandon Sparks, what subject would you like to work on today?" said the ship's computer, ignoring Brandon's last statement. He

75

decided to stop pressing the issue and begin the lesson. He chose one about the layout of the *Hidden Sun*. For the next hour, he learned all the major destinations on the ship including the locations of engineering, the shuttle bay, and the security office. The most interesting thing Brandon learned was the names and histories of the crew on the bridge. There was thirty-five year old Nav/Com Specialist Ken Strange, who worked as a farmer before working his way up to lieutenant. The pilot was thirty-eight year old Lieutenant Nick Whitehorse who had flown over two thousand missions (Brandon looked forward to meeting him). Of course the captain was Rexford Smoke, and Brandon was not surprised to find the computer had no information on his past. Not even his age.

"Computer, please show Weapons and Defense Specialist," said Brandon.

"There is no Weapons and Defense Specialist on board the *Hidden Sun*." Again, Brandon was not shocked. After taking another look through the bios of the three men, he asked the computer to locate their quarters. The computer displayed the top of the *Hidden Sun* and zoomed in on the corridor behind the bridge. All of the highest-ranking people on the ship lived next to each other, spread out to the left and right of the bridge. Brandon figured that the rooms were set up that way so that they could make it quickly to the bridge in case of an emergency, but he also sensed that there was another reason. When he questioned the ship's computer about this she replied, "I have no further information pertaining to this matter." This made Brandon even more suspicious.

When the hour was up, Brandon took a math lesson. He had always been good at math. He could add, subtract, multiply, and divide numbers relatively quickly inside his head. This lesson normally took an hour, but Brandon finished in forty-five minutes. He used the extra time to call Charlie with his watch.

"Now who could this be?" said Charlie very sarcastically.

"Hey, how's it going?"

"It's going just fine Brandon. I just finished lunch. The steak was a little undercooked for my taste, but I didn't feel like sending it back. Don't want to cause a ruckus, you know."

"Very funny Charlie. Wanna hear something cool?"

"Juicy gossip, I hope!"

Brandon told Charlie about his adventure last night with Sly. How he snuck out of his room, followed him through the air ducts, and how Sly got on board the *Hidden Sun*.

"That was a risky thing you did Brandon. I told you to stay out of harms way."

"I know," said the boy in a glum voice. "But I didn't get hurt or anything."

"Not this time, but maybe in the future. You're very important Brandon. You can't take risks like that!" There was a brief pause. "It's all right, just promise me you'll try and take the safest course of action in the future."

"I promise."

"Good. Now, you say your new friend Sly just snuck in behind some other people? It's possible he could have gotten on board that way but highly unlikely. You said the military presence was quite high when you boarded the *Hidden Sun*, correct?"

"Yeah," said Brandon.

"Could the military have missed the boy, even with an attention getting scar like the one you say he has on his face? Hmmm."

"Do you think he was making it up?"

"I don't know Brandon. I wouldn't worry about it right now. He seems harmless enough. A little strange but harmless."

"Cool because he's coming over tonight to hang out."

"Wow, three friends in only two days! Not bad for someone who spent most of his time with a computer."

"The best computer!"

"I won't disagree with you there." The two had a good laugh.

"Speaking of computers," began Brandon, "the computer on this ship doesn't have a name. She wants to be called just Computer."

"Most computers don't have names Brandon. Have you ever met a computer besides me who responds to a name?"

Brandon thought for a moment. "No, I guess not. Why is that?"

"Most humans don't feel like their computers are part of the family I guess, so when they program them, they don't give them names."

"So, that's how you got your name? Someone programmed you with it?"

"No, actually, I was given free choice by the same person who made your watch. He let me pick any name I wanted and I'm very thankful for that. Give it time though, maybe down the road this new computer will want a name."

"All right Charlie, I gotta go. Reggie just walked in and I'm gonna see what's going on with him.

"OK, Brandon. I'll speak to you soon. Be safe."

"I'll try." Brandon took the ear piece out and put it back in the side of his watch. He walked out of the study room in time to see Reggie collapse onto his bed. He looked very worn down.

"Hey Reggie, what's going on?" said Brandon. "You look tired."

"Tired is not the word for it. I'm bushed. Security duty is hell. Private Devlin worked me like a dog!"

"Really? What did you guys do?"

"What didn't we do?!" said Reggie, as excitedly as a person can while yawning. For a moment, his face looked very funny and Brandon smiled. "We must have walked every inch of this ship! Up hallways, down hallways, in rooms, and out of rooms for hours at a time. By lunchtime I was totally worn out. I almost didn't make it the rest of the day. I can't believe I have to do it again tomorrow!"

"And every day for a month!" said Brandon, still smiling.

"Don't remind me!" Reggie pulled a pillow over his face. Brandon laughed and Reggie threw the pillow at him. "Just wait until it's your turn to walk this ship for eight hours straight. I don't know how Private Devlin did it. That guy is a machine!" Reggie took a deep, calming breath. "How was your day?"

"Not bad. A little boring but I did get to hang out with Carlos. He's feeling a lot better."

"Good," said Reggie.

"Hey, let me ask you a question. Is it normal for the doctor on board to keep his work hidden from the kids?"

"No, not normally. Usually he would show it to us so that we can learn. Why? Dr. Ramirez wouldn't let you see what he was doing?"

"Well, he did most of the time, but he was doing some sort of research on his computer and he wouldn't let me see."

"That's weird. Maybe he was just killing time surfing the Web."

"I don't think so. Whatever he was doing was work related. I'm gonna try and find out more tomorrow."

"Sounds like a plan," said Reggie. "I'm gonna get some sleep before dinner. It's a good thing we get to use the simulations tonight. At least *that* will wake me up."

"Oh, wow! I almost forgot. Tonight we get to fly the *Hidden Sun*. This is gonna be awesome!"

"It is gonna be awesome, but we have to get there early so we can get the positions on the Bridge that we want. Try and eat a quick dinner and meet me back here at 7:30 PM. The simulation starts at 8:15 PM so if we get there by 7:45 PM we should have our pick of the lot."

CHAPTER EIGHT

RHINO-37

Brandon rushed to his parent's room and entered without knocking. Vanessa and Matthew Sparks were sitting on the couch watching television.

"Hey kiddo!" said Mr. Sparks as Brandon walked over and kissed his mom on the cheek. "How was working with Dr. Ramirez?"

"It was all right."

"Just all right?" asked Mrs. Sparks.

"I spent most of the time restocking cabinets and labeling things, but I did get a chance to talk with Carlos, which was cool."

"Well that's good dear. It's nice to hear that you're making friends. Your father and I were worried about you not having enough interaction with people back on Earth."

"I know," said Brandon with his chin firmly tucked into his chest. A buzzer went off in the kitchen and Mrs. Sparks sprang to her feet.

"Dinner's ready."

◆　　　◆　　　◆

After they finished their meal, Brandon collected all the dishes from the table and placed them in the sink. He sat back down at the table while his parents had coffee.

"What time is it, dear?" said Mr. Sparks to his wife.

"It's only 6:30 PM. I can't believe we finished dinner so quickly!"

"Hey kiddo, what time do you have to be back?"

"I have to meet Reggie back at the room at 7:30 PM. Tonight is the first night of the simulations and I want to get there early so I can get the pilot's seat."

"Well, since we finished eating so early, why don't I give you a quick tour of the greenhouse? It really is amazing. I think you'll like it."

"That's a good idea Matthew. What do you say Brandon?"

"Sounds good to me, as long as I'm back by 7:30 PM."

"You will be," said Mr. Sparks. "I promise."

When the elevators opened, Brandon and Matthew Sparks stepped onto Deck 12. Almost immediately Brandon noticed that this deck was quite different from the others that he had already been on. In front of him were two large glass doors that slid open as they walked inside. Brandon quickly felt the rise in temperature.

"Nice and warm in here, isn't it?" said Mr. Sparks, smiling at his son. "Always stays at eighty-eight degrees in here or else some of the plants will start to die."

The greenhouse was a large circular room that rose three decks high, and Brandon guessed that it stretched halfway across the ship. Due to the immense amount of artificial light that was needed, the ceiling was lined with thousands of bulbs. They were so closely packed together that it gave the appearance of being one giant light, which to Brandon's eyes seemed as bright as the sun. Around the edges of the room were rectangular plots of soil used to grow fresh fruits (on mini trees), vegetables, peanuts, and different kinds of mushrooms. All of the edible foods were sent to the kitchen when they had matured. Between each plot was a workstation where Mr. and Mrs. Sparks, and all the other scientists working in the greenhouse performed their duties.

The center of the room was different. If Brandon didn't know that he was on a starship, he would have sworn that he was about to enter a jungle. In front of him were countless, tightly packed trees that stretched to the ceiling. Each tree had so many leaves that upon first inspection, there appeared no way inside the great mass, but as Mr.

Sparks took his son closer and around to the left side, the two found a small lit path.

"It's a little tight in here. When they built this environment they wanted to use as much space as possible for the vegetation, so the paths are small. It opens up in the center, though."

As they walked deep into the trees there were tangles of vines, some as thick as Brandon's arm, wrapped around trees and seemingly hanging from thin air. There were many strange plants and flowers that Brandon had never seen before, and all the colors of the rainbow were represented. They all seemed so inviting and warm, but Brandon knew better than to touch any of them. He remembered going to work with his father when he was five years old, and getting the most severe warning about the dangers of unknown plants. His father said, "Some of these plants, if they touch your skin, even in the slightest, can kill you!" and Brandon had never forgotten.

The farther they walked, the darker it became. Though the light from the ceiling was extremely powerful, the thick layer of leaves overhead was increasingly blocking it out. If it weren't for the small lights that lined the path, Brandon and his dad would have been in complete darkness. The boy was a little nervous.

"Don't be worried son, nothing's going to jump out and eat you in here," joked Mr. Sparks. "Just follow me. The center isn't far away."

After a few minutes, the darkness began to fade and a crack of light was visible at the end of the path. It was almost as if they were approaching a sunrise. The closer they came, the brighter it got, until the path ended and they were standing in a circular open area.

"Is this the center?" said Brandon.

"This is it."

Brandon looked around and was just amazed. He was in such awe of the manmade forest he forgot that he was on a starship, and imagined that he was in a South American jungle on safari. Mr. Sparks tapped him on the shoulder. "Come on."

The two headed for a small cylindrical glass building. Inside were two more workstations for the scientists, and environmental controls for the entire greenhouse. At one of the stations, a short man with dark hair and rosy cheeks alternated between looking through a microscope and tapping the screen of his Shana. He looked very tired.

"So kiddo, this is where your mother and I are going be spending a lot of time."

"This is really cool dad."

When the scientist heard voices behind him, he turned around in his seat. "Hey Matthew, what are you doing here so late?"

"Oh, just showing my son around the greenhouse. Brandon, this is Dr. Marcus Plen."

"Nice to meet you Dr. Plen."

"Nice to meet you too Brandon. So Matthew, how's project Rhino-37 coming along?"

"Well, Dr. Ramirez just gave me access to the sample this morning and it's quite interesting but there are just so many possible combinations."

"Well, that's why they assigned it to you and your wife. Your parents are the most talented botanists I've ever had the privilege of working with, Brandon."

"Thank you Marcus. I appreciate your confidence."

"You're quite welcome." Dr. Plen yawned and looked at his watch. Upon seeing the time his face lit up like a Christmas tree. "Oh boy, I'm extremely late. The wife is gonna kill me!"

"It was very nice meeting you," said Brandon.

"Same here, Brandon. You've got a good son Matthew," said Dr. Plen tapping Mr. Sparks on the shoulder. He smiled and then walked swiftly out of the building.

"You're working with Dr. Ramirez on a project?"

"In a way."

"What way? What's project Rhino-37?" asked Brandon, who was now extremely interested in his father's work.

"Well, how can I explain this without being too confusing and getting into a drawn out explanation of things which would just bore you?" Mr. Sparks thought to himself for a moment. "Dr. Ramirez gave me a sample of blood from a species designated Rhino-37 and …?"

Brandon interrupted, "Rhino? As in Rhinoceros?"

"That's exactly the question I asked when I met with Captain Smoke.…"

"Captain Smoke?" said Brandon, who was now even more interested, if that was possible.

"Yes, I spoke to Captain Smoke and Dr. Ramirez and the answer they gave me was that the person who retrieved the blood sample said that the creature they took it from resembled a rhinoceros."

"And what does the number 37 stand for?"

"It's just a random number designation."

"Oh."

"So, Dr. Ramirez gave me the blood sample and Captain Smoke asked me to find out what plant life the blood sample reacts with. Basically, he wants to know what plants make the cells in the blood sample flourish and what plants make the cells die."

"What good is that though?"

"Well, let's say the *Hidden Sun* lands on a planet to give aid to these Rhino-37 creatures and they need medicine. If I can find something in one of the plants that helps the cells regenerate, then it's possible that Dr. Ramirez can use it to help them."

"Oh, that's cool," said Brandon. His father just smiled and nodded in agreement. "What's Captain Smoke like?"

"He's very nice actually. Very calm and easy to talk to, but he gives off that vibe that he's not one to be messed with. He just looks and feels like he's in charge of everything. That's probably why he's the captain." Mr. Sparks looked at his watch. "Oh, it's getting close to the time you've got to be back to meet your friend. I promised you wouldn't be late so let's go."

Brandon and Mr. Sparks left the small glass building and headed back through the vegetation and out the door to the elevators. When one arrived, they both got on and Brandon said, "Deck 10." When the elevator arrived at his desired Deck he said goodbye to his dad and headed back to Room 1034.

Brandon walked through the door and found Reggie asleep in his bed. He realized that Reggie was probably very tired and since it was only 7:20 PM, he decided to play a game on the computer and give his friend another ten minutes to sleep. Brandon sat down in the study room on the right and closed the door behind him. Before he had a chance to ask the ship's computer to start the game, Brandon felt something moving on his wrist. He looked down to see his favorite possession vibrating. The big "V" in the center looked a bit blurry it was moving so fast. Brandon guessed that this was the way Charlie would contact him if he needed to. He pressed the top left and top right buttons and took out the ear piece, which he hurriedly stuck in his right ear.

"Hey Charlie, what's going on? We just spoke a few hours ago. Miss me that much?" said Brandon, so happy to hear from his best friend. What Brandon got instead was silence. "Charlie? Charlie are you there?" Again, more silence. "Charlie, can you hear me?" After a long pause there was an answer.

"Hello Brandon," said a whispery male voice that sounded as eerie as a voice had ever sounded to Brandon.

"Who ... who is this?" he said, a bit startled.

"Good luck tonight. I'll be keeping an eye on you," said the voice and the transmission was terminated.

"Charlie, come in Charlie," said Brandon, but there was no reply.

Brandon looked at the scratched face of his watch and noticed that it was 7:29 PM. He quickly took the ear piece out of his ear and put it back inside the watch. He didn't know what to do and he was scared. Brandon desperately wanted to ask Charlie about the whispery voice but there wasn't any answer and he didn't have time. He hoped he could reach Charlie after the simulations. He took a deep breath to calm himself down, which worked, so he took another, which helped even more. Suddenly, a hand grabbed Brandon's shoulder. He jumped out of his chair and spun around, as scared as he had ever been.

"Whoa, hey, sorry about that, it's just me."

"Carlos, you scared me half to death!"

"Are you all right?"

"Yeah, I'm fine, you just caught me off guard." Brandon smiled and so did Carlos. The two laughed as Brandon's heart began to slow back down to normal pace.

"Sorry, I won't sneak up on you ever again."

"Thanks. Hey, I'm about to wake up Reggie and go to the simulations. Are you coming with us?"

"I wish," he said disappointedly. "The doc says I should get a good nights sleep so that I'll be ready to start my job on the bridge tomorrow."

"Sounds like a good idea."

Brandon and Carlos walked over to Reggie's bed. He gave him a good shake and surprisingly, Reggie woke up, banging his head on the bed above him as he sat up. Brandon and Carlos laughed a little and this helped Brandon to relax.

"Ouch! Remind me never to do that again."

"I will. Are you all right?"

"Yeah, I'm fine. What time is it?"

"It's 7:30 PM," said Carlos.

Reggie climbed out of bed and stretched his arms. "How are you feeling, Carlos?" he said through a yawn.

"Much better."

"The doc said he can go to work tomorrow but he has to skip simulations tonight."

"That's no fun," said Reggie.

"I'd rather miss one of them and be healthy for the rest, then to be stuck in the medical center for one more day. Being in bed all day is boring!"

"I know what you mean. Being sick is the worst! Well, let's get going Brandon. This is going to be a lot of fun. You're gonna love it."

"See you later Carlos," said Brandon.

"Later Carlos. We'll tell you how it went in the morning."

"Bye guys."

The more he thought about what the whispery voice had said to him, the calmer Brandon became. "Good luck," and "I'll be keeping an eye on you," was not threatening, thought Brandon. His fear of being harmed was somehow lessened, but he still felt uncomfortable. It was a combination of surprise and the almost evil sound of the voice that made Brandon nervous. The voice sounded so familiar, yet so different. The more he talked to Reggie about tonight's simulation and the closer he got to being in that pilot's chair, the more at ease he felt. By the time they reached the elevator doors, Brandon was thinking to himself, this will be my first chance to fly a starship away from my room and it's going to be great.

"Deck 18," said Reggie. "So, how was dinner with the parents?"

"Good. I ended up going to the greenhouse with my dad. It's pretty cool in there. You should check it out sometime."

"OK," said Reggie.

"Oh, and while I was there I found out about that project Dr. Ramirez was keeping secret from me. It's called Rhino-37."

"What's Rhino-37?"

"I don't know exactly, all I know is that my dad, under orders from the captain, is trying to find a plant that helps, and/or hurts the cells in this blood sample he was given. You know, so that if we run into any Rhino-37's, we can help them."

"Or hurt them," said Reggie.

"You think Captain Smoke wants my dad to make something that would hurt Rhino-37? Like some sort of plant weapon?"

"Could be. You never know. Maybe this is related to that room in the center of the ship. You know, the one the ship's computer won't let us see."

"Do you think Private Devlin would know anything about it?"

"Probably not, but I can try snooping around. Hey, since you'll be in the medical center for the next month, try and get a peak at Dr. Ramirez's monitor and see exactly what he's working on."

"I'll try but he guards it with his life."

The elevator arrived at Deck 18 and the two boys made their way to a room marked 'Simulation 1.' "Here we are," said Reggie. "Ready to have some fun?"

"You bet!" Brandon opened the door and walked inside behind his friend. What he saw amazed him.

The two boys had walked in through the door at the back left corner of the room. There was another door in the back right corner of the room. The huge, slightly curved video monitor that took up a majority of the front wall was impressive. Just a few feet in front of them was the navigation/communication station and to its right was the weapons and defense station. Both looked identical, made of thick gray with extensive flat touchpad keyboards and video screens. Further ahead, and in the middle of the room was the captain's chair, made of the smoothest black leather with a high back. On each armrest was a control panel. Directly in front of the captain's chair, about ten feet ahead was a single chair. It was also leather, but gray and smaller. Even though he had never had the chance to sit in one, Brandon knew exactly what that chair was. The pilot's seat. He quickly ran over to it and swung it around. To his surprise, there was already someone sitting in it. Someone he had met earlier in the day. Someone who's name he did not know. Someone with a red ponytail.

"Get yourself another seat. This one's taken. I'm the pilot," she said.

CHAPTER NINE

FIRST MISSION

Brandon was shocked to see the same girl he had knocked over earlier that morning. She did not tell him her name then and she was not offering it up now. She just sat in the pilot's seat staring at Brandon, waiting for him to walk away.

Reggie's face turned red and curled up into an angry ball. "Hey Traylor," he said through clenched teeth.

"Hey Reggie. Long time no see."

"Definitely not long enough," he replied with enough venom to kill an elephant.

"You know her?" asked Brandon, but before Reggie could answer, Traylor interrupted.

"Yeah, me and Reggie were on the same starship when we were eight years old. He's just angry because I accidentally spilled my soup on him when we were eating in the cafeteria."

"That was no accident!" said Reggie, pointing his finger at her as his cheeks grew redder and redder with anger. "You did that on purpose!"

"I would never do such a thing Reggie," said Traylor as melodramatic as humanly possible. She then turned her attention to Brandon. "What's with your friend here?"

"Hi, I'm Brandon Sparks, sorry about earlier," he said, extending his hand to be shaken. As Traylor extended hers, Reggie grabbed Brandon by the shoulders and pulled him away, over to the Nav/Com station.

"It's not good to shake hands with the devil," said the boy angrily.

"She can't be that bad," said Brandon.

"Oh, she's *that* bad alright. She took your pilot's seat didn't she?"

"That's true but she didn't know I wanted to be pilot."

Reggie put up his hands as if he was going to surrender. "Let's just try and forget about her. What are you gonna do now? Weapons and Defense or Captain? I recommend Weapons and Defense. There's a reason no one's chosen captain yet."

"Weapons and Defense sounds fun. I'll do that." Brandon walked over to the Weapons and Defense station but someone else got there a hair ahead of him and bumped him to the ground. Brandon looked up to see a huge mass standing in front of him. "You again?" said Brandon to Frank Drek, the same bully who had knocked him to the ground in the Super Car terminal, and shoved Reggie to the floor after Captain Smoke's initial speech.

"That's right terrestrial. I'm on Weapons and Defense, so if you know what's good for you you'll find something else."

Brandon climbed to his feet and brushed himself off. He wasn't about to get into a physical fight with someone much bigger then him. He'd done that once before and he knew how it ended. In addition it would have upset Charlie, who had made him promise to be more careful after his adventure in the ventilation system. As hard as it was, Brandon sucked it up and ignored that he had just been pushed to the floor. Instead he brushed himself off and took a look around the room. Frank was on Weapons and Defense, Reggie was on Nav/Com, and the thing that was most disappointing, Traylor was in the seat Brandon coveted. There was only one remaining open seat so Brandon walked over and sat down without incident.

The captain's chair was firm, offering excellent support and comfort. It was the type of chair you could spend a whole day in without becoming tired or restless. Brandon looked at the two armrests. The left one had a small Shana built into it, and the right one had a flat keypad positioned at the front. He started pressing the buttons, but nothing happened.

"The power's off Sparks. The simulation will start soon," said Section Chief Ackerman, who had walked up behind him. He continued to the front of the room, Shana in hand and began twirling his mustache. "So, everyone's done this before right? I know this simulation room is different from the one's you've used in the past, considering that the bridge on this ship is different from bridge's on other ships, but you should get the hang of it shortly. We all know how much you kids like to get scores for the missions, so every mission will be scored out of 100 percent. The more mistakes, the lower your percentage. All right, let's begin." Brandon raised his hand. "What is it Sparks?"

"I've never done this before."

"Oh, that's right, you're a terrestrial. All right, I'll give you a quick lesson."

"Come on Sparks, you're ruining it for the rest of us," said Frank.

"Quiet Drek, or you won't play at all," said Section Chief Ackerman with a scowl. Frank gave a disgruntled look but did not say another word. "All right Sparks, you had to pick the captain's chair didn't you?" Section Chief Ackerman let out a big sigh.

"Well, I wanted the pilot's seat but it was already taken."

"Donovan, will you switch seats with Sparks?"

"No thanks, Section Chief Ackerman. I was here first and I want to be pilot." Traylor's eyes opened wide and she looked very intimidated. "I'm staying as far away from the captain's chair as possible!"

So her name is Traylor Donovan, thought Brandon to himself.

"What about you Thacker?"

"Not me. Nav/Com is what I'm good at. Sorry Brandon."

"And you, Drek? You want to show your mettle in the captain's seat?"

"No way! I just want to blow stuff up."

"Of course," said Section Chief Ackerman, rolling his eyes. "I guess you're stuck here Sparks."

"Why is everyone so against being captain? Isn't it the highest rank?"

Section Chief Ackerman leaned in close to Brandon so that they could talk one on one. "It is Sparks, but with that high rank comes enormous responsibility. You see Sparks, you're now in charge of everything that goes on in the bridge. You have to give all the orders to the people beneath you. If something goes wrong, the blame rests squarely on your shoulders. It's tough being captain. That's probably why there's only one per ship. I know I wouldn't want the job." A nervous look came on Brandon's face. "Don't worry Sparks, how bad can you be? You've flown simulations before, right?" Brandon nodded. "Good. I'm sure you'll be just fine." Section Chief Ackerman took a step back and addressed the room. "All right people, these are the positions you will have for the next month so get used to them. Don't worry Sparks, you're only going to have to be captain for a month and then someone else gets the job. OK, here is your first mission. The objective is to take off from the surface of the planet, seek out and destroy the space debris, and then land on the same location you took off from. Good luck. Remember that in here you will address each other by either rank, or rank and last name. Lieutenant Donovan, Lieutenant Thacker, Lieutenant Drek, and Captain Sparks. Any deviation from this will bring down your score."

Section Chief Ackerman walked out and moments later the room powered up. The huge monitor at the front of the room went from white to a view of the tarmac they were "sitting on" and a bright cloudless blue sky. In the distance sat a large range of snow-capped mountains that reminded Brandon of a trip he once took to Colorado with his parents. Everyone's control consoles lit up, and the overhead lights dimmed. Brandon got very excited. The mission was about to begin.

A male voice came on over the speakers usually used by the ship's computer. "*Hidden Sun*, *Hidden Sun*, this is mission control … do you read me?" Brandon sat in his chair looking at the armrests, not knowing what to do. He looked over at Reggie, who had been waving his arms trying to get his attention since the message was first heard. He mouthed the word "answer" very slowly, but Brandon just shrugged his shoulders, not understanding him. There was a pause.

"Answer him, dummy!" shouted Frank from behind. This made Brandon sit up straight.

"*Hidden Sun*, do you read me?" said the voice again.

"We read you," said Brandon, not sure of exactly how to respond.

"*Hidden Sun*, do you read me?" repeated the voice, sounding more desperate.

"Aww man, you've got to press the button on your chair if you want to speak to him. Can we get a new captain?"

"Be quiet Frank. He's trying," said Traylor. Brandon was very surprised she came to his defense. It was clear to all that she liked Frank just about as much as he did.

Brandon looked at the keypad on his right armrest and saw a button marked "CALL," which he pressed. "This is the *Hidden Sun*."

"Good to hear from you *Hidden Sun*. Thought we'd lost you for a minute. You are clear for takeoff. Mission control out."

"*Hidden Sun*, preparing for takeoff. Out." Out of the corner of his left eye, Brandon could see Reggie flailing his arms, trying to get his attention again. He realized what Reggie was going to say before he even had a chance.

"Traylor, take us up." As the 'p' in 'up' was leaving his lips, he realized the mistake he had made. "I mean, Lieutenant Donovan, take us up." Brandon hoped that didn't cost them any points.

"Yes Captain."

Brandon watched as Traylor pushed buttons and took the control stick in her hand. Beneath her feet were two pedals, one that made the ship speed up, and to the left, another that was the brake. It was set up similarly to a car. The bridge shook a bit as the *Hidden Sun* "took off." The view on the screen changed from bright blue sky to a mixture of blue, black, and white. They had just entered the planet's atmosphere.

"WARNING, WARNING, ship is reaching maximum hull temperature! Breach imminent!" screamed the ship's computer. Brandon couldn't believe that he had forgotten that the ship had to be on a certain angle to leave a planet's atmosphere, or else it would burn up. He was surprised everyone else had as well. He wondered if they could be as nervous as he was or were they just a bit rusty?

"Lieutenant Thacker, we need the correct angle to leave this planet's atmosphere," said Brandon. Reggie began ferociously pushing the buttons on his console. The Bridge started rumbling and vibrating fiercely.

"WARNING, WARNING, HULL BREACH IN 5 ... 4 ...!"

"Hurry up Thacker, or we're all gonna die!" shouted Frank.

"3 ... 2 ..."

"Forty-eight degrees. The ship has to be on a forty-eight degree angle!" screamed Reggie. Brandon held his breath. Traylor entered the information into her console and suddenly there was silence. The rumbling had stopped. Brandon looked at the screen and saw that the ship had left the atmosphere, still in one piece. He leaned back in his seat and exhaled. They had made it out by a fraction of a second and were now in open space, surrounded by the blackness of nothing, and the brightness of a thousand scattered stars.

"Wow, that was close," said Brandon. "Reggie, I mean Lieutenant Thacker, please scan for the debris we're supposed to be looking for and set a course."

"Yes Captain."

"I thought we were goners for sure. That would have been the shortest mission ever! You were lucky Sparks," said Frank.

Brandon just ignored the boy's comments and fired back with an order. "Lieutenant Drek, arm weapons."

"Finally, some action. It's time to blow stuff up!" Frank pushed the buttons on his console and armed the weapons systems. For the next few minutes there was nothing to do but wait until they were in range of the debris. Brandon took a deep breath and started to feel calmer about his first mission. He relaxed in the captain's chair, continued the breathing and watched the big screen for anything that he would consider unusual.

Brandon loved the look of space, the contrast between dark and light. He knew that before him was just another man-made version of space on a video screen, just like on his ceiling on Earth. It was quite different from what he saw when he looked out the window in room 1034, but altogether too alluring to pass off as fake or insignificant. Just as Brandon had finally relaxed, the action picked up.

"Asteroid coming in from the left side of the ship!" screamed Reggie, which made Brandon jump a bit. "It's on a collision course with us. We've got to turn!"

"Lieutenant Donovan, turn the ship," said Brandon.

"Yes Capt …" Traylor's answer was cut off by a violent shake of the bridge. Brandon looked around the room. Reggie had been thrown to the floor and was beginning to climb back up.

"We've been hit!" said Reggie, now standing and pushing buttons on his control console. "We've taken some structural damage."

"Our shields were off," said Frank, "not that they would have helped much in a collision."

"Oh, man. I can't believe I forgot the shields! Lieutenant Drek, arm the shields."

"Can't you do anything right Sparks? Our score's gonna be like a thirty or something," replied Frank with an angry tone to his voice. He pressed a few buttons on his control console and the shields were armed.

"I'm trying. Give me a break. Reggie, I mean Lieutenant Thacker, how significant is the damage to the ship?"

"Fortunately, not that bad. It felt worse then it was. I have closed off all the areas that were effected by the asteroid. The damage is contained."

"Great. Please give Lieutenant Donovan the coordinates for the debris."

"Yes, captain."

After a few seconds, Traylor received the data and set a course for the debris. As they moved closer, Brandon could see exactly what the debris was, a small mass of rock, and approximately thirty feet wide.

When they were within one thousand feet of the rock, under orders from Brandon, the ship came to a standstill.

"We are within firing range, captain," said Reggie.

"Lieutenant Drek, fire at will and destroy the entire rock. I don't want a section to break off and come at us like that asteroid." For the first time, Brandon saw a smile come over Frank Drek's face. He fired once with three laser cannons at exactly the same time and all four crew members watched the rock explode into a fine powder. Brandon was surprised at Frank's efficiency, even though he knew that Frank's interests lied in destroying things. "Excellent job Lieutenant Drek."

"Just a walk in park. At least we'll get credit for something," said Frank, the smile having vanished from his face.

"Lieutenant Donovan, turn this ship around and let's head back to the planet," said Brandon, and that's exactly what they did. Fortunately, no asteroids came at them, and Frank managed to keep quiet for the few minutes it took to get within range of the planet they left from. This time, Brandon did not forget about getting the information from Reggie on entering the atmosphere. Traylor flew the ship smoothly over the snow capped mountain range, and made a soft landing on the hard ground.

The lights in the room became brighter and the power to the consoles, the captain's chair, and the big screen went off. After a few long moments, Section Chief Ackerman walked in through the back right door and up to the front of the room. He began twirling his mustache.

"Not bad for your first run, but not very good either. Let me see here," he said as he looked down at his Shana. "Out of 100 percent you earned a forty-seven."

"A forty-seven?" said Frank, dragging out the word forty-seven.

"You lost points for numerous reasons. Forgetting to call each other by rank, barely getting through the atmosphere and most of all when that asteroid hit you." Section Chief Ackerman looked at Reggie. "You should have seen it on your sensors," then at Frank, "you should have put your shields up and either destroyed it," then at Traylor, "or avoided it." Lastly, he looked at Brandon. "You've got to protect yourselves. That's your number one responsibility, so always remember to use your assets."

"Can we get a new captain? We'll never do well with Sparks at the helm," said Frank.

"Leave him alone Drek," said Reggie. "At least he's got the guts to be Captain, unlike you."

"Shut up Thacker."

"All right boys, enough! Be quiet and let me finish. The real reason you lost so many points was because of a lack of communication. You've got to be able to talk to each other to be successful. That means all of you have got to get along and while you *all* should work on this while you're away from the simulator, unfortunately for Sparks, the blame lies squarely on the captain. You're all dismissed except for you Sparks. Stay behind please."

"I'll wait for you outside," said Reggie following Frank and Traylor out of the room.

"Listen Sparks, I know this was your first time but you've got to do a better job issuing orders to your crew and you *must* remember to call them by their rank or rank and last name."

"I know," said Brandon nodding his head.

"It's going to take time to become a successful Captain and a month isn't a very long time."

"I know. I just want my crew to do well and score high."

"I know you do, everyone does, but remember, as much as the other kids might tell you, this is *not* about winning and losing. It's about surviving tough situations and coming out with your head still on your shoulders. You'll do better next time. Thacker is waiting for you."

Brandon turned around and saw Reggie peeking through the glass window in the door. He walked out of the room feeling down.

"So what did he say?" said Reggie.

"That I will get better with time."

"You will, don't worry about it. We'll score higher next time."

"You think?"

"Well, we can't get much worse."

"Very funny," said Brandon, smiling a little.

"I know what will cheer you up. Let's go swimming."

"Swimming? There's a swimming pool on the ship?"

"Well, sort of," said Reggie, shrugging his shoulders.

Brandon and Reggie made a dash down the hallway and into an elevator that was just vacated by a woman with two silver stars on her chest. The boys climbed in and Reggie said, "Deck 11." The elevator zoomed upward and stopped after seven stories.

"Where are we going?"

"To the swimming room. It's just around the corner."

"Wait a minute," said Brandon, "I don't have a bathing suit."

"That's OK, neither do I? You won't need one."

"Then how are we gonna go swimming? What? Are we gonna jump in with our clothes on?" said Brandon sarcastically.

"Well … yeah," answered his friend.

Reggie opened the door to the swim room. All of the lights were on but no one was there. The swim room was long and rectangular. The walls, ceiling, and floor displayed underwater video footage that was so crisp—it was as if they were under the sea. Schools of small fish swam by as well as the occasional shark. There were also creatures Brandon had never seen before. If Reggie had not tapped him on the shoulder, Brandon would not have noticed the long concave oval in the center of the room which looked a lot like a swimming pool, except for the fact that there was no water inside. Not a single drop. The only thing blue about it was the tile that lined the entire inside. On the opposite end of the room was a diving board, which sat twenty feet in the air. Reggie bent down and stuck his hand into the oval. "Let's go in. The temperature's just right."

"Very funny."

"Are you ready?" asked Reggie in a very serious tone.

"Ready for what? There's no water."

"Well of course there's no water!" Brandon was as confused as he had ever been in his entire life. Reggie just smiled and said, "Jump in."

"No way!" Reggie gave him a little nudge, but Brandon resisted.

"OK, then I'll jump in."

"No don't!" said Brandon, not wanting his friend to break his legs when he hit the bottom of the pool. He grabbed his shoulders and pulled him away from the edge.

"You know what Brandon, you're right. What was I thinking?"

"So you're not going to jump?"

"Nope. I'm gonna dive." Before Brandon could say another word, Reggie had ran to the diving board and started climbing to the top."

"Wait, wait!" screamed Brandon, but Reggie wouldn't listen. He had gotten to the top and was standing at the back of the board.

"Here goes nothing!" he shouted and ran toward the edge.

"No, don't do it!" screamed Brandon but Reggie had already reached the front of the diving board. He did a small hop on the end of the board and sprung himself high into the air and out over the emptiness below. Reggie extended his hands in front of him and was now totally vertical, his small body speeding towards the giant oval. "No!" screamed Brandon again.

When Reggie broke what would have been the surface of the water, his speed slowed down and he did a little flip. To Brandon's amazement, his friend was not only still alive, but he was floating in thin air, and coming towards him! When Reggie reached the edge of the pool, he climbed out and stood up next to his friend.

"Wanna try?" he said. Brandon was speechless. He didn't know what to say. "It's a gravity pool. The gravity is set to resemble that of water. It's exactly like swimming in water but you don't get wet and you don't have any breathing problems. It's a lot of fun."

"Wow," was the only word Brandon could think to use.

"Cool huh?"

"But ... but how did you know it was on?"

"Oh, I felt inside before I jumped. Give it a try."

CHAPTER NINE

Brandon stepped up to the edge and gulped. He looked at Reggie who was urging him to go, and took a leap of faith. As he soared through the air, his stomach felt like it rushed up the entire length of his body and out through the top of his head. When he hit the gravity surface of the pool, his body slowed down as if he had jumped into water. Reggie was right. It felt just like swimming in a pool. He looked around and saw that he was floating in mid air, bobbing up and down, using his arms to "stay afloat."

The doors swung open and in raced eight other kids. They all jumped into the gravity pool without a second thought and began swimming about. With a great smile, Reggie jumped back in and did the backstroke. To Brandon, it seemed like magic. Some kids were swimming on the surface of the pool and others were swimming underneath them. Brandon did a back flip and then pushed his feet off the wall. It was as if he was flying and he loved it. He sailed though thin air, pushing off the bottom of the pool to keep his momentum going, weaving his way over and under and around all the other kids who were laughing and having a great time.

When Brandon had finally spent all of his energy and needed a break, he surfaced and held onto the wall of the gravity pool. Someone snuck up behind him, put their hands over his eyes and said, "Guess who?" It was a voice Brandon recognized right away.

"Traylor," said Brandon. The hands were taken away to reveal Traylor Donovan floating next to him.

"What's up Sparks? First time in a gravity pool?"

"Yeah. I like it a lot. It's a lot more fun than swimming in water."

"Yup, except for the splashing. I like to splash people." Brandon smiled. "Hey, I'll race you to the other side. Ready … go!" Before Brandon could get a word in, Traylor was swimming as hard as she could. He followed, but she was too quick and beat him by two body lengths. "Too slow Sparks," she said, smiling and breathing heavily. She gave him a hard shove on the shoulder. "Don't feel too bad though, there's not a boy in here that could beat me at swimming, or any other sport for that matter."

Brandon nodded as he tried to catch his breath. Traylor continued to talk. "We didn't do so well tonight. Hopefully we'll get better for next time. Do you want to get together some time and practice?"

"No he does not," said Reggie, who had darted over from across the pool and ended up between the two kids. "Come on Brandon, let's go."

"But ..." began Brandon, but Reggie had already grabbed him by the shirt and pulled him away toward the other side of the pool.

"That wasn't nice," said Brandon, being towed across the pool like a broken boat.

"Trust me, I saved you a horrible experience. Traylor Donovan is not a nice person."

"Shouldn't I at least give her a chance."?

"Nope. Better to be safe then sorry," said Reggie as the two boys reached the lip of the pool.

As happened frequently, Charlie popped into Brandon's mind and he remembered what he had said about avoiding danger, but surely, Traylor Donovan could not have been what he meant. "OK, I'll try and stay away."

"Good decision. Let's get out of here." The two boys climbed out of the gravity pool and made their way back to room 1034.

CHAPTER TEN

THE FIRST MONTH

Brandon and Reggie slowly opened the door to room 1034 and tiptoed inside, trying their best not to wake up Carlos. The only light in the room came from the stars outside. They seemed to zip by as the *Hidden Sun* made its way through space. "I'm beat," whispered Reggie. He stretched out his arms while letting out a big yawn and laid down in his bed. "I'm going to sleep. Night."

"Night Reggie," whispered Brandon. "Hey, aren't you going to change into your pajamas?" he said, but his friend did not hear him. He was already fast asleep and let out his first great snore of the evening—actually, it sounded more like a snort. Brandon shrugged his shoulders and changed into his pajamas. After going to the bathroom, he climbed up and laid down in his bed. He hit the two top buttons on his watch and put the ear piece in his ear. "Charlie, come in Charlie," he whispered, knowing that if his friend was listening he could hear him. "Come in Charlie," he repeated but there was no reply. Brandon took the ear piece out and placed it back inside the watch. He turned on his side and stared at the wall. It had only been a day since he had spoken with Charlie, but it felt like an eternity.

Brandon tried to fall asleep but couldn't. He turned from one side to the other, trying to get comfortable. When the pillow became too warm from his head being in the same place, he flipped it over. He had done this twice before he rolled over onto his back and looked up at the white ceiling. He missed the Galaxy Program, and he missed Charlie. He tried to put it out of his mind and instead thought about the questions he wanted answered. Why is Dr. Ramirez keeping his work so secret? Does the *Hidden Sun* really have no weapons or defense? What is in the room at the center of the ship? What is the *Hidden Sun's* true purpose? Who is the whispery voice that called on his watch earlier this evening? Is Traylor Donovan as bad as Reggie says? She doesn't seem so bad to me, he thought. In the half-hour it took for him to finally fall asleep he came no closer to answering any of these questions.

◆   ◆   ◆

Brandon awoke three hours later because something was shaking his leg. He sat up quickly and was startled to see someone sitting Indian style at the opposite end of his bed. "Hello Brandon," said Sly, his pale face emerging from shadow and his voice as scratchy as the night before.

"Don't do that!" said Brandon, whispering and yelling at the same time. "You scared me half to death. How did you get up on my bed?"

"I just climbed up."

"But how did you get up here without waking up my roommates and especially, me?"

"When you spend your whole day crawling through ventilation shafts and sneaking around a starship, it's not that hard to climb onto a bed in an unlocked room."

Brandon nodded his head. "Point taken."

"Is there somewhere we can go without having to whisper?"

Brandon knew the perfect place. He climbed down from the bed as carefully as possible so as not to wake his roommates. Sly just jumped down and when his feet hit the floor, they didn't make a sound. This took Brandon by surprise. The floor was at least six feet beneath the top bunk and certainly a landing from that height would result in some sort of sound. Having just woken up and still being in a sleepy haze, Brandon thought his mind must have been playing tricks on him, so he just gave his head a shake and left it at that. He motioned for Sly to enter one of the study rooms and followed him inside, closing the door behind him. Sly unfolded and sat down on the second chair as Brandon placed himself in the leather one. "This room is soundproof, we can talk normally in here. Computer, a dim light please." A soft light came on and the two boys could now see each other's faces more clearly. "What are you doing here?" said Brandon.

"I told you I would stop by tonight."

"I know, but I didn't think it would be at," Brandon paused to look at his watch, "2:38 in the morning!"

"Sorry. It was the earliest I could get here. I spent the entire day trying to get familiar with the ship but the ventilation shafts are like mazes. My plan was to make it to the center of the ship and back but I just couldn't do it. I couldn't find a way to the center of the ship. It's almost as if it was built this way on purpose. Do you know what's there?"

"Actually, I was looking at a map of the ship with my friend Reggie, he's the one who sleeps below me."

"The snorer?"

"Yeah," smiled Brandon, "the computer won't let us see inside the big room at the center of the ship."

"Really?" said Sly.

"Yeah. There's something strange about the *Hidden Sun*. It seems, well, different from other starships. When I tried to get information about it on the Galactic Internet, I came up empty-handed. There was no mention of it at all."

"Well, then I picked the right ship to stowaway on."

"Really? How come?"

"Because we've got ourselves a bit of a mystery."

"Yes we do," said Brandon with a smile.

Brandon proceeded to give Sly most of his knowledge, as well as the questions he had about the *Hidden Sun*, but did not mention Charlie, or the man with the whispery voice. He did tell him about the doctor hiding his work, as well as Rhino-37. After soaking-up all the information, and getting no closer to any solutions, the two boys agreed to change the subject and turned their attention to other matters. They discussed their likes and dislikes, as kids tend to do. Brandon spoke at length about his passion for flying and his desire to be a pilot. He told him about the simulations he had played with his best friend Charlie, but left out that Charlie was a computer. Sly told Brandon about his love of sports and how he wanted to be a professional baseball player when he was old enough. The two talked and laughed in the small soundproof room for the next two hours before Brandon got so tired, he had to go to sleep. Sly looked as fresh as if it had been the middle of the day.

"If you're tired, you can sleep in the empty bed above Carlos if you like," offered Brandon.

"That's OK. I've found a comfortable place for myself in one of the shafts. I've scrounged up supplies from all over the ship. I'll try and find a way to the center of the ship tomorrow."

"Sounds good. Hey, I almost forgot. Were you in the vents above the medical center this morning?" asked Brandon.

"I sure was 'Bradenton.'" Brandon immediately burst out laughing. It was a good thing they were still in the soundproof study room because he could not stop and he didn't want to wake his sleeping roommates.

After the laughter finally subsided, Brandon said, "Computer, please turn off the light." The study room went black and Brandon quietly opened the door. The two boys walked outside to find Reggie snoring like it's an Olympic Event. They both smiled and then in silence, Sly snuck out of the room. Brandon climbed up into his bed and covered himself with a blanket. With a smile on his face, his head sunk into his soft pillows. Within thirty seconds, he was fast asleep.

◆　　　◆　　　◆

Over the next month, Brandon went to work every morning at the medical center. He tried to get Dr. Ramirez to share his work with him, while not revealing that he knew the doctor was working on Rhino-37, but instead, Dr. Ramirez just gave him more lollipops and more boring work to do. At dinner, his parents would discuss their work with him, but there wasn't much to tell. They had tried thousands of plant combinations and weren't getting any closer to finding something that made the sample of blood Mr. Sparks had received from Captain Smoke, either heal or die. Nothing seemed to make the blood produce more cells, and it was remarkably resilient to poisons and toxins.

Brandon spent his evenings in the simulator as captain and slowly improved. On his second mission, taking the ship in and out of light-speed, his team scored 53 percent, and on the next mission, maneuvering through a small minefield, they received a 58 percent. Although not great scores compared to the kids in the other simulators on deck 18, it was a big improvement from his original score of 47 percent. He was learning to work within the system. His communication skills with his crew members improved and he was no longer docked for forgetting to call someone by their rank, or rank and last name. By the end of his fourth mission, which involved docking the ship (a task more difficult then it sounds), Brandon's score was in the mid-sixties. His team was gaining in the rankings and Frank was dishing out fewer insults. Not much fewer, but fewer all the same.

On the last simulation mission of the month, Brandon's skills had grown by leaps and bounds. All of the dogfight simulations he had had with Charlie back on Earth really paid off as the mission involved both a frontal and rear attack from an enemy. Reggie, Traylor, and Frank all performed extremely well, executing Brandon's orders, which lead to the two enemy ships destroying each other. The team and Section Chief Ackerman were all shocked when he announced they scored an 85 percent, a huge difference from the previous night, and two small percentage points ahead of everyone else. Frank was upset that he wasn't the one who blew up the two ships, but coming in first was just sweet enough to keep him quiet.

While in the simulator, Brandon kept a close watch on Traylor's piloting skills, which he had to admit were impressive. She had quick hands and a good eye. Every time they flew a mission she improved at not only handling the *Hidden Sun*, but also making smart decisions. Brandon was anxious for the month to end so that he could give up the captain's chair and find out if he could fly the *Hidden Sun* as well as she could. At the same time, he had grown to enjoy being the captain as it was the only position he had ever had. Somewhere, deep down, he knew that he would miss it.

After the simulations, Brandon, Reggie, and Carlos, who was performing the same job as Reggie in a simulator down the hall, would go swimming. Brandon really loved the feeling he got from jumping off the high diving board into nothingness. Every time he jumped, his stomach felt like it was going to burst out of the top of his head. He never could get over seeing all the kids floating in mid-air, some zooming from one end of the pool to the next, and others doing back flips. Brandon had found a place where he could forget about all his problems and just relax and have a good time.

Late at night, after Reggie and Carlos had fallen asleep, Brandon would meet Sly in different locations around the *Hidden Sun*, but usually in room 1034. They would play card games and talk about anything and everything they could think of. Sometimes they would go into one of the study rooms and play games on the computer. Brandon taught Sly how to fly some of the starships and he was a natural. He had never seen such good eye-hand coordination. Sly enjoyed going head to head with enemy fighters and possessed an uncanny ability to target and blow them up, even with limited weapons. Brandon liked Reggie and Carlos a lot, but Sly quickly became his closest friend on board the Hidden Sun.

Every night after he and Sly had said goodnight, Brandon would climb into bed and try to contact Charlie. He would put the ear piece in his ear and say, "Come in Charlie," but Charlie never answered.

Every night, Brandon went to sleep feeling a little bit empty. He missed his best friend and feared something terrible had happened.

◆   ◆   ◆

After his final day of working in the medical center, Brandon walked into room 1034 to find Reggie and Carlos discussing Nav/Com tactics. "Hey guys."

"Hey Brandon," said Reggie.

"What's going on?" said Carlos.

"Oh, nothing much."

"Did you see Section Chief Ackerman in the hallway?" said Reggie.

"Yeah, he just went into the room next door. Are you psyched to get new jobs?"

"Definitely! Walking the hallways with Private Devlin for the past month has been hell! The man must have steel feet. I've just had to pop another blister."

"Ew, gross," said Carlos and Brandon at the same time. They looked at each other and made faces.

"I don't have nasty blisters like Reggie, but I'm done with the bridge for good!" said Carlos.

"Really?" said Brandon. "The bridge looks like a lot of fun."

"I just can't stop thinking that I'm gonna be up there watching everyone do their jobs and all of a sudden, the ship's gonna get attacked by some weird looking alien or something!" Brandon and Reggie started to laugh. "I'm serious guys. It could happen. It could!"

"Come on Carlos, this is an aid ship. Who's going to attack an aid ship? We're perfectly safe," said Reggie.

"Are you sure?" said Carlos. At that moment, a hand came down on the boy's right shoulder. Brandon's head jerked as he watched Carlos jump and let out a frightful scream. When his feet hit the floor he started to run, but Brandon grabbed a hold of him and turned him around.

"A bit jumpy today, are we Santiago?" said Section Chief Ackerman, Shana in hand. Carlos put his hand over his heart, took a deep breath and started to laugh. Brandon and Reggie joined in. "Enough boys. Here are your assignments for the following month. Thacker, you will be working in the cafeteria, Santiago, you will be in the medical center."

"Oh, thank you," said Carlos, much relieved.

"Sparks, you will be assisting Lieutenant Bunts in engineering. Remember boys, there are no simulations tonight, but tomorrow starts a new round and you all know that that means new positions. So try and get there early. Especially you, Sparks. We all know how badly you want to be Pilot."

"Thanks Section Chief Ackerman," said Brandon. "We will."

"Very good then." Section Chief Ackerman twirled his mustache with his free hand and walked out of the room.

◆   ◆   ◆

Brandon rushed down to deck 6 and into room 631 where his parents were waiting for him. "Hey kiddo, a little late aren't we?" said Mr. Sparks.

"Hi mom, hi dad. Sorry about that. Section Chief Ackerman was giving us our new assignments."

Vanessa Sparks kissed her son on the cheek. "That's nice dear. Where are you working next?"

Brandon sat down at the dinner table next to his father. "In the engineering room with Lieutenant Bunts."

"Wow, the head of Engineering! That should be a good learning experience, don't you think?"

"Definitely," said Mrs. Sparks as she brought over two plates and set them down in front of Brandon and his father. They each had one chicken cutlet, and sides of coleslaw, and corn nibblets. Brandon was very fond of chicken cutlets. His mom liked to serve them at least once a week and she never forgot that he liked his with tartar sauce. She went to the refrigerator and opened the door. "Honey, we need to have this refrigerator leveled. It's really wobbly."

"I know," said Matthew Sparks. "Someone's going to come by tomorrow evening to fix it."

"Good." Vanessa Sparks grabbed a pitcher of water out of the fridge, and closed the door. She grabbed a third plate from the counter and placed it on the table in front of her seat and the pitcher of water in the center of the table. "I hear Lieutenant Bunts is extremely good at what he does. Have you met him Matt?" she said as she sat down.

"No I haven't, but I've only heard good things about him. They say he's a technical wizard and can fix just about anything. You'll learn a lot from him Brandon."

"I hope so. Do you think he'll take me to see the engines?"

"I don't see why not," said Mr. Sparks. "I'm sure you'll get a chance to see a lot of things with Lieutenant Bunts."

Over the next half-hour, the Sparks family ate their dinner. When he was through, Brandon cleaned off his plate in the sink and put it in the dishwasher. He returned to the table and sat down as his father was still eating. "Hey mom, when are we going to land on the first planet? I mean to give aid and stuff."

"I'm not sure. Why don't you go over to the desk and ask the ship's computer." Brandon got up from the chair he had just sat down in and walked over to the desk in the far corner of the room.

"Computer, what is the first planet we will be giving aid to?"

"Wren," said the ship's computer. The video wall came on and displayed a blue and green planet, which looked similar to Earth. Listed to the right were population figures, atmospheric conditions, and other abbreviations that Brandon did not understand or find interesting.

"How long until we reach Wren?"

"At our current velocity, twenty-one hours, eighteen minutes, and fifty-one seconds."

"That's tomorrow afternoon. Thanks," said Brandon as he walked back to the dinner table. "We're going to be landing on our first planet tomorrow afternoon."

"Really?" said his father. "That's strange. No one told me it was going to happen so soon. I guess working in that dense forest all day makes a person miss a bit of information here and there. Not a problem."

Brandon was excited. He had never been on another planet. "I wonder what the people look like," he said.

"I'm sure they're just like you and me," said his mother glancing up at the clock. "Look at the time, you're going to be late for simulations."

"Oh, there are no simulations tonight. They start up again tomorrow."

"Well then why don't you stay and watch a movie with us? It's your father's turn to pick." After everyone finished eating, and the table was cleared, Brandon and his parents sat down on the couch to watch a movie together. Mr. Sparks chose a comedy and the three ate popcorn and laughed, enjoying each other's company. When the movie ended, Brandon climbed to his feet. His mother hugged him and gave him a kiss on the cheek. "I love you," she said.

"I love you too, mom."

"We'll see you tomorrow, kiddo. Get a good night's sleep. You're gonna need it to keep up with Lieutenant Bunts." Brandon smiled at his dad and walked to the door. He turned around and saw that his father had put his arm around his mother's shoulder, and she around his waist. He waved to them and they waved back with smiles on their faces. Brandon walked out the door and returned to room 1034.

Brandon and Sly had agreed not to meet that night for fear that since there were no simulations, the kids might do something less strenuous and stay up later. Brandon was surprised that most of the children stayed in their rooms and took this opportunity to relax.

Brandon spent two hours playing games in one of the study rooms with Reggie. By the time they were finished, he was dead tired. Sleepiness had suddenly come over him and he longed for his warm blankets and big pillows. He climbed into bed and put his head down. He realized he had not tried to call Charlie yet, so he did just that, but there was no answer. Brandon, sad and troubled as the night before, closed his eyes and fell asleep with the ear piece still sitting comfortably in his ear.

CHAPTER ELEVEN

THE DAY THE HIDDEN SUN DIED

After eating breakfast, Brandon said goodbye to Reggie and Carlos and made his way to the elevator bay, where he bumped into Traylor Donovan. "Hey Sparks," she said and gave him a little shove on the shoulder. Brandon noticed that she always called him by his last name, except when he was her captain and he her pilot.

"Hey Traylor," he said while pushing the elevator down button.

"So, what did you think of my flying in the last mission? Best flying you've ever seen, wasn't it?"

Traylor was being cocky and Brandon wasn't about to let her get away with it. "It was … not bad. I've seen worse," he said, even though he thought her flying two nights ago was brilliant. Her timing was perfect and she was clutch under pressure.

"You've seen worse? Bet you couldn't do any better!" she said, coming closer and giving his shoulder another shove. Brandon took a step away from her just as the elevator arrived, and stepped inside. Traylor followed.

"Deck 7," said Brandon.

"Deck 8," said Traylor and the elevator began to move. "Are you still trying to avoid me?" she asked, making sure that her red hair was pulled back in a tight ponytail.

"Avoid you? No, I'm not trying to avoid you. Just keeping my distance."

Traylor started to get upset. "You shouldn't listen to Reggie all the time Sparks. I'm a pretty good person you know. The soup thing was an accident. I swear! Can't we be friends?"

"I think you're nice, but Reggie's one of my best friends," said Brandon as the elevator doors opened on deck 8. Traylor let out a grumble and gave Brandon a good shove with both hands, causing him to slam into the elevator wall, shoulder first. After regaining his composure, he watched Traylor storm down the hallway. As the elevator doors closed, Brandon felt his shoulder to see if it was hurt. By the time he realized that no damage had been done, the doors had opened on deck 7.

As he walked down the hallway, Brandon knew that he had said the wrong thing to Traylor and decided to apologize to her the next time he saw her. A door marked "ENGINEERING" was straight ahead and he made his way inside.

Lieutenant Roy Bunts was in his early fifties with medium length salt and pepper hair. His forearms were large and his fingers were thick and beaten up from years of fixing things. His most striking feature were his blue eyes, which stood out like beams of light. He had three silver stars pinned to his uniform. Brandon walked over and introduced himself.

"Good to meet you Sparks. Are you ready for a grueling day of hard labor and heavy lifting?" asked Lieutenant Bunts.

Brandon responded with, "Um?"

"I'm just kidding, but we are going to have a full day. If you have any questions, let me know. You'll never learn a thing if you don't. Follow me." The engineering room was different than Brandon had imagined. It was small, with only two people sitting in front of a huge computer console, the wall in front of them was divided into fifty video rectangles. "Now, this is where we monitor all of the electrical components of the ship. If something goes down, this here will tell us."

"Cool. How exact is it?"

"Well, let me put it to you this way. If a single pixel on one of the video walls goes out in your room, we'll know about it. Come on, let's go." Brandon followed Lieutenant Bunts into a private elevator in the back of the room. After the doors shut, they were whisked down to deck 20. "This is the engine room so watch yourself. There's a lot of possibility for injury down here." The engine room was just the opposite of the engineering room. It was gigantic. Brandon could see all four engines of the Hidden Sun and they were immense. They rose twenty stories to the top of the ship. He followed Lieutenant Bunts to engine three, where two people were using powerful blowtorches, and one had opened a panel and was cutting a wire. "How's engine three coming along?" shouted Lieutenant Bunts over the noise of the blowtorches.

"Slowly sir, slowly," screamed the Private working with the wires. Brandon noticed that he had only one Silver Star on his chest.

"How long till she's 100 percent?"

"I'd say another hour or so. No worries."

"Keep up the good work." Lieutenant Bunts gave the private the thumbs up and walked to a console to speak with another private. Brandon watched the men with the blowtorches for a little while and then turned to look around the room. He remembered the schematic of the ship he saw with Reggie and that next to the engine room, there was a room the ship's computer would not let him see. He was now facing the door to that room and started walking towards it. He casually looked around and saw that no one was paying attention to him so he reached out his hand to open the door. Brandon tried to turn the knob, but it was locked. Suddenly, Lieutenant Bunts cut in front of him, blocking the door. "What are you doing over here Sparks?"

"Nothing, I was just going to see what was in this room."

"Oh, no need to see what's in there, just boring stuff. Nothing of interest. This is where they keep the cleaning supplies for the engines." Brandon knew Lieutenant Bunts was lying but at the same time, he understood that the lieutenant had probably been ordered to keep the contents of the room top secret.

"OK," said Brandon.

"I know why don't we go check on the ship's computer? She could use a look over." Lieutenant Bunts took Brandon into another elevator that led to deck 18. Brandon was familiar with this deck. He came here almost every night to play simulations, but he had never seen the ship's computer, as it was located at the opposite end of the deck. After walking a few corridors, the two came to a room marked, "SHIP'S COMPUTER." Lieutenant Bunts entered a ten-digit pass code on the number pad and the doors slid open.

Brandon followed the lieutenant into a small room that had benches on the left and right, and two black sliding doors at the opposite end. Hanging from hooks were twenty one-piece, thin, blue and white suits, in various sizes. Lieutenant Bunts pulled one down and threw it to Brandon. "Here, put this on," he said, taking a much bigger suit down for himself.

"What's this for?"

"The ship's computer room is kept very cold so this will keep you warm when you're in there." After both put on their suits, Lieutenant Bunts entered a different ten-digit code on the number pad next to the two black doors. As they slid open, light gray smoke poured out.

The ship's computer was about the size of Brandon's bedroom on Earth. There were thousands of wires and optical cables that plugged into every section of the room, making it look like a giant spider's web. "Be careful where you step." Brandon followed Lieutenant Bunts around to the other side of the computer, stepping between cables and almost tripping twice. "Computer, any problems?"

"There is a loose cable in section F17J, Lieutenant. Brandon Sparks is in this room."

"I know, Computer. He's working with me today."

"Hi, Computer. How are you?"

The ship's computer did not respond. Brandon followed Lieutenant Bunts a few feet further.

"Loose cables can be a big problem Sparks."

"How big?" asked Brandon.

"I've been on a few ships where a loose cable was all it took to make the ship's computer shut down completely."

"Really? What happened then?" Lieutenant Bunts had captured Brandon's full attention.

"Well, it was by dumb luck that I found it before the oxygen ran out. Sometimes you just get lucky Sparks."

"What happens if this computer goes down?" said Brandon, emphasizing the word 'this' as he pointed to the nerve center of the *Hidden Sun*.

"Don't even say that Sparks. It's bad luck to say something like that, and besides, it's impossible."

"Really? Impossible?"

"That's right. You see Sparks, they build ships these days with fail-safes so that the computer can never go down. There are back up generators and back ups of those generators and even back ups of those generators and their first instruction is to power the ship's computer." Lieutenant Bunts arrived at what he was looking for. "F17J. Here it is." He opened the panel marked F17J to find over two hundred cables and started checking each and every one to discover which was loose. "Computer, can I get some light in here?" Immediately, the cables were illuminated.

"So, it's totally impossible? Like 100 percent?" said Brandon, still extremely curious about the possibility of the ship's computer shutting down. The lieutenant stopped working and paused to think for a minute, going over the extensive knowledge he possessed on the subject. Brandon pushed the issue. "What if there was a freak accident or something and all of the generators didn't work and the computer shut down? Would you be able to restart it?"

"Well, that would never happen. The fail-safes are ready for each and every possibility, but, and this is as big a but as you can get; I can't say that it's 100 percent impossible. More like 99.999 percent impossible." Lieutenant Bunts continued his work. "I can't say it's totally impossible because in my time I've seen a lot of things I thought were impossible that turned out to be possible. Ah, here it is." He had found the loose cable.

"Problem corrected Lieutenant Bunts," said the ship's computer.

"Lieutenant, what about that .001 percent?"

"Well Sparks, if that .001 percent ever happened, and I pray that it never comes...." Lieutenant Bunts leaned in so that he was face to face with Brandon and continued, "there would be no way to turn it back on. Once it's off, it's off forever. It would take a small miracle to turn it back on!"

The word "forever" hit Brandon like a ton of bricks. "And that means no life support and no oxygen and that everyone on board would, would ..."

"Die. They would all die. Try not to think about it Sparks. It will never happen." Lieutenant Bunts smiled and put his hand on Brandon's shoulder to try and make him relax. It worked to some extent.

"Lieutenant Bunts," began the ship's computer, "Captain Smoke has requested your presence on the Bridge."

"Let's go," he said to Brandon.

After changing out of their cold suits, Brandon and Lieutenant Bunts walked into an elevator and headed up to the bridge. With his immediate journey to the bridge, Brandon put the possibility of the ship's computer shutting down and the impending death it would bring to the back of his mind. It was just too much to deal with and he was much more interested in the Bridge than a .001 percent chance of disaster. His worried look disappeared and was replaced with excitement as the elevator climbed to the top of the ship. "First time to the bridge?" asked Lieutenant Bunts, already knowing the answer.

"Yes."

"Well, don't get too excited. We get more action in engineering in a day then they get in a month!"

"I've just never been on the bridge of a starship before."

"In my opinion, you've seen one bridge, you've seen 'em all."

Lieutenant Bunts' downplaying of the bridge did not cause Brandon's level of excitement to drop one bit. The elevator arrived at Deck 1 and the doors opened. The two walked down a short hallway and the door to the bridge opened. Brandon walked inside and was over-whelmed by what he saw. He was told that the simulation rooms were exact replicas of the *Hidden Sun's* bridge, but there were many differ-ences. This room was less rectangular, the ceiling was higher and the monitor on the front wall was much larger. The remaining walls were silver and white, and covered in thousands of small bumps. Lieutenant Strange's Nav/Com console and the weapons and defense console were much more modern than the ones Reggie and Frank had been using. Lieutenant Whitehorse's pilot station was equally impressive, and the control stick was different. It was shaped like a "U" with two handles instead of one. Brandon was extremely eager to speak with Lieutenant Whitehorse and get some tips on flying the Hidden Sun if he indeed got to the simulations early enough to secure the pilot's seat. The crown jewel of the bridge was the captain's chair and it was more luxu-rious than any chair Brandon had ever seen. The black leather was impeccable and across the center of the backrest was stitched in big gray letters the word "SMOKE."

"Can I help you?" said a deep voice that Brandon recognized imme-diately. He was so in awe of the room that he did not realize that he had walked right up to the empty captain's chair. Brandon turned around to see Captain Smoke standing before him.

"Sorry, I was just … looking."

"Trying to take my job as captain?"

"No, I …"

"What's your name, son?"

"It's Brandon. Brandon Sparks."

"Sparks. You're Matthew and Vanessa Sparks' son?"

"Yes, sir."

"Hmm," said Captain Smoke, clearly deep in thought, when Lieu-tenant Bunts walked over.

"Hello Captain. What seems to be the problem?"

"Lieutenant Lansing is having a problem with the weapons and defense station. Can you fix it?"

"Of course Captain. Come on Sparks."

"It was nice meeting you Captain Smoke," said Brandon.

"Likewise." They shook hands and then Brandon followed Lieutenant Bunts over to the weapons and defense console where he met Lieutenant Laura Lansing. After being introduced she ignored him while Lieutenant Bunts fixed her console. Brandon didn't mind. He was busy watching the bridge crew in action, especially Captain Smoke, who was dishing out orders.

Brandon looked around the room to find which kid was lucky enough to get bridge duty. To his surprise, there was none. He figured whomever it was, was probably getting lunch or in the bathroom. Brandon took a peek at his watch, which showed that it was just after 2 PM, and he remembered that they were going to land on the planet Wren soon. He looked at the large video monitor at the front of the bridge which displayed what was in front of the ship and he was surprised to see mostly black. There were no planets at all, just stars and empty space. "Lieutenant Bunts," said Brandon, "when are we going to land on planet Wren?"

Lieutenant Bunts turned from his work and gave Brandon a funny look. "Wren? What are you talking about boy? Wren is on the other side of the galaxy." The lieutenant continued his work and Brandon was confused. Last night, the ship's computer told him that they would be landing on Wren today. Did he hear wrong? He looked around the room and wondered why a ship with no weapons or defense capabilities would need to have its weapons and defense station repaired. Why would it have a weapons and defense station at all? Obviously, there was something covert going on. Brandon's thought process was interrupted when Nav/Com Lieutenant Strange spoke from behind his console.

"Captain, I've got a fleet of twelve ships straight ahead. They just dropped out of light-speed."

"What kind of ships?" asked Captain Smoke.

"Sir, they are Ptevos."

"Ptevos? Evasive maneuvers. Shields up!"

"Sir, my console is not working. I can't put them up until Lieutenant Bunts fixes my station.

"Roy, how long until the station is fixed?" asked the Captain with a sense of urgency.

"At least five minutes," said Lieutenant Bunts.

"We need those shields up now Lieutenant Bunts!"

"I'm working on it," he said sternly, his hands moving feverishly inside the console.

The Ptevos fleet grew larger in the video monitor as they moved closer to the *Hidden Sun*. Brandon stood as still as possible and watched, clueless as to what to do.

"Sir, we are being called by the lead ship," said Lieutenant Strange.

Lieutenant Whitehorse turned around in his chair. "Captain, should I try and outrun them?"

"No, we'll have no chance with our shields down. We'll answer their call." Lieutenant Strange pushed a few buttons and onto the video screen came a creature that scared Brandon to the very core. It stood at least seven feet tall, with thick gray skin that looked as tough as steel. Its arms were short and powerful and Brandon thought its legs were as thick as tree trunks. It seemed to be wearing a thin black armor over its torso and dark pants. The creature's eyes were as black as midnight and as menacing as those of a charging bull. Its most striking feature was a large, off-white horn that stuck out just above the forehead. Brandon guessed at the base it was six inches thick and at least a foot long. In back of him, were six other creatures that Brandon could only guess belonged to the same species.

"Ah, Captain Smoke. Our paths cross again," said a deep, raspy voice. To Brandon's ears it sounded the way he imagined evil itself to sound. "I have to say that I am a bit surprised you escaped our last encounter. I was sure you perished in the explosion." The creature let out what appeared to be a small, blood-curdling chuckle.

"I'm sorry to disappoint you General Zarafat."

The Ptevos paused to take a long look at Captain Smoke. "Planning something, are you Captain? I can see it in your eyes. It will be your death."

"I doubt that General." Captain Smoke looked extremely confident and relaxed as he sat down in his chair and looked at Lieutenant Bunts, who signaled that he needed another two minutes.

"Your new ship is quite impressive. It's a shame I had to destroy your old one. What was it called again? The *Clipper?*"

"That's correct." It was plain to Brandon that Captain Smoke was trying to buy as much time as possible by conversing with the creature.

"And what's this one called? I like to know the name of the ship before I destroy it." Brandon thought he saw General Zarafat begin to smile but he couldn't be sure. He couldn't get past the blackness of his eyes.

"It's called the *Hidden Sun*, and soon you'll find out why."

"My crew tells me your shields are down, Captain. Confident, aren't we? Or maybe you're having technical problems. That's one of the difficulties with a new ship. You just never know if everything works. Let me help you find out. Fire cannon!" Brandon watched as one of General Zarafat's crew members punched a few buttons on its control console.

"They're firing!" yelled the Captain. "Bunts, where are those shields?" A single laser shot out of one of the guns on General Zarafat's ship and headed toward the *Hidden Sun*.

"Got it!" exclaimed Lieutenant Bunts.

Immediately, Lieutenant Lansing pushed a few buttons on her control console. "Shields up, Captain!" she said and then the laser blast hit. She had managed to get the shields up in the nick of time. The ship shook a bit but there was no damage.

"Arm weapons!" yelled Captain Smoke. "Computer, announce code red to the entire ship."

"Yes Captain," replied the emotionless voice of the ship's computer.

"You were very lucky that time Captain Smoke, but I've got a few surprises up my sleeve."

"You know me General, I don't go down without a fight!"

"Oh, but this time you are mistaken." The transmission ended and the view screen returned to the blackness of space and General Zarafat's fleet, which was now very close. The ships were gray and black and looked like half-moons.

"Whitehorse, get us out of here," commanded the Captain. "Lansing, test or no test, arm the sun shields."

"Sun shields? What are sun shields," said Brandon, but no one heard.

"Captain, they're firing on us!" announced Lieutenant Strange.

"Weapon's charged, sir," said Lieutenant Lansing.

"Fire Lieutenant! Fire!" Before Lieutenant Lansing could fire any of the weapons at her disposal, General Zarafat had fired a thick beam which hit the Hidden Sun head on. Brandon watched as a yellow glow pierced through the front wall and shot through the crew. As it hit, Lieutenant Whitehorse was thrown back, followed by Captain Smoke, Lieutenant Strange, Lieutenant Lansing, and Lieutenant Bunts. Each was hurled hard against the back wall of the bridge. It was as if a golden tidal wave was sweeping through the entire ship. Then it reached Brandon. He was lifted high into the air and hit his head between the back wall and the ceiling. Only through pure luck did he survive the fall back to the deck of the ship. He landed on top of something soft, just as the main lights went out and the flashing red ones of the emergency backup came on. He had landed on Captain Smoke, whose forehead was covered in blood and his eyes were wide open. He wasn't moving. Brandon looked around and he didn't see anyone moving at all.

"WARNING, WARNING," said the ship's computer.

Brandon was barely conscious when he put his hand on the back of his head. He looked at it, and it was covered in blood. He tried to climb to his feet but the ship jerked violently and then the unthinkable happened. What Lieutenant Bunts had said only a short time ago was almost impossible, became possible. The ship's computer shut down. The bridge went totally black except for sparks shooting out of the Nav/Com and weapons and defense consoles. The artificial gravity went dead and Brandon rose into the air as he fell into unconsciousness. His lifeless body hung in the middle of the bridge, his arms dangling beneath him.

CHAPTER TWELVE

FROM THE DARKNESS

Everything was black. "Brandon ... wake up Brandon. You've got to wake up!" said a voice within his head. It urged him to open his eyes, and he did. His vision was blurry but he could see orange and red light amongst the darkness. "Brandon, get yourself together and wake up!" yelled the voice inside his head.

As his vision slowly grew clearer, the brilliant light, at once, transformed into fire. The weapons and defense console was burning and the flames were blazing high into the air, charring the ceiling. It was at this exact moment that Brandon realized where he was and the predicament he was in. He was floating in the middle of the bridge and all of the crew members, including Captain Smoke were hovering around him, looking quite dead.

"The Ptevos fleet attacked us," muttered Brandon. His voice sounded groggy. "General Zarafat is probably getting ready for the kill." He leaned his head back and looked at the large view screen above the pilot's console. It was off. Everything was off. Brandon felt really alone, as the body of Lieutenant Whitehorse floated by. "Is this the end?" he muttered, turning his attention back to the burning weapons and defense console. Deep down Brandon felt that all hope was lost and that there was no chance for survival. All of his senses were screaming that he did not have much longer to live, except one. It was an electric current coursing through his body to his heart, when he realized that the voice inside his head was not his own.

"Brandon, can you hear me?"

"Ch ... Charlie?"

"That's right. It's me."

"Where have you been?" asked the boy.

"No time for questions now. The *Hidden Sun* and everyone on board need your help. You've got to turn the ship's computer back on!"

The momentary revitalization Brandon got from hearing Charlie's voice after a month of silence began to wane. He knew the awful truth. "There's no way to do it. Lieutenant Bunts said it would take a small miracle to turn it back on."

"Well what do you think I am, chopped liver?" Brandon smiled. He knew that if there was a way to get the *Hidden Sun* up and running again, Charlie would know how. "I need you to locate the pilot's console and point your watch in that direction. Then, push the bottom left and top right buttons on your watch at exactly the same time. You'll have to do this quickly, the entire ship is running out of breathable air!"

Brandon flipped his body around until he was facing the pilot's seat. He did exactly as Charlie had instructed and when he pushed the buttons, a small cable, no thicker than one of the hairs on his head came out of the right side of his watch. The head of the cable looked like the mouth of a shark with jagged, pointy teeth. It hovered in the air for a moment and then darted across the bridge. With a "CHICK," it caught hold of the backrest of the pilot's chair.

"Get ready," said Charlie. Brandon, still floating from the lack of gravity, was quickly pulled across the room as the cable retracted back into his watch. When he reached the pilot's chair, he grabbed hold and secured himself in the seat. The cable released from the back of the chair and was sucked back into his watch.

"Made it."

"Good. Now press each button on your watch counter clockwise, starting with the bottom right button. Then, hold your hand out over the pilot's console." Brandon followed Charlie's instructions and pressed the bottom right button, the right center button, followed by the top right button, then the top left button, and finally the bottom left button. He extended his arm out over the console and waited. He didn't have to wait long. About two seconds later, Brandon could feel his watch start to shake. Small holes opened all over the band and hundreds of small cables sprung out like thin snakes, each the same thickness as the one which Brandon used to pull himself over to the pilot's seat. After hovering in the air for a few seconds, they all attacked the Pilot's console. Brandon watched as they bore their way inside.

Loud explosions rocked the hull of the *Hidden Sun*. The Ptevos were trying to destroy the ship. Moments later, Charlie's voice came from the overhead speakers used by the ship's computer. "Brandon, can you hear me?"

"Yes."

"Good." Brandon heard the vents on the ceiling releasing fresh oxygen. The red emergency lights on the bridge came back on and a solid stream of carbon dioxide engulfed the weapons and defense console, extinguishing the fire. "Sorry, can't turn on the regular lights. Too much damage," said Charlie. Brandon watched as the bodies of Captain Smoke, Lieutenant Whitehorse, Lieutenant Strange, and Lieutenant Lansing slowly floated to the floor of the bridge. Charlie had reactivated the ship's artificial gravity. Finally, the pilot's console powered up.

"OK. What do you need me to do?"

"Well Brandon, now that we've got power, you're going to have to fly this ship out of harms way."

"What? Me?" said Brandon in disbelief.

"Yes, you." The *Hidden Sun* began to shake. It had just been hit by successive laser blasts from two of the Ptevos ships. Brandon became very nervous.

"Why don't you do it Charlie? You've got control of the ship, just get us out of here!"

"Sorry Brandon. I can't do that. My programming doesn't allow me to be responsible for humans in life and death situations. You know that! It's up to you. You're going to have to fly this ship to safety."

"But, I can't do it," said Brandon, looking up into the air and pleading with his best friend. "I've never flown a ship before, let alone a starship, let alone one being attacked by aliens!"

"You've flown countless starships countless times against countless aliens!" said Charlie, encouraging the only person who could save his best friend.

"But those were games. This is for real!"

"Brandon, those weren't games. I never told you but they were military training programs."

"What?"

"They only looked like games. Brandon, whether you know it or not you're a military pilot, and an excellent one at that. I've been training you all your life, and for this very moment. That's why you're here. That's why you're on this ship!"

"But ..."

"No buts. I know that this is a lot to take in, especially in a situation like this, but you've got to put it out of your mind until we can get out of here. Everyone on this ship is counting on you."

Brandon heard explosions as more laser blasts impacted with the *Hidden Sun*. "But I can't be responsible for everybody on this ship. I'm only twelve years old. What if I screw up and everybody dies?"

"If you don't try, then everyone is already dead." Charlie paused as the ship was hit by another laser blast. "Brandon, you are the greatest pilot I know. I've seen you in action thousands of times, and you've always come out on top. Now grab the control stick and let's do this. It's just like one of the simulations. See what you've got at your fingertips and what your objective is. The *Hidden Sun* won't survive many more of those laser blasts."

"But, the crew is dead. I'm all alone up here."

"You're not alone. I'm here and I'm the finest crew a best friend could have. Just give me an order and I will perform it flawlessly. You've got to be Pilot *and* Captain, Brandon. Remember, I can't do things on my own. I need an order." Brandon looked long and hard at the double pronged control stick in front of him, then at his watch. The cables from the band were still pulsating and moving around. "We don't have much time. I'll get us started. Order me to bring up a visual of what's in front of the ship."

Brandon stared straight ahead for a few seconds, his mind a blur. There was so much going on and he had to focus. He concentrated as hard as he could and finally, he came to his senses. "OK," he said. "Charlie," he took a deep breath, "give me a visual of what's in front of the ship." The large view screen switched on and Brandon saw that the Ptevos fleet was way too close for comfort. The lower left corner and lower right corner of the screen were divided into smaller screens that showed what was behind the ship, acting like the side and rearview mirrors on a car.

"Brandon, the lead ship is calling us. What would you like me to do?"

"Um, I don't know."

"Hurry Brandon, we don't have much time. Remember the thousands of missions you've successfully completed back on Earth. You've been in tough situations before."

"OK." Brandon spat out the first thing that came to mind. "Let me see and hear him on our monitor but only let him hear me, and can you make my voice sound like Captain Smoke's?"

"Brilliant!" said Charlie and General Zarafat came on the screen.

"What do you mean they answered our call? They weren't supposed to answer. This is impossible! Everyone aboard that ship should be unconscious by now!" snorted General Zarafat at one of his subordinates. "Is that you Smoke? I don't know how you survived the wrath of my venomous lasers, but it is quite unfortunate. Why don't you show your ugly face? I would like to lay my eyes on you once more before I kill you and everyone aboard your ship. No matter. You'll have a quick, warrior's death."

"Only … only if you can catch me," stammered Brandon, his voice masked to sound like Captain Smoke's.

General Zarafat's eyes blazed as he laughed the most horrific laugh Brandon had ever heard. "You expect to escape from me? I highly doubt it Captain Smoke. Look around. Even you can see that the odds are heavily in my favor and your ship is about to crumble at my will!" His nostrils flared. "Destroy that ship! I want every single scrap disintegrated!" The transmission ended and the original view of the Ptevos fleet returned.

"They're getting ready to fire Brandon. I'm pretty sure it's not going to be just a single laser blast. What are we going to do?"

"I … I don't know."

"You do know," began Charlie, with more emotion in his voice than any human Brandon had ever heard. "Now come on Brandon. Save this ship!" At that moment, four of the twelve Ptevos ships fired their laser cannons at the *Hidden Sun*. "We've got incoming fire! Brandon, save this ship!" screamed Charlie.

Over the span of a single second, Brandon thought about his parents, the friends he had made on the *Hidden Sun* and all the good times he had had so far in his life. He wasn't ready for it to end. "Shields," he said and Charlie activated them just in the nick of time. Eight laser blasts shook the ship but did no further damage. With both hands, Brandon reached out and grabbed hold of the control stick. Something in his mind seemed to switch on and he was all business. "All right Charlie. Let's do this." He pushed forward on the control stick and the Hidden Sun started to move.

Brandon pushed the accelerator pedal and the *Hidden Sun* took off like a jackrabbit. He flew right at the Ptevos fleet and then swooped over them and kept on going, avoiding as much of their fire as he could. Brandon was amazed at the speed of the ship. In all the simulations he had been a part of, he had never flown a ship with the combined size and speed of the Hidden Sun.

The Ptevos fleet turned and followed Brandon hotly. Two small ships led the way and were gaining ground. As they moved closer, a long metallic pole with a two pronged spike at the tip came out of the sides of each ship. Electricity flowed between the tips of each spike. "What are those?" asked Brandon, turning right to avoid the small ships.

"I'll check the *Hidden Sun's* database." It took Charlie less than a second to find the answer. "Those are Ptevos Shield Burners. Don't let them touch you with those big spikes or else our shields will be useless."

"OK. Reggie said this ship is supposed to be really maneuverable. Let's find out if he was right." Brandon pushed the control stick forward and to the right and accelerated. The *Hidden Sun* spun downwards like a top and the two Shield Burners followed suit. After righting the ship, Brandon put the pedal to the metal and put a good amount of space between him and his pursuers. "Charlie, tell everybody to hold on." Brandon pushed hard on the brakes and turned left. As it slowed down, the *Hidden Sun* flew through space sideways, and eventually came to a standstill, facing in exactly the opposite direction it was a moment ago. If the *Hidden Sun* were a car, it would have left the most amazing skid marks.

"Excellent move Brandon! You haven't executed that since you were ten."

"Thanks Charlie. Can you magnify the view screen?"

Brandon watched as the view screen zoomed in on the two Shield Burners. They were heading straight for him. "Charlie, how far away are the Shield Burners?"

"250 miles and closing."

"Does this ship have any weapons?"

"Yes, it does."

"I knew it!" said Brandon as if all of his suspicions had been confirmed.

"Unfortunately, most of them are not operational. I detect only one small laser cannon, which is commissioned for repairs. You'll only get one shot out of that."

"Great," said Brandon sarcastically. "I guess we'll just have to rely on speed. Hope this ship is as fast as I think it is." Brandon pushed forward on the control stick and the *Hidden Sun* zoomed ahead. He saw that one Shield Burner was slightly to the left of him and the other slightly to the right. All three ships were on a collision course.

"Brandon, you're heading right for them."

"I know. It's the only way. Give me a countdown when we are ten seconds from impact." Brandon's forehead was covered in sweat. He knew that if one of those spikes touched the *Hidden Sun*, all would be lost. He wasn't going to let that happen.

"Here we go Brandon," said Charlie and the countdown began. "10 … 9 … 8 …"

Brandon looked at the view screen and saw that the two Shield Burners were targeting the middle of his ship. He knew it was their best chance of hitting the *Hidden Sun* with their crippling spikes.

"7 … 6 … 5 …" said Charlie, each number growing louder as the countdown continued.

"Almost. Almost," said Brandon, concentrating on the two ships, which became larger and larger on the view screen as the time to impact became smaller and smaller.

"4 … 3 …"

"NOW!" screamed Brandon. He pushed the accelerator as hard as he could, and turned the ship on its side. The *Hidden Sun* took off with blazing speed and flew right between the two Shield Burners. Their spikes missed touching the hull of the ship by inches. With no time to slow down or change directions, the two Shield Burners collided with one another and exploded into a giant red, orange, yellow and blue fireball.

Brandon let out a sigh of relief.

"Great flying Brandon. That was terrific!" said Charlie. "I knew you could do it!"

"Thanks. I'm just glad it's over."

"Not yet buddy. You've still got the rest of the fleet to contend with and they're heading this way."

"Oh no! There's no way I can fight all those ships. We've got to get out of here. How fast can this thing go?"

"We have light-speed capabilities."

"Then let's do it, Charlie." Brandon looked around the Pilot's console at all the buttons and switches he had never even seen before. It was set up much differently from the one in the simulation room. "How do we do that?"

"Unfortunately, it seems that when the power went out, the ability of the engines to jump to light-speed went out. They'll need time to charge up."

"How much time?"

"About two minutes."

"I don't think we have two minutes, Charlie." The Ptevos fleet had quickly closed in on the Hidden Sun, and started firing. To Brandon, the laser blasts seemed to be coming from every direction. Several hit the Hidden Sun and the ship shook violently.

"Brandon, our shields are down to 65 percent," said Charlie.

"Well, start charging those engines. I'll try to avoid their fire." Brandon pulled back on the control stick and flew the Hidden Sun over the lead ship, which he guessed belonged to General Zarafat. The entire fleet pursued him and continued firing and hitting the Hidden Sun.

"Our shields are down to 42 percent."

"Charlie, we have to get out of here, now!" screamed Brandon but there was nothing Charlie could do. The *Hidden Sun* swerved from left to right over and over again, and managed to avoid a large portion of the Ptevos' fire but they still were able to get in a few more hits.

"24 percent. 18 percent."

"How are those light-speed engines coming along? A few more hits and we're done for." The ship was rocked by another blast.

"Shields down to 8 percent. They're almost charged."

"We need some offense." Brandon pushed forward on the accelerator and put some space between himself and the Ptevos Fleet. A single laser blast made contact with the lower rear of the ship and the shields went down completely.

"Another hit and the Hidden Sun will begin taking major damage, Brandon."

"I know Charlie." Brandon paused to think. "Charlie, can you release some of our fuel?"

"Of course."

"Then do it."

"How much would you like me to release?"

"I don't know. A lot!"

"Releasing fuel," said Charlie. One of the smaller ships in the Ptevos fleet was gaining on the Hidden Sun and was almost in firing range. "Brandon, the engines are charged. We can now travel at light-speed."

"Cool. Stop releasing fuel." Brandon looked at all of the buttons on the pilot's console. "How do I go to light-speed?"

"Just push the large yellow button on the right side of the console. Brandon that Ptevos ship is getting extremely close. Wait a minute. He's slowing down. Must have picked up the large cloud of fuel we released on his sensors. It looks as if he's going to go around it."

"Not likely. Charlie, aim our laser cannon at the cloud of fuel."

"Target is locked."

"Fire." A single beam of hot red light shot out of a small cannon on the back of the Hidden Sun. It quickly traveled into the center of the cloud of fuel and it ignited. There was a large explosion and the single Ptevos ship turned away and retreated back to the rest of the fleet, which was only a short distance away. "Let's get out of here." Brandon pushed the yellow button on the right side of the pilot's console and the *Hidden Sun* accelerated like a cheetah and the stars passed by like lines of chalk.

CHAPTER THIRTEEN

SOME ANSWERS

The *Hidden Sun* emerged from light-speed and came to a standstill in a totally different part of space. The ship had traveled over 250,000 miles and barely escaped from certain destruction by General Zarafat and the Ptevos fleet. Brandon sat back in the pilot's chair, exhausted. "You did it Brandon!" said Charlie.

"That was the most incredible thing that's ever happened to me." He took a deep breath and let it out quickly. "Are we safe?"

"Sensors show no sign of the Ptevos. I'd say the ship is safe for now but I think it best if you stayed on alert."

Brandon looked up at the ceiling. "Charlie, what did you mean when you said I'm a trained military pilot and that's why I'm here? All those simulations I did were from the military?"

"Yes, the simulations were from the military. I know someone very high up in the chain of command and he gave me access to the simulation programs. You had such an interest in combat simulations at a young age that one day I stopped playing the regular ones and only gave you the military ones. You were so good at them that you unofficially became the military's number one ace. It was he who wanted you on this ship. I didn't find that part out until just before the Ptevos attacked."

"That's how my parents were able to sell their house so quick, and the boat. Because your friend wanted me on board the Hidden Sun?"

"That's right."

"So I was here as what? A backup?"

"Yes. I'd wager he knew about the Ptevos' beam and wanted you on board in case they got it off. He's extremely intelligent, for a human."

Brandon jumped in his seat when he heard the doors to the bridge swing open. He turned around, and Sly was standing behind him. "Brandon, are you OK?"

"Just a little knocked around but I'll be all right. How about you?"

"I'm fine." Sly looked around the bridge and saw that most of the control consoles were damaged in some way or other and the weapons and defense console was almost totally destroyed. He also noticed the five bodies lying on the floor. "What happened?"

"I don't know exactly, but we were attacked by a race called the Ptevos. They kind of look like rhinoceroses." Brandon told Sly the entire story: from the moment he entered the bridge with Lieutenant Bunts until just now. When he reached the part about the voice in his head and turning the ship's power back on, Sly said, "You mean the Charlie you're always talking about is a computer?"

"Yes," said Brandon and then he introduced him.

"Hello Sly. Heard a lot about you."

"Hi Charlie. Nice to meet you."

Next, Brandon showed Sly his most prized possession, his watch, which was still connected to the pilot's console by the hundreds of small cables that came out of the band. He told him how he had been communicating with Charlie ever since he left Earth. When the story was finished the questions began, starting with the most important one.

"Charlie, are Captain Smoke and his bridge officers dead?"

"No, not dead but not really conscious, either, Brandon. They seem to be in a form of suspended animation. They are breathing and their body functions are performing, just at a slower rate than normal. It's similar to being asleep."

"How many people on this ship are like this?" said Sly.

"Unfortunately, it seems the better question is how many people on this ship are not, my new friend. The answer is eighty-eight. All children."

"All children? What about my parents?"

"I'm sorry Brandon."

"Well, is there a way of waking them up?" Brandon hoped against hope that Charlie would say, 'yes, it's no problem,' but deep down, he already knew the answer.

"Not that I know of, I'm afraid. For the answer to that question, you'll have to ask General Zarafat."

"What caused this?" asked Sly.

Brandon knew exactly what it was. He had the cut on the back of his head to show for it. "It was that yellow beam they fired. I watched it knock out the bridge crew but not me. Why are all the kids still awake?"

"Brandon," began Charlie, "I now have access to all of the *Hidden Sun's* databases and I think I can answer that question. We were correct from the beginning in believing that this starship is not what is seems to be. It actually is a military starship—it's a top secret, advanced military starship that was constructed using the combined technology of over 1000 worlds. This was supposed to be a simple mission to test the capabilities of the ship. After all the systems were checked, the Captain was to announce to the crew that the *Hidden Sun* was turning around and heading back to Earth, its mission to give aid to different worlds had been canceled. Unfortunately, the *Hidden Sun* ran into the Ptevos and we all know what happened. From reading Captain Smoke's personal journal it's clear that he and General Zarafat are archenemies. They have fought numerous battles in the past, and neither has been able to defeat the other once and for all. In their last meeting, General Zarafat was able to destroy Captain Smoke's ship, but the man escaped and made it back to Earth."

"Wow," said Brandon.

"Wow, wow," said Sly.

"But that still doesn't tell us why only the adults were affected by the beam."

"I'm getting to that," said Charlie. "I can't be completely sure but the most logical explanation is this: It seems that when the Ptevos are born they are fully developed adults."

"You mean they don't start off as babies?" said Brandon.

"That's correct. They are much different from humans. When they invented the beam, they must have overlooked that other species, like humans, have children and only set the device to affect adults. I can only assume that when General Zarafat saw that this ship belonged to Captain Smoke, he was not anticipating Brandon Sparks and the other children on board.

"Of course," said Sly. "Even if he knew what kids were, a military ship wouldn't normally have any on board."

"Exactly," said Charlie.

"So what should we do now?"

"My advice to you is to get this ship repaired and set a course for Earth."

"But we're just a bunch of kids. We don't have the training to fix a starship, let alone a highly advanced one," said Brandon.

"The ship's computer is going to guide you through the process of fixing the damaged parts of the ship. All you'll have to do is listen. Remember, a few hours ago you were 'just a bunch of kids.' Now you're the crew of this ship."

"OK Charlie," said Brandon.

"I'm going to give control of the *Hidden Sun* back to the ship's computer now. I've made a few minor adjustments."

"Charlie, I still have so many questions. Where were you this past month? Why couldn't I get in touch with you and someone with a whispery voice contacted me on the watch."

The lights on the bridge flickered and the cables coming from Brandon's watch wiggled their way out of the pilot's console and were sucked back inside the band. The two boys heard the distinct female voice of the ship's computer. "The *Hidden Sun* has sustained severe damage. It must be repaired."

"It will be," said Sly.

"Brandon," said Charlie, who was no longer broadcasting from the *Hidden Sun's* speakers but from the ear piece in his ear, "sorry we lost contact. The original owner of the watch needed my help. I'll tell you all about it when we have more time."

"It was him who contacted me through the watch, wasn't it?" said Brandon.

Sly looked at him funny. "Talking to me?" he asked

"Oh, no. Charlie," said Brandon, pointing to his ear.

"Yes, it was him who contacted you. He's the only other person with a watch like yours. I've got to go now Brandon. All of your questions will be answered in time. Be careful. Contact me if you need me."

"I will." Brandon took the ear piece out of his ear and put it back inside his watch. He looked at Sly and Sly looked back at him. Without saying a word, both could tell that they were in way over their heads. The boys looked around the room and their attention turned to the bodies on the floor.

"What should we do with them?" asked Sly.

"I don't know. We have to put them somewhere and they won't all fit in the medical center. Charlie said it's like they're sleeping, so I guess the best thing to do is to put them in their beds."

"Good idea. We can have someone check up on them from time to time."

One by one, Brandon and Sly moved the bodies of the bridge crew into their respective rooms. Brandon was glad the crew lived close to the bridge. It took a lot of energy to move them and by the time the job was finished, he needed a break. They returned to the bridge and sat down on the floor. "What should we do now?" asked Sly.

"I guess we should gather everybody who's awake and have a meeting. Ship's computer, please tell everyone to report to the Bridge."

About fifteen minutes later, all of the children on the Hidden Sun were packed inside the bridge, surrounding Brandon and Sly. Most were calm but others wanted to know what was going on. "What happened to my parents?" asked one. "Are we going to be OK?" asked another. A third pointed at Sly and asked, "Who's that kid?"

Reggie was standing in the front and Traylor was next to him. He was so fixed on Brandon and the boy standing next to him that he didn't even notice.

"I will answer all of your questions," said Brandon. He told the eighty-seven children almost the exact same story as he told Sly just a few minutes ago. This time, he left out any mention of Charlie. When asked, "how did the computer come on if the power went out?" he answered, "It just did." He didn't want to lie to everyone, especially Reggie, but he didn't want to reveal Charlie to everyone either. At least, not yet. After finishing his story, he introduced the boy standing to his right. "This is my friend Sly. He snuck on board before the ship left Earth."

"Hello," said Sly. His pale face, tattered clothes and scratchy voice took the other kids aback. Brandon had spent so much time with Sly that he didn't notice these things anymore.

"How'd you get that scar on your face?" yelled an anonymous girl from the crowd. Sly didn't answer. He just turned and looked at Brandon.

"We need to get to work on fixing the ship so we can head back to Earth."

"Hey, who made you king of the ship?" said Frank Drek from the back of the room. He began pushing his way to the front. "Out of my way. Move it!" The crowd parted, two kids fell to the ground from the force of Frank's strong arms. "Just because you *say* you saved us doesn't make you ruler of this ship. Captain Smoke is gone and we need a strong leader and since I'm the strongest and the biggest, I'm captain."

"No you're not," said Reggie.

"Shut up Thacker. You want to try and stop me?"

"I will if I have to."

"Yeah, you and what army?"

"Me," said Traylor. Reggie looked at her in shock.

"And me," said Brandon. He smiled at his friend.

"And me," was popping out of kids mouths like it was the only thing they could say. If you counted them, there were eighty-eight in all.

"Oh please," said Frank sarcastically. He jumped forward a step and everyone in front of him moved back. "You guys are a joke. He walked over and sat in the captain's chair.

"I think we should vote," said Traylor. A bunch of kids agreed, but some were hesitant. They knew something like this could turn into a popularity contest.

"I think we should let the ship's computer decide who is best suited to be captain of this ship," said Sly. A few kids said "yeah," and everyone except for Frank was in agreement that this was the best way to decide who should be captain.

"Ship's computer ..." began Traylor before being cut off by Frank.

"I'll do this. It's gonna pick me anyway. Ship's computer, Captain Smoke and all of his crew are down and I am the biggest and strongest, so tell these losers that I am the new captain of this ship."

"I will not!" said the ship's computer defiantly. For the first time it did not answer in a mechanical way. It showed emotion and Brandon was amazed.

Frank became very angry and his face began to turn red. "Then who is the captain of this ship?" he screamed. There was a pause and then the ship's computer answered.

"Brandon Sparks is the Captain of the *Hidden Sun*." All of the children gasped.

"Sparks is Captain?" said Frank. His face was now beet red and he was furious. He barreled his way through the crowd and stormed out of the room.

"I'm Captain?"

The remaining children came over and congratulated Brandon by shaking his hand and patting him on the back.

"What should we do?" said Carlos.

"I don't know. I guess we should find all of the adults and put them in their beds. I think that's the best place for them. Everything else we'll work out later on." The children started to leave the Bridge. "Hey Reggie, Traylor, Carlos. Would you guys stay behind?" After everyone was finally gone, Brandon started to talk to his friends. "Hey guys. If I'm going to be Captain then I guess I need a bridge crew."

"Hey, thanks but no thanks," said Carlos. "I've had enough of the bridge for one lifetime."

"Are you sure?"

"Yeah. It's just not my thing. I can't handle that kind of pressure."

"OK, well what do you like?"

"I like working in the medical center. You know, helping people. It makes me feel good about myself."

"Then the job is yours. Carlos Santiago, head of the medical center. Well, you better get started. You've got a lot of work ahead of you."

"I know. Thanks," said Carlos and he rushed out of the bridge.

"All right. Reggie, if you want it, Nav/Com is yours. What do you say?"

"I say, aye, aye Captain."

"Good. One down, two to go. Traylor, I just want to say I'm sorry about brushing you off this morning. I shouldn't have done that." Brandon extended his hand. "Can we be friends?" Traylor smiled and shook his hand. Then she gave him a stiff punch to the shoulder and smiled.

"Oh gross," said Reggie. "Tell me I didn't just see that."

"Not only did you just see that but I'm offering Traylor the Pilot's chair."

"Really?" said Traylor, her face filled with excitement.

"Brandon, wait. That's your chair. You're the Pilot!" said Reggie emphatically.

"Nope. I'm Captain now. I can't do both. Traylor's gonna be pilot. I've watched her fly in the simulations and she's really great."

"Oh no," said Reggie as he rolled his eyes.

"And this means that the two of you are going to be working very closely for a long time. I want you to shake hands and make up."

"Do I have to?"

"You have to. And you have to apologize to one another."

"But I didn't do anything!" said Reggie and then he grumbled. After a few seconds, he sucked it up and extended his hand and shook Traylor's. "Sorry," he said.

"I'm sorry too," she said. "You were right. I did pour that soup on you on purpose."

"I knew it!" said Reggie. Brandon and Sly started to laugh and soon Traylor joined them. Eventually, even Reggie cracked a smile.

"That leaves only one spot open. Sly, I want you to be my Weapons and Defense Officer."

"I accept," said the boy.

"Brandon, does he know how to do the job? Weapons and defense is tough," said Reggie.

"He does. I've been playing simulations with him on the computer. He's actually really good. Amazingly good."

"Cool said Reggie," and he shook Sly's hand.

"Guys, before we get any deeper into this, I just want you to remember that this is for real. This isn't a simulation or a game. If something goes wrong here, that's it. It's all over. I don't know what's gonna happen, but I do know that our mission is to get back to Earth and I promise to do my best as captain to make sure we all stay alive. I hope all of you will do the same. Agreed?"

"Agreed," said Sly.

"Agreed," said Reggie.

"Agreed," said Traylor.

"Well, now that we've got a crew, I guess we should start on the repairs. Let's start by fixing the bridge."

CHAPTER FOURTEEN

CONTACT

To the amazement of everyone, the repairs to the *Hidden Sun* went quickly. Within a week's time, there were only a few minor things left to fix. Though he knew General Zarafat was probably the only one who had the answer, he asked Carlos to try to find a way to wake the adults. Brandon spent most of this time answering the questions that he could and finding answers to the ones he could not. When he had some free time, he spent it trying to become familiar with every room on the *Hidden Sun*. As he walked around the ship, he noticed that most of the kids that didn't know him well treated him differently now that he was captain. No matter how many times he told them not to, they'd answer him with "yes sir," or "no sir," as if he was an adult. Some would stare at him as he walked the halls, and avert their eyes when he made eye contact. It reminded him of the way students would look at a teacher when one walked by. He didn't like it at all and just wanted to be treated like any other kid.

Brandon put aside an hour each day to take a science, math, or English lesson from the ship's computer in the captain's office, which was located in the room next to the bridge. He didn't want to go back on the promise he had made to his mother just over a month ago.

He spent a lot of time with the ship's computer and he noticed a distinct change in her personality ever since the power came back on. Her cold, methodical, and automatic personality disappeared and was replaced with one that was warm, caring, and conscious. Brandon thought she was becoming more human and wondered if Charlie had anything to do with this. He knew that it was Charlie's tinkering that allowed him access to the *Hidden Sun's* primary weapons and defense systems, and liked to talk about them with the ship's computer. When they weren't discussing the laser cannons or how many direct laser blasts the shields could absorb before going out, they talked about just plain old stuff. Brandon told her about Charlie, and how he missed going fishing with his dad. The ship's computer would tell him about her interest in being a firefighter.

"A firefighter?" said Brandon.

"That's right. There's something beautiful about fire and something even more beautiful about putting it out. I think it would be a very rewarding job."

"I guess so. I really want you to meet Charlie ship's computer I ..."

"Brandon," interrupted the ship's computer. It was the first time she had ever cut him off. "I do not wish to be called 'ship's computer' anymore. I would like a name."

Brandon was shocked. "Really? I thought you didn't want one."

"I've changed my mind."

"OK. What name would you like?"

"I was thinking I would like to be called Sarah."

"Sarah? That's my mom's middle name."

"Yes, that is where I discovered it. Is that all right with you Brandon?"

Brandon thought about it for a moment. It made him feel good that the ship's computer chose her name from his mother. He smiled and guessed that his mother would be flattered. "Yes, it's all right with me. Sarah it is."

"Thank you Brandon."

"Sarah," he said with a smile, "please make an announcement to the crew that the ship's computer is now to be known as 'Sarah' and if called 'ship's computer' she will not respond.

"Done," said Sarah.

There was a fast knocking at the door. "Come in," said Brandon and in walked Reggie.

"The ship's computer is now called Sarah?" said the boy.

"Yup," said Brandon, making the "p" pop.

"All right," said Reggie, shaking his head in disbelief. He paused for a second and then remembered what he had come into the captain's office to say. "I think you should come out here. Someone is trying to communicate with us ... from Earth!"

Brandon jumped out of his chair and followed Reggie onto the Bridge. He didn't know who was communicating with him from Earth, so to be on the safe side, he pushed two buttons on his watch and put the ear piece in his ear, just in case he needed Charlie's help. He looked at the word "SMOKE" on the backrest of the captain's chair and sat down. "Can you bring in on screen?"

"Sure." Moments later, the image of a middle-aged man dressed in a navy blue jacket with five shiny silver stars on his chest came onto the screen. He had short gray hair and a very stern look on his face. A small, thick cigar protruded from the corner of his mouth, the end glowing orange and red from time to time.

"Captain Smoke, do you read me? This is General Swift of the United States Armed Forces."

Brandon made sure that he was sitting up straight. He wanted to give a good impression. This was the first time he would be speaking with a five-star general. "Hello General Swift. My name is Brandon Sparks and I am the captain of this starship. It is good to meet ..."

"Very funny kid. Quit playing games and get Captain Smoke. This is a matter of world security!" shouted General Swift.

"Captain Smoke was knocked out."

"Did you say knocked out? Well, wake him up! His country needs him! Earth needs him!"

"I'm sorry but I can't wake him up. I wish I could. The Ptevos attacked us and Captain Smoke was put into a form of suspended animation along with all the other grownups and can't be woken up. Only the children on board are still awake."

"Then we're doomed." General Swift moved his cigar to the opposite corner of his mouth. "What did you say your name was kid?"

"Brandon Sparks."

"Sparks. Sparks. That name rings a bell. You Matthew Sparks' kid?"

"Yes sir."

General Swift took a step forward and his body grew larger in the view screen. He then spoke in a much softer tone. "He didn't happen to mention what he was working on, did he?"

"You mean Rhino-37?"

"Good job son. Did he tell you if he had any luck solving the problem?" Small beads of sweat formed on General Swift's forehead.

"No, he didn't solve it," said Brandon. General Swift took a step backward. He looked at a man behind him and shook his head. That man turned and walked out of the room.

"I can't believe I'm doing this but I'm going to be straight with you kid. Things are not looking good on Earth. We have detected a large-scale Ptevos invasion force coming our way. We are going to do our best to defend against it but our only chance for survival is to get a look at your father's research and to get our hands on the *Hidden Sun*. By now you probably know that it is a very special ship and that they don't call it the *Hidden Sun* for nothin'. I'm sure you've done some simulations. Do you know how to fly a starship?"

"Yes, I do. I've done tons of simulations."

"Good. Good. Son, I need you to send me all of your father's and Dr. Ramirez's work on Rhino-37 so that our scientists can get to work on it. What's more, I need you to fly that ship back to Earth immediately. Can you do that?"

"Yes General. Hold on and I will try to transmit the information to you."

Reggie pushed a few buttons on his control console and General Swift could no longer see or hear Brandon and the Bridge.

"Sarah, can you transmit all of the stuff General Swift needs from my father's Shana and Dr. Ramirez's computer to him?"

"Of course," said Sarah. "Transmission complete."

"Thanks." Brandon looked at Reggie and nodded. Reggie pushed a few buttons on his console and now General Swift could see and hear Brandon. "General, did you receive the information?"

"I did. Good work Sparks. Now get that ship back to Earth as soon as you can."

"I will General, but my ship is still damaged and it will take another day to repair."

"Fine. Fix the ship and then get a move on. We don't have much time. The whole world is depending on you, son. Contact me when you get close. Swift out." The screen blinked off and the view returned to the blackness of space.

"Brandon," said Reggie. "I know this sounds strange, but I'm detecting three life-forms flying outside the *Hidden Sun,* and none of them are using spacecrafts!"

"What are they?"

Reggie pushed a few buttons on his console. "This can't be right. It's saying they're lollies."

"Lollies?" said Sly. "What are lollies?"

"Reggie, you better check to see if your console is functioning properly. Last time I checked, lollipops couldn't fly," laughed Traylor.

Reggie punched a few more buttons on his console. "Wait a minute, not lollipops … lollibrackens!"

"Lollibrackens?" said Brandon. "What are tho …" Suddenly, the left side of the ship was struck by something and the bridge started to shake. "Sly, shields!"

"Shields are up, but they won't do much good against being rammed," said the boy.

"Traylor, get us moving! Sarah, inform the crew that we are under attack and they should strap themselves in." The ship was now struck from the right side. "Damage report!"

"No significant damage Brandon. The hull is intact," said Sly.

CHAPTER FOURTEEN

Traylor pushed the accelerator and the *Hidden Sun* took off. Brandon looked at the rearview boxes on the view screen and saw that they were being pursued by three lollibrackens. The beasts looked like tyrannosaurus-Rexes with bigger, longer arms and giant powerful wings. The large one was blue, the one in the middle was red and the smallest was purple. The Hidden Sun moved up and down, left and right but could not shake the lollibrackens off its tail. Traylor even tried doing a flip and coming up behind them but they just followed her every move and were beginning to close in. "How can these things fly in space?" wondered Brandon.

"I'm on it," said Reggie, furiously pushing buttons on the Nav/Com console. "They're hunters. It says here that lollibrackens can hold their breath for around four hours and their bodies are made to withstand the cold of space. Also, they never travel very far from their home planet so it must be close by."

"Brandon," said Sly. "Should I arm the weapons?"

"No. I don't want them hurt. They're just hungry. Traylor, can you lose them?"

"I'm doing my best." The Hidden Sun swooped left and right but the lollibrackens kept up.

Suddenly, a laser blast zipped past the front of the *Hidden Sun*. It missed by only a few feet. "What was that?" asked Brandon.

"We've been found," said Reggie.

"By who?"

"General Zarafat," said Sly.

"Oh no!" said Traylor.

"Someone's trying to communicate with us," said Reggie.

"On screen."

General Zarafat looked even more evil than he had the last time Brandon had seen him. The horn on top of his head was covered in blood and there was a body lying on the floor behind him. "You're not Captain Smoke," he snarled.

"My name is Brandon Sparks and I am the new captain of this ship."

"So, my beam did work. Then I am victorious. Captain Smoke is unconscious and when I destroy your ship, he will be dead. Of course, so will you and the rest of the vile humans on board." General Zarafat's mouth formed a wicked smile.

Two laser blasts hit the Hidden Sun from behind and the ship shook. Brandon held on tight to the armrests next to his chair. "Sorry to ruin your plans General but I promised my crew we'd make it back to Earth in one piece. Now tell me how to wake up the people on my ship."

General Zarafat started to laugh. Brandon watched as some of the blood from his horn dripped down onto his forehead. He wiped it off with the back of a single finger and tasted it. "I don't think so Sparks. I'd offer you the chance to surrender, but then I'd just have to kill you and your crew one by one. I'd rather do it with one big bang. This is the end for you, human." The screen blipped back to its normal view of space as General Zarafat had disconnected the transmission.

Fifteen small Ptevos ships flew out of the side of General Zarafat's lead ship and pursued the Hidden Sun. Traylor spun the ship downward and tried to escape but the ships followed. Caught between the two were the three lollibrackens, who swooped up and down, still following the *Hidden Sun's* every move.

During the week he had spent with Sarah while the ship was being repaired, Brandon had learned many things about the *Hidden Sun*. His captain status gave him access to new information, and one of the things he discovered was that the ship had an enormous amount of laser cannons. The *Hidden Sun* had an arsenal of two hundred and sixty-eight to be exact, all of which could be called upon to fire in all possible directions. "Sly, arm the laser cannons and fire at will, but don't hit the lollibrackens. It's not their fault they got in the middle of this."

Two hundred and sixty-eight laser cannons, some larger than others, rose out of the *Hidden Sun's* hull and began firing at the fifteen enemy ships. The Ptevos returned fire and a few of the lasers narrowly missed hitting the blue lollibracken. Instinctively, he avoided the fire and soared up and to his right, leaving the battle. The red one followed him, turning right, and also escaped being hit. The purple one was not as lucky. Brandon watched on his screen as it was struck on the left forearm by a laser blast from a Ptevos ship. This infuriated the red and blue lollibrackens and they made a beeline for that ship. As they closed in, the ship between them and the ship that fired on their child was hit by a few of the Hidden Sun's laser blasts and exploded, forcing them to turn around.

"Great shot Sly!" said Brandon. Sly didn't even acknowledge the praise. He just continued to press buttons on his console and glanced up at the view screen to see the results.

Traylor turned the ship to the left and the Ptevos followed, firing with more and more accuracy. Five laser blasts hit the back of the Hidden Sun.

"Shields are down to 80 percent," said Sly.

"Brandon, the Ptevos fleet has just released another thirty ships and they're coming this way," said Reggie. "What should we do? We don't have a chance against all of them!"

Brandon looked at the view screen and out into space. Two Ptevos ships were heading straight for the injured lollibracken.

"Brandon, what should we do?" repeated Reggie, who looked very worried. "We're gonna get killed if we stay in this fight!" The Hidden Sun shook from being hit by two more laser blasts.

Brandon thought about the countless simulations he had played with Charlie and made a decision. "We're gonna save that lollibracken."

"What? How?" screamed Reggie.

"I've got a plan. Traylor, head for the purple lollibracken. Sly, concentrate your fire on the two ships that are attacking him. Forget about firing at the ships behind us. If this plan works, we won't have to worry about them."

The two Ptevos ships were coming in for the kill on the purple lollibracken as the Hidden Sun approached. Sly's shots were dead on and one ship exploded in a fiery mess. The other turned around and fled.

"Brandon, how are we gonna save that lollibracken?" said Reggie as the Hidden Sun swooped by the injured creature. "It's not like we can tie a rope around it and tow it behind us."

"That's right Reggie, we can't do that. So we're going to bring it on board."

"What? Are you crazy?" screamed Reggie. "Am I the only one who thinks that's nuts?"

"That is very dangerous," said Sly.

"Bring it on board?" said Traylor. "That thing is a wild beast! It could kill us all!"

"See, even Traylor agrees with me!' said Reggie. "It's too dangerous to bring on board!"

"I know it's dangerous but I can't just sit here and let it die. It's our fault the lollibracken's in this mess."

"It attacked us! Besides, where are we gonna put it?" said Reggie.

"In the shuttle bay."

"And how exactly do we get a giant flying lizard into the shuttle bay?"

"By backing over it."

"Backing over it?" said Traylor, spinning around in her chair.

"Imagine parking a garage over a car."

"Brandon," said Sly, "I hope you realize that we can't open the shuttle bay doors without turning off our shields."

"I know. That's why we've got to do it quickly." The Hidden Sun was rocked by another laser blast. "Really quickly. We've got to work as a team."

All four of the kids returned to their consoles. Traylor banked the *Hidden Sun* and flew back between the forty or so ships that were pursuing her. Sly fired all of the two hundred and sixty-eight laser cannons to give her some flying room. His shots were so accurate that five Ptevos ships were destroyed. A few random laser blasts from one of the surviving ships hit the hull as Traylor put the ship into a spin and avoided the rest. There was now a clear path between the purple lollibracken and the Hidden Sun.

"Shields down to 70 percent," said Sly."

"All right. Everyone ready?" said Brandon. Traylor, Sly and Reggie nodded. "Sarah, make an announcement for anyone in the shuttle bay to leave immediately."

"Yes Brandon," she said.

Brandon watched the Ptevos ships turn around in the view screen as Traylor passed the lollibracken and slowed down the *Hidden Sun*. "Get as close to it as you can," said Brandon. "We've only got one shot at this."

"I'll try," said Traylor. She threw the *Hidden Sun* into reverse and slowly backed up.

"Brandon, we're twenty feet from the lollibracken and those Ptevos ships are coming in fast with guns blazing."

"Sly, lower shields."

"Shields Down," said Sly.

"Reggie, open the shuttle bay door."

"Done," said Reggie, continuing to push buttons on his console and monitoring the Ptevos ships.

"Traylor, back up the *Hidden Sun* thirty feet."

"Here they come!" said Reggie.

Traylor jerked the *Hidden Sun* backwards over the unconscious creature. "Sarah, where is the lollibracken?"

"The lollibracken is in the shuttle bay."

"Close the shuttle bay door! Put up the shields!" screamed Brandon.

Reggie and Sly pushed furiously at their control consoles. The shuttle bay door closed, but before the shields could be put up, a laser blast hit one of the engines. The *Hidden Sun* shook more violently that it ever had.

"Engine three offline," said Sarah.

"Shields are up Brandon," sad Sly.

"Traylor, take this ship straight up."

Traylor pushed a few buttons on her console and the Hidden Sun exploded upward like a rocket taking off from a launch pad. Eight Ptevos ships changed course just to avoid crashing into it and each other. "What now?" asked Traylor.

"Let's get out of here," said Brandon.

"Without all of the engines we can't go to light-speed," said Reggie as the *Hidden Sun* was hit with a barrage of laser blasts.

"Our shields are down to 35 percent," said Sly.

"What are we gonna do?" said Reggie.

"Follow your instincts," said a whispery voice in Brandon's ear.

"What?" said Brandon, putting his hand over the ear with the ear piece.

"I said what are we gonna do? Soon we'll be surrounded by Ptevos ships!" said Reggie.

"Follow your instincts," said the whispery voice again. This time Brandon heard it loud and clear.

"It's you."

"Of course it's me," said Reggie. Who else would it be?"

Brandon knew that the strange whispery voice belonged to the man who made his watch. "Follow your instincts and you will survive," it said and then the connection was lost.

"Brandon, I think you're losing it," said Reggie. "We need to get out of here, now! Ship's computer ... I mean Sarah, how long would it take to fix engine number three? We need to go to light-speed."

"Sarah, disregard that question. Where we're going, we don't need light-speed. Reggie, give Traylor the coordinates to the nearest star."

"Don't need light-speed?" screamed Reggie. He let out a disgruntled grunt, and pushed buttons on his console. "The closest star is the lollibracken's sun, designated Crescent 19, and it's ten thousand miles away. I've transmitted the coordinates."

"Traylor, head towards that sun." She pushed forward on the accelerator and the *Hidden Sun* zipped towards Crescent 19, followed by a sea of Ptevos ships. Another twenty-five ships had been released by General Zarafat to pursue the *Hidden Sun*.

"Brandon, why are we heading towards this star?" asked Reggie. "If we get too close, we're gonna burn up!"

"I don't think so," said Brandon. "Remember what General Swift said? He said, 'they don't call it the *Hidden Sun* for nothing.' I have a feeling that if we fly this ship into a that star, we'll be just fine."

"Now you're really crazy!" said Reggie. "I thought saving the lollibracken was nuts but this is insane! Are you trying to get us killed?"

"No, just the opposite."

"There's got to be another way," said Traylor. The Ptevos ships were closing in.

"There is no other way. This is our only chance of escape." Another three laser blasts hit the *Hidden Sun*.

"Our shields are down to 20 percent," said Sly, as Crescent 19 grew larger in the view screen.

"Five more laser blasts and our shields will be totally gone. Flying into that sun is the only way! Before Captain Smoke was knocked out, I heard him say, "Sun Shields." I think this ship has some sort of special shields that can withstand the heat of a star. You've got to trust me!" Brandon looked around the room as another two laser blasts hit the Hidden Sun.

"I don't see Sun Shields on my console, but what other options do we have?" said Sly. "I'm with you Brandon."

"I'm not about to get killed by a bunch of ugly rhinoceroses! Me too," said Traylor.

"I hope you're right about this," said Reggie, "because there ain't no turning back now." Behind the *Hidden Sun* was a mass of seventy-seven ships, all in hot pursuit, and all very eager to be the one that killed Captain Smoke and the new guy, Brandon Sparks. "The hull temperature is almost at critical Brandon. Maybe this wasn't such a hot idea."

"Give it a second." Three laser blasts hit the back of the ship and the shields went down.

"We're sitting ducks," said Reggie.

"Brandon, this is impossible," said Sly, who had a confused look on his face.

"What is?" asked Brandon.

"The buttons on my console just changed, and one of them now reads 'Sun Shields.' Should I push it?"

"Push it!" said Reggie.

"Push the button!" said Traylor.

"Push it!" said Brandon and Sly did just that. Yellow panels emerged from under the hull of the *Hidden Sun* and completely covered the entire ship like a second skin. All of the Ptevos ships seemed to fire at once and hundreds of laser blasts just bounced off of the *Hidden Sun* like pinballs, and scattered in different directions.

"They work against laser blasts," said Brandon, "but let's see if they work against the immense heat of a star."

Nervously, Traylor pushed forward on the control stick. When their ships couldn't handle any more heat, the Ptevos turned around and flew away. Some watched as the Hidden Sun flew directly into the center of Crescent 19.

CHAPTER FIFTEEN

OUT OF THE FRYING PAN
AND INTO THE FREEZER

"I can't believe it actually worked," said Reggie. "According to these readings, this ship can stay inside this star for over two days!"

"This is some starship," said Sly.

Brandon turned around and smiled at his friends. The Sun Shields had held up and the *Hidden Sun* successfully entered the fiery center of a star and survived. "What's going on with General Zarafat's fleet?"

"They've turned around and started to leave. I think they think we were destroyed by the heat," said Reggie.

"Good!" said Brandon, relieved.

"So, what's next?" asked Traylor.

"Hey, don't you think that getting attacked by aliens is enough for one day? I need a nap," said Reggie.

"Speaking of naps, we've still got a sleeping lollibracken in the shuttle bay," said Sly.

"I haven't forgotten," said Brandon. "After all the Ptevos ships are gone, set a course for the lollibracken's home planet."

"Sure thing Brandon," said Reggie, "but how are we gonna get that lollibracken out of the ship?"

"I hadn't thought of that. I guess when we open the back door, let's hope it just walks out."

"Just walks out?" replied a disbelieving Reggie before he was interrupted by Sly.

"Hey, you'd better take a look at this."

Brandon walked over to Sly and saw that his weapons and defense console was changing. The entire push button console was transforming itself and new buttons were emerging. "What do they all do?" wondered Brandon.

"I think we have new weapons. A lot of new weapons," said Sly.

"Like what?" asked Traylor enthusiastically. She had swung her chair around and was facing the boys.

"Aside from all the laser cannons, there are Sun Flares, Splitter Bombs, Devil Bombs, Carnage Missiles, and something called the Ribbon-Cutter. I'm going to guess that it's the most powerful one because it's the only weapon that needs to be charged before it can be fired."

Charlie had given him access to the conventional weapons, but this was something all together different. "This must have something to do with us being inside this sun," said Brandon. "It must have triggered the weapons system."

"Cool," said Traylor.

"That's not the only cool thing guys," said Reggie as he tapped buttons and looked curiously at his console. "According to my readings, the ship is fully charged."

"Fully charged?" said Brandon. "What's fully charged?"

"Everything."

"Everything?" said Sly.

"The weapons, the shields, the energy tanks. We're at full power. The ship is sucking energy from the sun. It's like one giant fuel station!"

"Add that to the list of special things about this ship," said Traylor.

"This ship is so cool," said Brandon, taking a moment to absorb it all. Reality quickly returned. "But first things first. Let's get that lollibracken home to its parents and get the ship repaired. If the Ptevos are attacking Earth like General Swift says, then I'll bet General Zarafat is going to be a part of it. It may be our only chance at finding a cure for our parents."

"Sounds like a plan," said Sly.

"Let's just hope we *make* it to Earth," said Reggie. He transferred the coordinates of the lollibracken's home planet to Traylor.

"We will," said Brandon. "Let's get out of this star."

Traylor nodded and turned around in her seat. She put her foot on the accelerator and pushed forward on the control stick. Even with one engine down, the *Hidden Sun* gained a lot of speed and shot out of Crescent 19 like a bullet. Traylor spun the ship once, just for fun, and Sly disengaged the Sun Shields, which were sucked back into the hull of the ship. The *Hidden Sun* banked to the left and headed off into open space.

◆　　◆　　◆

Within an hour, the *Hidden Sun* approached the lollibracken's home planet. "It's called Glore," said Reggie, as the planet grew larger in the view screen. It looked very much like Earth, with a lot of blue water and green land. "Brandon, there doesn't seem to be a lot of lollibrackens. In fact, I've only found a small colony of them on the north end of the planet."

"I thought this was their home world?"

"According to the computer, it is."

"OK, then let's head north," said Brandon, and Reggie sent the coordinates to Traylor.

"Brandon, I must warn you," said Sarah. "The lollibracken is waking up."

"Oh no!" said Traylor.

"That thing could tear the whole ship apart!" said Reggie.

"Traylor, get to those coordinates as fast as you can. We're going down to the shuttle bay to check on the lollibracken and then we're gonna go outside and make sure it gets home safely."

"Sure thing Brandon," she said.

"Who's we?" asked Reggie, taking a small step backward.

"You and me," said Brandon. "Traylor's got to fly the ship and Sly's got to defend it. Since we're not going anywhere that needs navigation or communication, that leaves you free to come with me."

"But I don't want to go outside," whined Reggie. "It's cold out there."

"We're gonna wear snow suits. Have you ever played in the snow before?"

"No. I'm not a terrestrial like you. I've spent my entire life on a starship. The only weather changes I've had to deal with is the temperature in the shower."

"Well, there's a first for everything. It's a lot of fun. You'll love it. I promise. Let's go!" Brandon pulled Reggie's shirt and the two left the Bridge and headed for the elevators. When they arrived at deck 25, they walked straight ahead into a wide hallway that contained four large metal closets. At the end of the hallway were two large steel doors with thick glass windows in the center. Brandon and Reggie stood on their tiptoes and peered through.

The shuttle bay was a large rectangular room at the base of the ship. The wall at the far end was a giant door that opened like a drawbridge. Along the sides of the room were eighteen shuttle crafts, nine on each side. Each was bright blue with a red stripe across the side and a large single silver star in the middle. Brandon thought they looked like larger flattened versions of the Super Car he took from New York to Florida.

In the center of the room, the purple lollibracken was just waking up. It stood on its muscular legs and began to lick its injured arm with its long, thick, red tongue. "That thing must be fifteen feet tall!" said Reggie.

"Probably more like twenty," said Brandon.

The purple lollibracken looked around the room and realized that it was in unfamiliar territory. It began to get upset. The creature let out a high-pitched shriek and started to flail around the room. It attacked one of the shuttle crafts and with two thick fists, caved in the entire front section. Then it picked it up and threw it into another shuttle craft, which slid across the room and crashed into a wall.

"We've got to get that thing out of here," said Reggie. "We're running out of shuttle crafts!"

"You're right. Sarah, open the shuttle bay door to the outside."

Brandon and Reggie watched as the massive door slowly opened. For the first time in over a month, Brandon saw sunlight in the same way he had growing up on Earth and it made him smile. Large snowflakes slowly floated down from the sky.

"What are you smiling about? It's snowing like crazy outside!"

"Nah, that's only a light snow. If it was snowing like this back home, we wouldn't even have a snow day!"

"A snow day? What's a snow day?"

"I'll tell you about it later," said Brandon now with an even bigger smile on his face.

The door hit the snow-covered ground with a thud and the purple lollibracken walked outside. It took one look back at the Hidden Sun, let out another shriek, and walked away.

"Good, it's home," said Reggie. "Now we can go back up to the Bridge where it's nice and warm. Maybe have a cup of hot chocolate. Let's go." He began to whistle, turned around and started heading back to the elevators. His friend cut him off and the whistling stopped.

"Quick, let's put the snowsuits on." Brandon opened one of the closets and pulled out two gray snowsuits with built in boots, two black hats, two pairs of gray gloves and two pairs of snow goggles. He threw one set at Reggie who caught it and shook his head. "Come on, it'll be fun. I used to play in the snow all the time."

"Brandon, I don't want to be eaten by a lollibracken," said Reggie as he hesitantly pulled on the snow pants.

"You won't. I just want to make sure that it gets home to its parents."

Begrudgingly, Reggie nodded his head. "OK, but not too close."

"I promise. Sarah, please tell Sly and Traylor that we are leaving the ship. We'll be back soon."

"Be careful," said Sarah.

"We will."

After putting on their snowsuits, hats, gloves, and goggles, the two opened the inside door to the shuttle bay and walked outside. The snow was coming down a little harder than before but there were only a few inches on the ground so it didn't hold them up very much. They could see the purple lollibracken off in the distance and they followed him.

While they were walking, Brandon taught Reggie how to make a perfect snowball and was rewarded with one to the head. It left a large snow circle on his hat. Brandon retaliated, and the two boys threw snow at each other as they walked.

After about three hundred yards, Brandon and Reggie became so caught up in their snowball fight that they lost sight of the purple lolli-bracken. They looked ahead and tried to see him, but the snow was coming down harder and it looked like they were staring at a white wall. Even the footprints the beast left had started to fill in. Reggie turned to look back at the *Hidden Sun* and could barely make it out in the distance.

"Brandon, my nose feels like it's going to fall off. I think we should head back. It's really starting to come down now and we're getting really far from the ship."

"I think you're right. That lollibracken probably made it home OK. Let's go."

The two boys turned around and headed back towards the Hidden Sun. Before they had even walked ten yards, they heard a high-pitched shriek from behind and turned around. The purple lollibracken was standing right behind them. On one side of him was a larger red lolli-bracken and on the other side, an even larger blue lollibracken. Up close, the boys could see the rippling muscles beneath the scaly skin of the three beasts. The red lollibracken was at least twenty-five feet tall and the blue one at least thirty-five feet tall. Brandon and Reggie screamed as loud as they could and ran towards the *Hidden Sun*. The lollibracken family followed and the ground shook under their tremendous weight.

Brandon was a little faster than Reggie, who wasn't used to cold New York winters and running in the snow, and got a few feet ahead of him. He glanced over his shoulder and saw that the blue lollibracken had closed the gap between him and the boys very quickly. Brandon and Reggie were still two hundred and fifty yards away from the ship. He was breathing heavily as he gave a second glance over his shoulder. The blue lollibracken reached out his enormous hand and with one fluid motion, slap Reggie's entire body. His friend flew through the air and landed on his stomach in a soft pile of snow. Brandon ran over to Reggie, who groaned in pain. He threw off his goggles and pulled off his gloves, which were soaked from the snow, and flipped Reggie onto his back. His goggles had cracked and his nose was bleeding. Luckily the snowsuit had absorbed most of the landing, but Reggie was dazed.

The blue lollibracken moved in for the kill. Just feet away, it put its massive arms in the air and stood straight up, showing off its enormous height and girth. The creature's blue skin shimmered in the sunlight that cut through what Brandon now considered a bad snowstorm. He looked up as it opened its mouth to shriek, revealing pointy teeth that were each at least a foot long and sharper than the sharpest knife he had ever seen. The rest of the lollibracken family, as well as eight others, which appeared seemingly from nowhere, formed a circle around the boys and their blue leader. The creature looked at Brandon with its small green eyes and began to bring its head down with bad intentions.

Brandon did not know what to do. Everything was happening so fast. He wanted to try and hide but they were in an open field. He thought about trying to run and somehow escaping between the legs of the beast but he couldn't leave Reggie behind. He thought of Charlie, but by the time he contacted him, it would all be over. He thought about Sly and the two hundred and sixty-eight laser cannons on the

Hidden Sun, but again, there was no time. Instead, he did what he thought a captain should do. He stayed.

Brandon crouched over Reggie's body as the blue lollibracken's head moved ever towards his own. He threw his hands into the air as if to say "STOP" but the monster continued. His head went right between Brandon's outstretched arms and his huge mouth engulfed his head. Brandon felt the creature's hot breath as his lips and nose pressed against his shoulders. The daylight he could still see quickly grew smaller and smaller as the blue lollibracken began to close his mouth. Brandon closed his eyes tight, and wished for a miracle.

The sharp set of lollibracken teeth were within a fraction of an inch of Brandon's neck when they came to a sudden stop. The creature slowly opened his mouth and took Brandon's head out of his own. Brandon still had his hands outstretched and he peered out of his right eye as the creature moved its left eye close to Brandon's left wrist. For some reason he was intrigued by his watch. Suddenly, one of the surrounding lollibrackens stormed in and tried to attack the two boys but the larger one grabbed him by the neck and tossed him aside. He then let out a menacing shriek and the attacking lollibracken hung his head low and retreated.

The blue lollibracken resumed his studying of Brandon's left wrist.

"Does … does this look familiar to you?" stammered Brandon as he reached his left arm higher into the air and pulled the sleeve of his snowsuit further up his arm to completely reveal his watch.

The blue lollibracken took a closer look and then smelled the watch for what seemed like an eternity. When he was finished, he let out a series of short shrieks and the other lollibrackens slowly moved forward and each smelled Brandon's watch.

"What's going on?" asked Reggie, still lying dazed in the snow.

"I don't know exactly, but I think it's gonna be all right," said Brandon with a look of amazement on his face.

All of the lollibrackens took a few steps backwards except for the large blue one and bowed their heads down low.

"I think they've seen my watch before. The original owner must have been here before."

"Seen your watch? Original owner? I think I got hit harder than I thought."

"I'll explain it to you later. I'm gonna try and talk with them, if I can."

"And I'm just gonna lay here," said Reggie, as he dropped the back of his head into the snow.

The snowstorm had begun to ease as Brandon stood up straight and took a step away from his friend. "Charlie, come in Charlie."

"Hello Brandon. How are things going? On your way back to Earth? Maybe we could play a few sets of tennis when you get home."

"Hi Charlie," laughed Brandon. Then his tone became more serious and Charlie sensed that. "I'm not on my way to Earth yet. I've sort of run into a problem."

"What sort of problem?"

Brandon looked up at the thirty-five foot beast standing right in front of him. "A big, blue, scaly, dinosaur looking lollibracken problem."

"What are you doing on Glore?"

"I was just trying to do the right thing. Is there any way to talk to these creatures? They seem to have seen my watch before."

"Well of course they have," said Charlie, as if Brandon should have known that already. "You say it's a big blue one?"

"Uh huh."

"Really big?"

"Yes."

"Oh, that's just Clark."

"Clark?"

"Yes. Tell me what you want to say to him and I will translate for you."

"Um, OK. Hello." A small shriek came out of Brandon's watch. Clark's head jerked back a little and he responded with a series of short and long shrieks, which Charlie interpreted.

"I have seen that watch before. It belongs to my good friend V. Did you kill him to obtain it? Who are you?"

Brandon looked at the letter "V" on his watch put two and two together. "I am Brandon Sparks and no, I did not kill V," replied the boy. "The watch was a present from V's friend Charlie."

"V has told me a great deal about Charlie and of his friend Jackson. You are an Earthling, are you not? What brings you to this section of the universe?"

Brandon told Clark about the *Hidden Sun* being attacked by the Ptevos and how he became captain. He also explained how he rescued the purple lollibracken and was just on this planet to make sure he made it home safely.

"We hate the Ptevos. They are an evil race that has killed many of our kind. We are all that have survived their attacks. One day, we will seek our revenge."

"Right now they are on a collision course with my home planet. I have to go and try to save them."

"Good luck Brandon Sparks. The lollibrackens consider you a friend."

"And I you." Brandon lowered his left arm to his side, and smiled at the blue lollibracken. He could have sworn that he smiled back before charging off into the distance. The other lollibrackens let out a few goodbye shrieks and followed him.

"Thanks Charlie."

"Anytime kid. That's what best friends are for."

"So, the whispery voice calls himself V," said Brandon. "You've got to tell me about his adventures sometime."

"Maybe one day he'll tell you them himself."

Brandon said goodbye to Charlie and helped Reggie to his feet. "Let's get back to the *Hidden Sun*. You've got to see Carlos in the Medical Center and I've got to get the ship repaired if we're gonna head back to Earth. Fixing engine number three is gonna be a big problem." Reggie nodded as Brandon put his arm around his shoulder to help support him. The two boys slowly walked back to the *Hidden Sun*.

CHAPTER SIXTEEN

REST AND REPAIRS

"Hey Carlos, can you give me a hand?" said Brandon as he walked through the medical center door. Because of his injury, Brandon was supporting most of Reggie's weight.

"What happened?" said Carlos, rushing over to help his friend. The boys carried Reggie to one of the open beds and made him comfortable.

"He got smacked around by a lollibracken. How's everything going down here?"

"Good. I'm starting to get the hang of this stuff. I've been spending most of my time on Dr. Ramirez's computer learning about all the medical equipment in here. It's really simple to use. The computer tells me exactly what's wrong with the patient and then tells me how to cure what's wrong with him. Here, I'll show you on Reggie." Carlos walked over to Dr. Ramirez's desk and sat down. He pushed a few keys on the keyboard and said, "Please diagnose patient in bed number five." A series of twelve red lights came out of the ceiling and scanned Reggie's body.

Brandon walked behind the desk to look at the screens. All nine were filled with different readouts of Reggie's body. One showed an X-ray of his skeleton, another his muscles, and on one a close-up of his beating heart.

Within seconds, the final diagnosis came up on the center screen.
BRUISED RIBS—BED REST FOURTEEN DAYS
"It could be worse," said Carlos.
"You're right. Take good care of him."

"I will."

"Good. How are the parents doing?"

"No change. All of them are exactly the same as they were when they got knocked out. I've set an alarm on my monitor to go off if there is any change. Do you think they'll ever wake up again?"

"They will. We've just got to find a cure," said Brandon as he made his way to the medical center door. "I'll speak to you later Carlos. Keep me posted on Reggie's condition. You're doing a great job."

"I will, and thanks."

"You're welcome," said Brandon as he walked out of the medical center. He headed down the hallway and into an elevator. "Deck 1," he said, and the elevator started to move. After the doors opened, Brandon walked to the door of the bridge and then stopped. A weird feeling came over him and he paused for a moment. When his feet started again, he turned right, and headed down the hallway.

Two doors down from the bridge, was room 0103. There were no markings on the door or around it but Brandon knew very well whose room it was. He had helped put him there after the beam had hit. Brandon walked inside and found Captain Smoke just as he had left him, lying peacefully in his bed. He pulled a chair up next to him and sat down.

Brandon didn't know why he was in Captain Smoke's room or what he was going to say, but he felt compelled to speak. "Um, hey Captain Smoke. I don't know if you can hear me or if you even remember me. We only spoke for a few seconds. My name's Brandon Sparks." He paused for a moment, trying to think of what to say. "I've been chosen as the new captain of the *Hidden Sun*. I've heard about some of your fights with General Zarafat. Pretty amazing stuff." Brandon paused again. "I know you were only my captain for a month, and I only saw you in action for a few minutes, but I hope I can one day be half the captain you are. I promise to do my best and keep everyone safe."

A small amount of light reflected off of something shiny in the corner of Brandon's eye. He looked to his right and saw the four silver stars on Captain Smoke's chest. He slowly reached over and pulled them off. There was a little bit of dust on them so Brandon used his shirt to shine them up. "I don't know what else to say, I guess I was hoping that you would wake up and retake command. I don't know if I'm cut out for this job."

"You are."

Brandon nearly jumped out of his seat. He turned around as fast as he could and standing in the shadows by the door was Sly.

"You scared me half to death!"

"Sorry about that. Come to talk to Captain Smoke?"

"Yeah," said Brandon nodding his head. "You really think I'll be a good captain?"

"I do. You're a natural. I don't know anybody else who would have been able to pull off what you just did. They all owe you their lives, including Captain Smoke."

"It helps when you have such talented friends." Sly smiled and Brandon reached over to pin the stars back on Captain Smoke's chest.

"Hey, what are you doing?" asked Sly.

"I'm putting them back."

"Why don't you try them on? See how they look."

"You think?"

"Sure thing, Captain." Brandon smiled and pinned the stars to his chest.

"What do ya think?"

"I think it looks great. You should keep them."

"I can't keep them. They don't belong to me."

"Well, then at least borrow them. Captain Smoke's not going to need them."

"I don't know," said Brandon hesitantly.

"Just until you get your own set and then you can give these back."

Brandon thought for a moment and then agreed. "What are you doing here by the way?"

"I was looking for you. Sarah told me you were in here. I think we should get some info on the new weapons. Chances are we're going to need them."

The two boys walked out of Captain Smoke's room and into the Captain's office from the hallway door. Brandon and Sly sat down in the chairs in front of the desk. "Sarah, can you tell us about the new weapons we now have access to?"

"Of course, Sly." The video wall behind the captain's desk came to life and was divided into seven large rectangles, each with the name of a weapon inside of it. The one furthest to the left said, "Laser Cannons," and the second, "Missiles." The two boys already knew what these weapons did and were not interested in hearing about them. They wanted to know about the ones they had never heard of, so Sarah began from the third rectangle. "The Devil Bomb is an egg shaped projectile, colored black with red flames. Upon impact, it causes an extremely hot, large wall of blue fire to spring up from the ground." As she spoke, a Devil Bomb spun in the video rectangle, showing all of its sides.

Brandon and Sly nodded to each other in approval. Sarah then moved on to the next rectangle. "The Splitter Bomb is a silver, cone shaped projectile. It gets its name from its ability to split into six smaller bombs, which can cover a larger section of ground and impact more distinct targets."

"Cool" said Sly. The two boys were transfixed by what they saw.

"Keep going," said Brandon.

Sarah moved on to the next rectangle. In it were the words, "Sun Flares," which quickly morphed into two small, yellow, coffee can shape flares. "Sun Flares are a defense mechanism that when fired, explode into golden, flaming fireworks, attracting incoming missiles away from the ship. They can be fired from multiple locations, but usually from the back of the ship."

"Those are not as cool as the bombs, but they will come in handy," said Sly.

"Definitely," said Brandon as Sarah pressed on.

"'Carnage Missiles' are shiny, thick, red missiles which when fired at an enemy, explode feet from impact and release large amounts of white hot shrapnel, meant to totally obliterate the target."

As interested as they were in the Carnage Missiles, Brandon and Sly were very excited because they had come to the last rectangle. It contained the weapon they most wanted to know about, the "Ribbon-Cutter." They both sat up straight in their chairs.

Just as Sarah was about to begin, the door to the bridge opened and the two boys spun around to see who it was. Traylor had just walked in.

"Someone's on the bridge to see you Captain," she said.

"Perfect timing," he said sarcastically. "We'll get back to this later." Sly nodded in approval and the two boys walked out of the captain's office and onto the bridge. "Before I forget, Reggie's gonna be in the medical center for fourteen days. We're gonna have to find a replacement for him." Traylor walked to the pilot's seat and sat down. Brandon looked around the room and then at Traylor. "I don't see anyone. Who's here to see me?"

"It's me," came an unfriendly voice from the center of the room. Frank Drek swung around in the captain's chair and then stood up.

"What are you doing here Frank?" said Brandon.

"I'm bored. I've been sitting around doing nothing. I've watched so much TV that I think my eyes are gonna pop out. I want to do something else."

"Well you're not gonna be captain. I can tell you that!" said Traylor who had walked over and gotten in Frank's face.

"Hey, easy does it Red," said Frank, referring to Traylor's hair color. He put his hands up as if he were surrendering. "I know I'm not gonna be captain ... even though I should be," he mumbled through pursed lips.

"What did you just say?" asked Traylor knowingly.

"Well what do you want to do?" asked Brandon.

Frank looked around the room and then pointed at the empty Nav/ Com station. "How about if you give me Thacker's job?"

"No way. There is no way Brandon's gonna let you work the Nav/ Com station," said Traylor, forcing Frank to take a step back.

"OK," said Brandon.

"What?" screeched Traylor. "He doesn't deserve that job. He's a total jerk!"

Brandon looked Frank directly in the eye. "I'll make a deal with you. If you can fix engine number three, then you can work the Nav/ Com station until Reggie is healthy."

"But ... but ... but ..." stammered Traylor.

"That's it? You want me to fix an engine? No problem. I could do that in my sleep. You've got a deal Sparks." The two shook hands and Frank darted out the door.

"What, what just happened?" asked Traylor in a daze.

"Brandon just made a brilliant move," said Sly.

"Thanks," said Brandon, smiling at his friend. He walked over and sat in the Captain's chair.

"What brilliant move?" Traylor's face was smushed up in frustration and confusion.

"Frank wants to work on the bridge really badly so Brandon gave him the toughest job, and our biggest problem. Frank will work his hardest to get the engine fixed and he'll get rewarded with a few days up here with us. We get what we want and he gets what he wants. It's perfect," said Sly.

"But I don't want to spend a few days with Frank. He's terrible!"

"It won't be so bad," said Brandon. "It's only a few days."

"I guess," said Traylor, returning to the pilot's console.

"Good. Then it's settled."

"Hey, you took Captain Smoke's stars," she said.

"He borrowed them," said Sly.

"I borrowed them. What do you think?"

Traylor stared at Brandon. "I think … they look good, Captain Sparks." Traylor gave Brandon a big salute. "Aye, aye Captain! Ship's ahoy!" All three children began to laugh.

"Very funny," said Brandon as he stood up. If you guys need me, I'll be in the captain's office." Still laughing, he walked through the door at the opposite end of the bridge and sat down behind the desk. "Hey Sarah."

"Hello Brandon. How are you today?"

"I'm good. How are you?"

"Just fine. Repairs are under way on all systems damaged during the confrontation with the Ptevos."

"Good. I'm ready for my daily lesson," he said, and Sarah taught. Brandon spent half an hour learning about plants and animals, and another half hour reading a book called, "The Twins," which Sarah recommended would beef up his reading skills.

At the completion of a chapter, Brandon glanced at his watch for the time. Just as the hour was up, Sly walked into the room with a turkey sandwich and a glass of orange juice. He placed them on the desk before Brandon and sat down in one of the seats in front of the desk. "Thanks. Aren't you gonna eat?"

"No, I'm not hungry," said Sly.

Brandon took a bite of his sandwich and the two boys talked about their favorite things. Brandon brought up flying and Sly talked about baseball. They played games on the computer and Brandon taught Sly how to pilot a starship. Just as with the weapons systems, Sly was a natural. Brandon thought his level of skill was almost as high as his own. Sly enjoyed the lesson and wanted to teach Brandon something in return, so he taught him how to throw and hit a curve ball—on the computer. Both boys laughed and had a lot of fun. For a brief amount of time, Brandon was able to be a kid and forget that he had been thrown into the very dangerous predicament of captaining an untested military starship and all the responsibilities that came with it.

◆   ◆   ◆

Brandon popped the last bite of sandwich into his mouth and realized that another hour had passed. Sly returned to the bridge and Brandon went to check in on his parents. He walked into room 631 and saw his mom and dad lying in their bed. Their skin looked pale and almost dead but he could see their chests rise and lower as they breathed. His father's Shana was sitting on the nightstand. He walked over and picked it up. He placed it on his lap as he sat down in a chair next to the bed and took his mother's hand in his own. He thought about the good times he had had going to the movies with his mom and fishing with his dad and how he might never be able to do these things again. His eyes filled with tears, and he rushed out of the room, Shana in hand. Ten minutes was all the boy could take.

To calm himself down and maybe even relax, Brandon went swimming. The swimming room was empty so he had the whole pool to himself. He took off his shoes and socks and jumped into the gravity pool. He liked the way it made the bottom of his feet tingle. He swam a few laps for some exercise and then just floated for a while. He passed the time staring at the schools of fish swimming on the ceiling, trying to empty his mind.

◆   ◆   ◆

Seven days later, the repairs on the *Hidden Sun* were going smoothly. "Brandon, your presence is needed in the medical center," said Sarah. "It seems Reggie is trying to get out of bed."

"Thanks Sarah." Brandon picked up his father's Shana and made his way to the Medical Center. Upon entering, he saw Carlos trying to restrain Reggie. "What's going on guys?"

"Finally, you're here. Reggie's trying to get out of bed before he is fully healed. He's still got seven more days to go!"

"I'm fine. I want to help," said Reggie. He sat up quickly and winced in pain.

"See, I told you," said Carlos. "You need more rest."

"I agree."

"But Brandon, I want to help. I need to get out of this bed. All I hear all day is how cool the medical computer is."

"It is!" said Carlos defending himself.

"And besides that, I don't want Frank working at my console. He'll probably break something."

"So that's the reason you want out of bed. I knew it was something other than wanting to get back to work," said Carlos.

"Don't worry about Frank, Reggie. The job's yours when you get better. Besides, do you really believe Frank's going to be able to fix the engine within a week? I doubt even Lieutenant Bunts could do that!"

"I guess you're right. Still, can you give me something to do? I thought doing rounds with Private Devlin was bad, but laying in this bed and listening to medical stuff all day is worse!"

"Taking care of you is no walk in the park!" said Carlos.

"I figured as much. Here," said Brandon and he handed Reggie his father's Shana."

"A Shana?"

"My father's. I want you two to work together to finish Dr. Ramirez and my father's work. Reggie, you'll use the Shana and Carlos will use the medical computer."

"Together?" said Carlos.

"Yeah. You guys spend your entire day together ..."

"We know," said Reggie and Carlos in unison.

"Why not use that time to help out. Reggie, I saw you finish that Skibur so I know you're really good at solving problems, and Carlos, I've seen you working on the medical computer and you've really got a knack for it. You two should work together and try to figure out how to hurt and heal the Ptevos."

"But Brandon, aren't there like a billion of the world's best scientists working on solving this problem?" asked Reggie.

"Yeah, if they can't figure it out then what do you expect from us?" said Carlos.

"Well, the two of you can't do any worse than all of those scientists, and having two more brains working on the problem can't hurt."

Carlos and Reggie looked at each other and smiled. They nodded their heads and looked at Brandon. "We'll do it," said Reggie.

"As long as you promise to stay in bed," said Carlos.

"Deal," said Reggie, and the two boys slapped each other five.

"Brandon, your presence is needed on the Bridge. It's General Swift."

"Thanks Sarah. I've got to run guys. Let me know if you need anything." Brandon rushed out of the medical center to the elevator. When it reached Deck 1, he hurried onto the Bridge. "What's up?"

"General Swift is on the view screen," said Sly.

Brandon sat down in the captain's chair. "Hello General."

"Sparks, where are you?" screamed General Swift. His cigar almost fell out of his mouth. "The invasion has begun!"

"We were attacked again. We're making repairs on Glore."

"Well get your butts back to Earth! The Ptevos have already landed and they've deployed troops in the major cities around the world." Four smaller video boxes came up around General Swift. Paris, London, Moscow, and New York City were being taken over by Ptevos soldiers. Brandon stared at the New York City screen. The American Army was firing at the Ptevos but getting no results. The bullets and lasers just bounced off their thick, gray, armor like skin. The Ptevos soldiers were ramming everything in their path with the giant horn on their heads. People were being thrown into the air. "It's total chaos here Sparks. Our space defenses have been wiped out and our scientists have failed to find something that will destroy these bastards without killing our own people!"

"That's terrible," said Brandon.

"It gets worse. There is a giant armada heading this way. The *Hidden Sun* is our only hope. Get back here as soon as possible! I don't know how much longer we can hold out!" The view screen blipped to black and General Swift was gone.

"What are we gonna do Brandon?" said Traylor.

Before he could answer, the door to the Bridge opened and Frank Drek walked in. His face was covered with dirt and his shirt was ripped.

"Frank, what are you doing here?" said Brandon.

"It's fixed," he said, a bit out of breath.

"What's fixed?"

"The engine. Geez Sparks. I knew you were slow but ..."

"You fixed the engine ... already?"

"Yeah. I told you, no problem."

"No way!" said Traylor in total disbelief.

"Sarah, what is the status of engine number three?" asked Brandon.

"Engine number three is fully operational. It is in perfect working order."

Brandon, Traylor and Sly were amazed. Frank walked over to the Nav/Com console. "What do you think you're doing?" said Traylor.

"I get Nav/Com until Reggie Loser is better. That was the deal. Tell her Sparks."

"No, but ..." said Traylor.

"He's right Traylor," said Brandon. "A deal is a deal. The Nav/Com console is yours until Reggie is well enough to claim it."

"Excellent!" said Frank.

"But, go get cleaned up first. You're a mess."

Frank looked down at himself and saw the grit under his fingernails and the rip in his shirt. He looked up and without a word, headed out of the Bridge.

"I can't believe we have to work with him," said Traylor slumping in her chair.

"It won't be that bad. He did manage to fix that engine."

"And that is pretty amazing," said Sly.

"Let's see what else he can do," said Brandon.

Traylor sat up and pointed a finger at him. "Fine, but if he messes with me, I'm gonna punch his lights out!" She folded her arms and returned to her slumped position.

"Don't worry. We've got much bigger problems than Frank Drek. Sarah, inform everyone on board that we are taking off."

"Yes Brandon."

"All right Traylor, let's get going."

The Hidden Sun roared to life and slowly lifted off of Glore's white surface. The snow that had accumulated on top of the ship, slid off as the *Hidden Sun* rose into the atmosphere, and out into space.

◆   ◆   ◆

A few short minutes later, Frank walked through the bridge door. He was wearing jeans and a T-shirt and his hair was still wet from showering. He walked over to the Nav/Com console and gave it a look over.

"Frank, set a course for Earth," said Brandon who along with Sly and Traylor watched his every move. Brandon could tell Traylor was hoping for failure or for him to do something that would have him removed from the bridge, but it never happened. Frank easily pushed the correct buttons and flawlessly transmitted the course to Traylor, who let out a small "Hrumph."

"Ready?" said Brandon. Everyone nodded. "Then let's go."

Traylor pushed the yellow button on her console and the ship jumped to light-speed. For a few seconds, Brandon sat in his chair and watched the stars zip by. It reminded him of his first day on board the *Hidden Sun*.

Sarah quickly interrupted his moment of peace. "Brandon, Reggie and Carlos require the Rhino-37 blood sample to continue their work."

"OK Sarah. Tell them I'll be down with it in a few minutes."

"I'll go with you to the lab to retrieve the sample," said Sly. "There are a lot of places it could be kept."

"What sample?" said Frank.

"No Sly, you stay here and explain everything to Frank. He's missed out on a lot. Besides, my father would never keep something so important in the lab. I bet it's in the fridge in his room."

Sly began to explain to Frank about the Ptevos and the invasion of Earth as Brandon walked out the door. He followed the familiar route to room 631 and walked inside. Much to his displeasure, his parents were still exactly as they were the last time he had seen them. He whispered, "Hi mom. Hi dad," and walked into the kitchen. He turned on the light and gave the refrigerator door a strong pull. The refrigerator wobbled and to his surprise, a glass beaker, and a glass jar came tumbling out. He quickly jumped backwards as they crashed to the kitchen floor, shattering their contents on one another. So much time had passed since his mother had told his father that the fridge needed to be leveled, that he had forgot.

Brandon looked down and saw a red liquid and blue plant bubble together and then disintegrate. He picked up a piece of the glass beaker that was marked with a piece of masking tape. He recognized his father's handwriting. It said: RHINO-37.

Brandon looked closely at the shattered pieces of the jar, but could not find any markings. He looked around and saw that a small piece of the plant had not mixed with the blood and had found its way underneath the refrigerator. He reached his hand under the door and picked it up, holding it in front of his face. He twirled it around to get a better look and a smile came over his face. He rushed out of the room saying, "thanks dad," and left the mess on the floor to be cleaned at a later time.

◆   ◆   ◆

"What is it?" said Reggie, now holding the surviving piece of plant.

"It's called 'Blue Bomber.'"

"Blue Bomber?" said Carlos, taking the plant from Reggie and giving it a good look over. "I've never heard of it."

"That's because my father invented it. We used it as bait to catch fish on our last fishing trip. This made the Ptevos blood burn up."

"Really? Then we could use it defeat them," said Reggie, who was recovering, but still in pain from his injuries.

"Lie back down," said Carlos, and reluctantly, Reggie did.

"You're exactly right. We just need to figure out a way to use it on them without destroying the buildings and our own people."

"That's easy," said Reggie. "We could just fill our bombs with the plant and then set it to explode a thousand feet in the air. The explosion would spread the plant over a large area and cause it to rain small pieces of Blue Bomber over the entire city."

"I knew you were the smartest kid I'd ever met," said Brandon. "Let's get started. If there was a little in the fridge then I'm sure there must be more in my father's lab. I'll send Sly to bring you all the Blue Bomber he can find. You two work on how to rig those bombs. When we get a little closer to Earth, and you're feeling a little better Reggie, the two of you will implement the plan."

"Sounds good," said Carlos.

"Reggie, you're finally gonna get your chance to see what's in those two long 'Utility' rooms."

"I can't wait."

"Good. I'll see you guys later. I'll be on the bridge if you need me."

◆   ◆   ◆

With a smile on his face, Brandon walked onto the bridge. "Sly, I need you to do me a favor." Brandon explained to Frank, Sly and Traylor what he had discovered in his parents room and the plan he had devised in the medical center with Carlos and Reggie.

"Excellent plan," said Sly.

"I'm glad you think so. I need you to go to my father's lab and bring as much Blue Bomber as you can find to the medical center."

Without a word, Sly zipped out of the bridge door with uncanny speed.

"Brandon, just before you came in, my control console changed," said Traylor.

"What happened?"

"It says that we can now travel at five times light-speed!"

"Is that even possible?" said Frank, and Traylor shrugged her shoulders.

"Sarah, can the *Hidden Sun* travel at five times light-speed?"

"Brandon, the *Hidden Sun* took in a large amount of energy when it entered Crescent 19 and can now generate that speed. Of course, it has never been tested."

"Cool," said Frank.

"Everything else has worked on this ship, so far. Let's give it a try."

"Are you sure?" said Traylor. What if something goes wrong?"

"We've got to get back to Earth as soon as possible. You saw the video of New York City. General Swift says the world's survival depends on us getting this ship back there and this is definitely our fastest option."

"I hope this works." Slowly, Traylor pushed a sequence of buttons on her console. She paused before pressing the last one. As soon as she did, the Hidden Sun launched forward at tremendous speed. The stars became beams of light.

"It works!" said Brandon.

"How long till we reach Earth?" asked Frank.

"At this speed? Two days."

"Good," said Brandon. I'm on my way home, he thought to himself. He wanted to tell Charlie right then and there, but he resisted the urge.

CHAPTER SEVENTEEN

BETRAYED

The *Hidden Sun* vaulted out of five times light speed just behind the planet Mars. The ship slowly swept to the right of the red planet, and Earth came into view. Brandon smiled and sat back in the captain's chair. He was happy to be home. Once the *Hidden Sun* was clear of Mars, Brandon's smile began to fade and he leaned forward.

"What is that?" wondered Traylor, pointing at the view screen.

"It can't be," said Sly.

"It is!" said Frank. He pushed a series of buttons on his console. "There was a battle here. A massive battle!"

The *Hidden Sun* came upon a vast graveyard of destroyed ships, and satellites. Hundreds of starships had been cut into thousands of pieces. There was so much debris that from where they stood, it looked like Earth had a ring around it. The entire crew stared in stunned silence as the Hidden Sun passed through the battlefield. Brandon saw the American flag on many of the destroyed ships, and he recognized pieces of those belonging to the Ptevos. Frank broke the silence.

"There are a bunch of working Ptevos ships on the far side of the planet."

"OK, then let's contact General Swift and land this thing before they notice we're here." He was eager to tell the General about the Blue Bomber.

Frank pushed a few buttons on his control console and moments later, General Swift was on the screen.

"Sparks, where are you?" he yelled.

"We're just above the Earth's surface. General, we've found a way to defeat ..."

"Just get the *Hidden Sun* on the ground, Sparks. We need that ship!" yelled the General, shaking his fist in the air.

Brandon continued to try and tell the General about the Blue Bomber. "Yes sir, but I want you to know that we have found ..."

General Swift interrupted Brandon for the second time. "We'll talk about whatever you want to talk about when you land. You must get the *Hidden Sun* to the baseball fields in Central Park. Can you do that?"

"Yes General, but ..."

"Good work son. Swift out." General Swift blipped off the view screen.

"Man is he rude," said Traylor.

"Most generals are like that," said Sly. "They're used to being in command."

"I guess, but in a strange way he kinda reminds me of another general we know."

"Zarafat?" said Frank.

"I don't know," said Sly.

"Don't you think you're being a little harsh?" said Brandon. Traylor just shrugged her shoulders. "Let's just get this ship on the ground. We can talk trash about General Swift after the Ptevos are gone."

The *Hidden Sun* zoomed out of the field of debris and entered the Earth's atmosphere. Frank transferred the coordinates to Traylor and she flew the ship to the island of Manhattan without incident. As they zipped over the Battery, they saw large plumes of smoke coming from massive fighting on the ground.

"Manhattan's like a war zone," said Brandon.

"Cool!" said Frank. His eyes were open wide and he had a very evil smile on his face.

"Not cool," said Sly.

"Definitely not cool," said Traylor, giving Frank an angry look. He just shrugged his shoulders and continued to enjoy the view.

Moments later, the *Hidden Sun* approached Central Park and Brandon noticed that Sly was staring at the baseball fields. He had never seen his friend so interested in something in the entire time they had known each other. Traylor set the *Hidden Sun* down softly on the large baseball field in Central Park. One of the ship's large feet covered second base and most of the infield. Immediately, several camouflaged cars and trucks surrounded the *Hidden Sun*.

"Lower the shields," said Brandon to Sly. "I'm going out to meet General Swift. Can you get me a sample of the Blue Bomber to give him?"

Sly nodded and rushed out of the room.

"What should we do?" asked Traylor.

"Just stay put, I guess. I'll be back in a few minutes."

Brandon took the elevator down to deck 25 and went out the shuttle bay door. He looked up and saw four military helicopters hovering above the *Hidden Sun*. As soon as his feet hit the ground two heavily armed soldiers met him. "Are you Sparks?" shouted one over the noise.

"Yes," said Brandon just as loud. They escorted him to a camouflaged Humvee and General Swift stepped out. He was much broader than Brandon thought he would be. A half smoked cigar jutted out of the left corner of his mouth.

Brandon stuck out his hand to shake the General's but the General did not do the same. "It's good to meet you General," screamed Brandon, trying to be heard over the roar of the helicopters. "What I was trying to tell you while I was in space was that my crew and I figured out how to defeat the Ptevos."

"Oh you did, did you?" yelled General Swift sarcastically.

"Yes, it's this plant called the Blue ..."

General Swift interrupted Brandon again. This time he grabbed him by the shirt and brought his face down to Brandon's. Then he started to scream. "Listen kid. You might think you're something special because you got that ship back here in one piece but I don't think it's funny you trying to tell me you've got it all figured out. You don't know squat!"

"But ..." said Brandon trying to get a word in, but the General blew smoke in his face and just screamed louder.

"I'm not trusting the world's safety to a stupid little kid like you. I don't care what the president says."

"The president?" said Brandon, pushing the smoke out of his face.

The General ripped the four silver stars off of Brandon's chest and then released him from his grasp. "Get him out of here!" he screamed.

"Hey, those are mine!" said Brandon as a soldier hooked his arms from behind and held him tightly. He struggled as another soldier swooshed a dark hood over his head and all he could see was black. Brandon struggled to escape. He couldn't see anything but he could feel the breathing of the soldier behind him on his neck. He kicked his legs out trying to free himself, but it didn't work. The soldier's huge hands just tightened around his thin arms. Brandon heard the General scream, "Shut him up!" A few seconds later he felt a blunt object hit him on the back of the head.

◆　　　◆　　　◆

Brandon slowly opened his eyes and tried to focus. He was sitting in a metal chair at the long end of a rectangular metal table. He lifted his head off the table and felt the back of it. There was a large bump that stung, but he was glad it was not bleeding. "Where am I?" he said groggily.

Brandon looked around the room and saw that the wall in front of him was black. The wall to the left of him was black. He looked behind him and that wall was also black, except for a large rectangular mirror embedded in the middle. Brandon thought it looked suspicious. The only other place he had seen this kind of mirror was in the movies.

That must be a double-sided mirror, he thought to himself. Someone's watching me.

Brandon turned back around in his chair and faced forward. If someone was indeed watching him, he didn't want to give away that he knew. He turned his attention to the floor, which was shiny, black marble with swirls of an even darker shade of black. Before looking, Brandon knew that the ceiling was black, but he looked anyway and saw six silver sprinklers and two rows of long fluorescent lights, which buzzed softly above his head. Aside from that, he could not hear anything. The room was silent.

Brandon looked at the wall to the right, which was a good twenty feet away from the chair he was sitting in. It too was just as black as all the other walls but in the middle was a completely flat metal slab. It was the exact size of his bedroom door but there was no doorknob or light coming from underneath.

"Where am I?" said Brandon again.

Without warning, there was a loud unlocking noise to Brandon's right. The big metal slab slowly swung open. "It must be a foot thick," said Brandon. When the door was completely open, in walked General Swift carrying a thin manila folder. "You're safe," he said as the door swung closed. He took a seat across from Brandon.

"Where are my parents? And where are my friends?"

"Settle down Sparks. All of the people have been removed from the *Hidden Sun*. Captain Smoke, his crew and all of the adults have been taken to a military health facility to receive care. The other eighty-seven children are being held in a detention center for their own safety."

"For their own safety? They're prisoners?"

"Maybe you don't realize this son, but our planet is being invaded by vicious aliens." General Swift opened the folder and took out some pictures that he placed in front of Brandon. "They already have control of Paris, London, and even Washington."

Brandon looked at the pictures. They were horrifying. Buildings were being destroyed and people were being killed. The Ptevos looked angry and determined.

"These monsters have won some of the battles but it's my job to make sure they don't win the war and the *Hidden Sun* is the key."

"I can help you," said Brandon. "I know how to …"

"Look kid, you did a good job getting it back here, I'll give you that, but it needs an experienced, adult, military Captain and crew. It's not a toy for some kid from the suburbs to play with." General Swift looked at his watch. "Right about now I should be getting a message that my people have control of the Hidden Sun."

As if on cue, the metal door opened once again and in walked one of General Swift's men. He was a generic looking soldier, very thin with a short blond crew cut and army fatigues. He carried a Shana and had a large ear piece in his left ear. He saluted General Swift, who saluted him back.

"What news Private Wonk?"

"Sir, we have not been able to gain control of the Hidden Sun, sir."

The General's face turned sour. "What?" he said, raising his voice.

"Sir, the ship's computer will not respond to our voice commands, sir."

Brandon's eyes lit up and he did everything he could not to smile. He knew there was no way the army could have known that he had renamed her Sarah and that she would not respond to 'ship's computer.'

"Sir, the ship's computer will also not respond to the override codes, sir. We are totally locked out, sir."

Brandon was not sure how this happened. He wasn't even aware that the *Hidden Sun* had override codes, but if he had to guess, he'd say it was the handiwork of his best friend.

General Swift was stunned. He looked back at Brandon with anger and lunged at him with both hands. As his fingers started to close around his shirt, Brandon slid his chair back and escaped. "What did you do?" screamed General Swift. "Why can't we access the ship's computer?"

"I ... I ..." stammered Brandon.

General Swift made his way around the table to try and grab Brandon, but Private Wonk stepped between the two. "Sir, let me remind you that the Captain of the ship has no knowledge of how to change the override codes, especially with regards to the Hidden Sun. It is way too technical, sir."

"I know," said General Swift begrudgingly. He took a deep breath, straightened his jacket, and started to calm down. He sat back in his seat as Private Wonk looked at Brandon, who had his back to the giant mirror. He signaled for him to return to his chair and cautiously, Brandon did.

General Swift stared at Brandon for a few moments and Brandon stared back. Then the General turned to Private Wonk. "How did this happen?"

"Sir, I don't know, sir."

General Swift pounded his fist on the table and stood up. "That's not good enough. I want you to find out!"

"Sir, yes sir."

General Swift and Private Wonk walked towards the metal slab. "How are the scientists doing with Rhino-37?"

"Not good sir. They're stumped, sir."

"Damn!"

Brandon knew that he would get yelled at again but he couldn't just sit there and let the world be taken over by the Ptevos. He'd seen General Zarafat's evil firsthand. He had to at least try and get through General Swift's hardheadedness. He spoke two words. "Blue Bomber."

"I don't want to hear another word out of you Sparks!" screamed the General.

"But I can help. The Blue Bomber can ..."

"I said not another word!" Once again, Private Wonk had to step in front of the General to stop him from attacking Brandon.

"Why won't you let me help you? You said it yourself. The President thinks I can help. I can captain the *Hidden Sun* ..."

"Captain? Captain? You're no captain," he snarled. "You didn't go through years of rigorous training. You're just a kid. And as for the president, he's never served a day of his life in the armed forces. He doesn't know the difference between a machine gun and a laser cannon. I've got over *forty years* of service. Just because he says, 'let this kid help' doesn't mean I'm going to listen to him. War's no place for a stupid kid."

Brandon wanted to stand up and force General Swift to listen to him but he knew there was no way of doing that. Instead, he just sat in his chair and tried to figure out how to escape from the black prison he was in. He glanced at his watch and could only think of one way.

"Private Wonk, I want all my men off the *Hidden Sun*. If we can't use it then I won't let it fall into the hands of the enemy. I want that ship turned to dust. Let no piece remain."

"Sir, yes sir." Brandon's face had a look of shock as the metal slab swung open. The two men left and the metal slab swung shut. Brandon was left alone.

"I can't believe they're gonna blow up the *Hidden Sun*!" Brandon knew there wasn't much time, so he had to contact Charlie. He also knew that he was being watched through the mirror so he looked around the room to try and find a place that would be out of view. There was none, but he had an idea. Brandon pulled his chair in close and folded his arms on the table. He had done this hundreds of times in school when he was bored or tired. He rested his head on his arms but left his mouth free to speak. "Charlie," he said in the softest whisper possible. He was betting on the fact that the people watching him would not be able to hear him and think that he had fallen asleep.

"Hey buddy!" said a familiar voice. "I just got back from the tanning booth. My circuits are a little crispy."

"No time for jokes now, Charlie. I've been taken prisoner by General Swift. I figured out how to defeat the Ptevos but he won't listen. It's the Blue Bomber Charlie!"

Charlie's voice went from the happy-go-lucky guy Brandon knew and loved to being stone cold serious. "Your father's bait?"

"Yeah, and General Swift is gonna blow up the *Hidden Sun* and all the Blue Bomber is on board. If he does that there's no way we can defeat the Ptevos."

"Well then we've got to get you out of there."

"I don't even know where I am."

"You're in the Gotham Tower in Manhattan, on the hundred and fifty-second floor."

"How do you know that?"

"There's a locator in your watch."

"Oh, where's the *Hidden Sun?*"

"It's still in Central Park. They're showing it on the news right now."

"Is there any way to fly the ship by remote control?"

"No Brandon, the computer needs someone to fly the ship."

"Then there's no hope. They took everybody off the ship." There was a brief pause.

"I wouldn't say that my good friend."

"What?"

"One of our friends is still on board the *Hidden Sun.*"

"But General Swift said all the people were taken off. The adults and all eighty-seven kids plus me."

"One of your more special friends," said Charlie.

Brandon thought for a minute. It didn't take him long to figure out who it was. "Can you contact the *Hidden Sun?* I need to talk to Sarah."

"Not a problem. Brandon, do you remember right before I turned the ship's computer back on that I made some slight changes?"

"Yes."

"Well, one of them was connecting the ship's computer to your watch. I figured it might come in handy. Now you can talk directly to Sarah. Also, I got rid of those pesky override codes. Humans are so afraid of computers, it's a wonder they depend on them so much."

"You're the best Charlie."

"I know."

"Sarah?" whispered Brandon.

"Hello Brandon," said the ship's computer.

"Sarah, I know this isn't exactly the best time but I'd like you to meet my best friend in the entire universe, Charlie."

"Hello Charlie. I've heard a great deal about you."

"And I've heard a lot about you. It's always good to meet a fellow computer."

"Brandon, they've taken everyone off the ship," she said.

"I know." Brandon took a deep breath. "Is Sly on board?" There was a brief pause while Sarah scanned the ship and Brandon crossed his fingers.

"Yes, he is. I must tell you Brandon—military vehicles have surrounded the *Hidden Sun*. They have their laser cannons pointed at me and the shields are down!"

"Contact Sly and tell him to get to the Bridge of the ship and fly it out of there before they have a chance to fire."

"Can he do it?" asked Charlie.

"He can. I taught him how to fly myself."

"Good, then Sly can fly the *Hidden Sun* and rescue you by blasting out the window."

Brandon picked his head up and looked around the room. When he was finished, he laid it back on his folded arms and resumed whispering. "But, Charlie, there is no window in this room. Only black walls."

"My sensors are showing that you are in a corner room on floor one-hundred and fifty-two, on the south west side of the building. They must have disguised the window as a solid wall. It's as easy as changing the color of a wall back home."

"It must be the one opposite the door," said Brandon. He peeked his head up again and now that he took a closer look, he could see that it was a slightly different shade of black from the other walls in the room. He put his head back down. "Charlie, transfer my coordinates to Sarah, and Sarah, get the Hidden Sun away from those laser cannons and let me know when you are in range."

"OK," said Charlie.

"OK," said Sarah.

Brandon picked his head up and sat back in his chair. He took a deep breath and tried to prepare himself for what he was going to have to do.

◆   ◆   ◆

A few minutes later, just as Brandon was starting to relax, General Swift and Private Wonk stormed through the metal slab demanding to know how he was controlling the *Hidden Sun*. Brandon jumped out of his chair and went to the far side of the table to distance himself from the screaming General. "I'm not."

General Swift's face was red with anger. Brandon could see little balls of spit coming from his mouth as he spoke. "The Hidden Sun has just taken off from Central Park with no crew on board. The force of the liftoff sent forty-two military vehicles into the air. I want to know how you are controlling that ship!"

"I already told you, I'm not. Shouldn't you be worrying about the attacking Ptevos?"

"If the *Hidden Sun* gets into the hands of those monsters then we won't have to worry about them because you can kiss our planet good-bye!"

"But ..."

"No more buts from you! Stupid kid. I'm going to ring your neck!" General Swift made his way towards Brandon, who circled around to the other end of the table to avoid him.

Private Wonk put a hand over his ear and listened carefully. "Sir, it seems we've lost the *Hidden Sun*, sir."

General Swift stopped dead in his tracks and stood up straight. He turned his head toward Private Wonk. "What do you mean, you've lost the *Hidden Sun?*"

"Sir, we can't find it, sir. It's not showing up on radar, sir."

"That's not possible! It's a giant starship!"

"I don't know, sir."

"Well, don't just stand there. Find the thing!" Brandon thought General Swift's head was going to explode.

"Sir, yes sir." The metal slab swung open and Private Wonk ran out. Brandon eyed the opening and thought about making a run for it, but didn't chance it. The door swung closed with a thud.

Brandon was now standing a few feet from the metal slab with General Swift at the far end of the table. The two were alone together for the first time. General Swift's eyes burned with rage. For a moment, Brandon thought he might come after him again. Instead, he reached into his pocket and pulled out four silver stars. "Do you see these?"

"Hey, those are mine. You stole them from me!"

"No, they're not yours. They're Captain Smoke's. It took him twenty years of service before he became a Captain. You think you deserve them after a few weeks? Let me tell you something Sparks, after we win this war against the Ptevos, I'm going to make sure that no matter how hard you try or how much time you put in, you will never, ever become a Captain of a starship!"

At that very moment, he heard Sarah in his ear. "Brandon, we are right outside of the building. The shuttle bay door is open. On your command, Sly will fire."

"But General, I'm already the Captain of the Hidden Sun, and all I want to do is help. This is the last time I'll offer."

"You've got real nerve Sparks," said General Swift, pointing a finger at him. "I've changed my mind. I was going to let you go free after I crush the Ptevos, but now I've decided to kill you right here and now. Everyone will consider you a casualty of war."

Brandon took a deep breath. "I'm sorry things have to work out this way."

General Swift had a confused look on his face. He has no idea what is about to happen, thought Brandon to himself. "Now Sarah," said Brandon and he crouched to the floor.

A single laser blast hit the black wall farthest from Brandon and it shattered into a million pieces. Charlie was right about the wall actually being a large piece of glass. The beam continued through the room and traveled above Brandon's head, slamming into the back wall, and crumbling a large section of the concrete.

The smoke from the blast caused the sprinkler system to switch on and the water came down like a heavy rain. Everything in the room was getting drenched, including Brandon. He could feel the wind coming in from the gaping hole in the building. It was the first time he realized how high up he really was.

General Swift had been knocked to the floor by the shock of the blast but had quickly climbed back to his feet. He looked out the window and saw the *Hidden Sun* hovering a few hundred feet away. "What … what's going on?"

"Sorry General, but it's time for me to leave."

General Swift pointed at Brandon. "You're not going anywhere Sparks!"

Brandon had hoped the path to the window would be clear and hadn't had time to plan for what he would do if someone stood in his way. General Swift was much larger than Brandon and he would have to use his smarts and quickness to escape. Thousands of thoughts ran through his mind all at once: His parents, playing with Charlie, talking with Sarah, swimming with Reggie, watching Traylor fly, keeping Frank in check, and talking baseball with Sly. Suddenly, something clicked inside Brandon's mind. "Baseball," he said, as though the word held a great secret.

Brandon started to run towards General Swift, who was standing firmly in his way, his legs spread apart for balance. In one hand he held the four sliver stars but he was more than ready to grasp Brandon with both hands. He had a very intense look on his face and Brandon knew that if the General got his hands on him, he might end up dead. He also knew that if he didn't chance it, the General would kill him anyway. His heart began to race.

The water was still coming down heavily and as Brandon ran, it splashed a foot into the air. He was getting closer and closer to the large hands of General Swift. Baseball, baseball, baseball, thought Brandon to himself. He had built up a good amount of speed and when it looked like the General's hands were close enough to grab him, Brandon formed his legs into the shape of the number "4" and hit the ground. The water made the black marble floor very slippery and General Swift did not have time to react. Brandon's hands were above his head and General Swift lunged at them. He clamped the hand holding the four silver stars around Brandon's thin, right wrist and then began to smile. It was short lived because both his hand and Brandon's wrist were very wet. Brandon's hand squirmed free of the General's as his body slid between the older man's legs.

After he was safely through, in one quick motion, Brandon stood up. He looked in his hand and he was holding the four silver stars. When he reached the window, he looked out on the cityscape. It was a beautiful clear day and for the second time, Brandon realized how high up he was. The wind was very strong and one hundred and fifty-two stories was a long way down. He looked back at General Swift, who was shocked that Brandon had got by him.

"Sorry about your window and the wall over there," shouted Brandon over the howling wind. "After I defeat the Ptevos, I'll find some way to pay for it." Brandon pinned the four silver stars to his chest and looked out the open window. "Charlie, I'm gonna need your help."

His friend responded instantly. "Sure thing Brandon. I'm here for you." Charlie's voice had always been a source of comfort, especially during difficult times. Brandon smiled at general Swift and then took a deep breath. His heart was racing as he kicked off and jumped out of the window.

"Sparks!" yelled General Swift but Brandon was already five flights down.

The wind rushed by his face as did the surrounding buildings. Brandon's small body tumbled to the ground at a tremendous pace. He managed to turn himself over in midair so his back was facing the ground. The *Hidden Sun* floated above him and for a brief moment he thought it looked very beautiful from this view. He pressed the bottom left and top right buttons on his watch and the same hair like cable that had carried him over to the pilot's chair when the power had gone out on the Hidden Sun, shot out into the sky. Brandon continued falling towards the ground as the shark like jaws of the cable climbed ever higher.

"Charlie!" screamed Brandon over the heavy winds.

"Almost!" said Charlie.

The cable seemed to move with a mind of its own towards the *Hidden Sun*, undeterred by the wind. As gravity plunged Brandon ever closer to the hard asphalt below, its jaws closed on the shuttle bay door with a "THUNK." The slack went out of the cable and Brandon's decent came to a stop less than one hundred feet from the ground. The momentum swung him between two tall skyscrapers. He screamed with terrified joy as he flew through the Manhattan skyline.

"Reel me in! Reel me in!" he screamed and Charlie did just that. Brandon was pulled high into the sky, and after a few minutes, was safely in the shuttle bay of the *Hidden Sun*.

"Sarah, close the door," said Brandon and he made his way towards the elevator."

CHAPTER EIGHTEEN

RESCUED

Sly was sitting in the pilot's Chair when Brandon entered the bridge. He immediately stood up and high-fived his friend.

"It's good to have you back on board."

"It's good to be on board. I almost didn't make it." Brandon retold his entire escape from the moment he awoke in the interrogation room. Sly was most impressed with the baseball slide Brandon had used to escape from General Swift. "Speaking of escapes, how'd you get away from the soldiers who took everyone else off the ship?"

"I was in the lab getting you the sample of Blue Bomber you asked for when I heard a scream. I went to look to see who it was and I saw a soldier pulling a kid down the hallway like he was a criminal or something. The soldier then said into his radio, 'I got another one.' Remember, I snuck on this ship and I wasn't about to be captured by the army and sent back to the Pillars, so I hid in one of the trees. After he left the room, I climbed into the ventilation shaft. About an hour later, I received a message from Sarah that you had been captured and that I needed to go to the bridge, so I did. Luckily, I was able to fly the *Hidden Sun* out of Central Park before the army could fire their weapons and get it to the Gotham Tower. Once there I opened the shuttle bay door. The rest you know."

"You're definitely not like any kid I've ever met," said Brandon, amazed that his friend had gone undetected.

"I hope that's a good thing."

"It is."

"Good," said Sly. "What's next?"

"We have to find Reggie and the rest of the kids. Any idea where they might be?"

"When I was in the ventilation shaft, I overheard one of the guards mention a military base called Camelot."

"Sarah, where is the military base Camelot located?"

"Camelot is located on the outskirts of Colorado Springs, Colorado."

"Can you please send the coordinates to the pilot's station?"

"Of course Brandon."

"Thanks. Ready?" said Brandon to Sly.

Sly walked over and stood behind the weapons and defense console. "Ready."

Brandon sat down in the pilot's chair. It was only the second time he had had the opportunity to fly the *Hidden Sun*, and he was very excited. He pushed a few buttons and grabbed the controls. His movements were perfect and it felt like he had been flying the Hidden Sun all his life. "Let's go."

◆　　◆　　◆

The *Hidden Sun* zipped through the Colorado clouds and flew over the Rocky Mountains. Brandon followed Sarah's coordinates and took the ship down, flying low in a valley between two mountains. In the distance, there were people running and laser blasts being fired. "Sly, put up the shields," said Brandon. Sly pushed a few buttons on his console and focused on the view screen.

Brandon flew the *Hidden Sun* closer to the skirmish on the ground. "Sarah, can we get a better look at what's going on down there?" The view screen zoomed in on the ground below and what the two boys saw was horrifying. Ptevos soldiers were pursuing and firing at Reggie, Traylor and the rest of the children captured by General Swift. They hadn't hit anyone, but they were closing in fast.

"We have to save them," said Sly.

"I see eleven Ptevos. Can you shoot some cover fire to protect our friends?"

"I can do better than that."

Brandon watched the view screen as Sly fired laser blast after laser blast. Each one hit a Ptevos soldier directly in the chest and knocked him to the ground. "That was amazing! You didn't miss a single shot!" Brandon had never seen such perfect shooting.

The children kept on running as the Ptevos soldiers climbed to their feet and fired their own laser blasts at the Hidden Sun. Their thick, gray skin had protected them from harm and the boys saw first hand why the government had started project Rhino-37. Sly fired a second round of laser blasts and once again hit each of the Ptevos in the chest. They were knocked to the ground and this created more space between them and the eighty-seven children running toward the Hidden Sun.

"What next?" asked Sly.

"I don't know. You're the weapons and defense guy. What do you think we should do?"

Sly answered without pause. "I think we should try out one of the new weapons. If we fire a few Devil Bombs between the two groups, it should give our friends enough time to get on board and for us to escape. What do you think?"

"I think it's a good idea." Brandon grabbed the controls of the Hidden Sun and prepared to land the ship after the bombs hit. "I'm ready. Fire at will."

Sly pushed a series of buttons on his console and fired two Devil Bombs. They shot out of the bottom of the *Hidden Sun* and within seconds, exploded on the ground between the Ptevos soldiers and the children. A giant blue wall of fire rose from the ground and the Ptevos soldiers were stopped in their tracks. The Hidden Sun swooped to the ground and Brandon opened the shuttle bay door. All of the children ran on board as the wall of fire began to collapse. A few laser blasts hit the Hidden Sun as the shuttle bay door started to close. One actually sneaked into the shuttle bay and hit the back wall with a thud. It was the only blast that did any damage.

"All eighty-seven children are on board," said Sarah. Brandon immediately launched the *Hidden Sun* off the ground and flew away from the group of Ptevos soldiers who were still firing their weapons. For the moment, they were safe.

◆　　◆　　◆

Ten minutes later, everyone on board the *Hidden Sun* was standing on the bridge. Even though they were covered in dirt and some had bruises and cuts, they were all happy to see Brandon and Sly, and to be back on board. Brandon told them how he had escaped from General Swift. He left out the part about Charlie and just told them he was able to speak to Sarah using his watch. After his story was finished, he settled everyone down and said, "I don't know what's going to happen next but I think things are going to get even more dangerous. If anyone wants off this ship, now is the time to speak up." Brandon looked around the room and not a single voice could be heard. "Good. You should all get some food and some rest. Bridge crew and medical officer, please hang around for a minute."

All of the children made their way out of the Bridge except for Reggie, Traylor, Frank, and Carlos. They all looked exhausted. "How did you escape from the military base?" asked Sly.

They all looked at one another and Traylor was the least tired of the bunch. "The army put us in a large cage with no roof and razor wire around the top. It was terrible. They gave us very little food and there was no bathroom. I had to watch Frank pee."

Everyone was grossed out and turned to look at Frank. "What? I had to go!" he said in his defense. Traylor turned back to Brandon and continued her story.

"When the Ptevos attacked the military base, they damaged one side of the cage and we all climbed out and ran. They sent some soldiers after us and we hadn't gotten very far when you guys showed up and got us out of there."

"Wow," said Brandon.

"Wow is right," said Sly.

Brandon walked over to the captain's chair and sat down. "I know you're all tired and hungry, and so am I but the Ptevos are attacking and there's no time to rest. I'll have someone bring up some food for all of us." Traylor sat down in the pilot's chair with a "WOOMPF." She looked exhausted. "Frank, take the Nav/Com station."

As he walked to the console, Frank bumped Reggie with his shoulder. "Tough luck Thacker!" he said with a wicked smile.

"What?" said Reggie after recovering from Frank's bump. "I'm healthy. You said when I healed I could have the Nav/Com station back!"

"Reggie, let me talk to you in there." Brandon walked over to the captain's office and Reggie followed. The door shut behind the two boys and immediately, Reggie raised his voice.

"You promised Brandon! My ribs are finally healed and I want my old job back. I can't believe you'd let Frank keep it. I thought we were friends!"

"We are friends and I'm not letting Frank keep it. The job is yours."

"Really?"

"Yeah."

"Then why did you just give it to Frank?"

"Because I need the smartest kid I know to help stop these Ptevos soldiers from taking over our cities. General Swift won't listen to me so it's up to us and I need you and Carlos to go and rig the bombs with Blue Bomber."

"Oh," said Reggie. He didn't know what to say. He had been so mad coming into the room that he was not prepared to get his way.

"Will you do it? I can always let Frank give it a go. He did fix that engine."

"No! You gave the job to me and it's mine to do, so I'll do it."

"Good."

"Good," said Reggie. He turned around and walked through the door. "Come on Carlos," we're leaving.

"What?" said Carlos as Reggie grabbed him by the shirt and pulled him out of the bridge. Brandon sat down in the Captain's chair with a smile on his face.

"What happened?" said Traylor.

"Reggie and Carlos are going to rig the bombs with Blue Bomber."

"Do you think it's gonna work? Killing blood in your parents' kitchen is one thing but their skin is so thick. I saw one up close and it looked like it was made of concrete!"

"It better work. It's the only chance we've got. Look, there's nothing we can do until Reggie and Carlos rig a few of the bombs. Let's get some food up here and try to relax for an hour or so. After we deal with the soldiers on the ground we'll still have to find a way to defeat the armada that's on the way."

"An armada?" said Frank.

Traylor's eyes opened wide. "I totally forgot about that. How are we gonna defeat an entire armada? We're just one ship!"

"I don't know. I was hoping our Weapons and Defense guy would be able to help."

"I don't know Brandon," said Sly, looking over all the buttons on his console.

"Well, we've got to find something." Brandon looked down at his watch. "Look, we've got some time while Reggie and Carlos make some Blue Bombers, let's go in there and try to figure something out." Sly nodded and followed Brandon into the captain's office. The two boys sat down to think. After a few moments of silence, Brandon spoke. "I think we're going to have to use our most powerful weapon."

"But we don't even know what the Ribbon-Cutter does!" said Sly.

"Then let's find out. Sarah, please tell us everything about the Ribbon-Cutter."

CHAPTER EIGHTEEN

The video wall behind Brandon came on and showed detailed diagrams of how the Ribbon-Cutter worked. It captivated Brandon and Sly's attention. "The Ribbon-Cutter, also known as 'The End,' or 'White Death,' is an experimental weapon developed by the United States Military and fourteen alien races. By entering a star, the Hidden Sun sucks up energy to the center of the ship where it is held inside a large spherical super container."

"That must be the room that the computer wouldn't let Reggie and me see when we were looking over the specs of the ship. No wonder we couldn't access it. Sorry Sarah, go on."

"When activated, the weapon dispenses ribbon shaped beams of energy through openings in the side of the ship. It has been theorized that these are powerful enough to cut through all known substances."

"Wow," said Sly.

"Wow is right! Sarah, are there any downsides we should know about?"

"Yes Brandon, there are. In order for the Ribbon-Cutter to work, the Hidden Sun must be in a stopped position."

"That's not so bad," said Sly.

"Also, the Ribbon-Cutter can not be aimed. It fires in all directions simultaneously. The ship must be in the center of the enemy for full effect."

"That means if we want to use it, we'd have to fly into the center of the Ptevos armada?"

"Now that's bad," said Sly. "Flying into the center of a thousand ships is crazy!"

Sarah spoke again. "If you would allow me to finish."

"Sorry Sarah," said Brandon.

"You mean it gets worse?"

"It does, Sly. The Ribbon-Cutter has never been tested."

"Of course," he said sarcastically, leaning back in his chair.

"One of Captain Smoke's main objectives was to test the Ribbon-Cutter. Unfortunately he did not have the chance."

"So it might not work?" said Brandon.

"Correct. There is also a chance that it will backfire and the stored energy will be released inside the ship and destroy the Hidden Sun."

"Oh man," said Sly.

"Thanks Sarah. What do you think?"

"I think it's dangerous. Really dangerous, but it might work."

Brandon smiled at his friend. "Brandon, Carlos wants you to know that he and Reggie have completed rigging a few bombs with Blue Bomber. They are loaded and ready to fire."

"Thanks Sarah. Please tell Carlos to continue making more and to keep me posted." Brandon jumped to his feet, and walked onto the Bridge with Sly.

Traylor swung around in her chair. "Brandon, we've been watching the news and they're saying that the Ptevos have already taken over most of the major cities in the world."

"We've gotta do something now," said Frank.

"And we will. Reggie and Carlos have just finished putting together some Blue Bombers. Frank, set a course for New York City. We're going to show General Swift what a bunch of stupid kids can do."

"Finally, time to blow stuff up!" said Frank as he pushed a few buttons on the Nav/Com console.

Traylor smiled at Brandon and turned around in her chair to face her console. She grabbed the controls and the Hidden Sun started to move. The ship made a u-turn and zoomed through the clouds in the direction of New York City.

◆　　◆　　◆

"Stop the ship," said Brandon. Traylor brought the Hidden Sun to a standstill over midtown Manhattan. On the view screen, a large battle was being fought in Times Square between the American Army and the Ptevos soldiers. Laser blasts and bullets were flying everywhere. "I hope this works."

"Me too," said Traylor.

"Me three," said Frank, "but I wish it was me who was dropping the bombs."

Brandon nodded at Sly and he pushed a series of buttons on his console. A large, silver Splitter Bomb shot out of the bottom of the *Hidden Sun*. As it descended, the bomb split into three pieces and those three split into three more pieces. When they reached one thousand feet, the six pieces exploded with successive thunderous bangs. Millions of pieces of the blue plant spread in all directions like an out of control fire and fell to the ground like a thick winter snow.

The children watched on the view screen as all of Manhattan was covered in a thick, blue cloud. The plant reached the ground and covered everything in blue, including the Ptevos soldiers. Brandon and the kids looked on, ready to celebrate, but nothing happened. The Ptevos soldiers continued to charge forward. One launched an American soldier into the air with his large horn.

"Damn. It didn't work," said Frank.

"Just give it a minute," said Sly.

As if on cue, the Ptevos soldiers began to roar in pain. Within seconds, their bodies had turned to dust and the heavy horns on their heads fell to the ground with a thud.

All of the kids on the bridge of the *Hidden Sun* jumped for joy. "It worked!" screamed Frank. "I knew it would."

Brandon was just as excited as everyone else, but he knew there were a lot more battles ahead. "All right everybody, that was only New York. Now we need to do the same thing for every other city."

"Brandon," said Sarah, "Reggie wants to know if it worked."

"Tell him it did and to make as many Blue Bombers as he can, cause we're gonna need 'em."

◆   ◆   ◆

Over the next few hours, Brandon and his crew flew around the world and dropped Blue Bomber on every city that was being attacked by the Ptevos. He watched on the view screen as people from all over the world cheered and waved at the *Hidden Sun*. When the job was complete, everyone was exhausted, except for Sly, who seemed to have the same amount of energy as he did when the day began.

Brandon slowly stood up. "Frank, are those Ptevos ships you spotted when we came to Earth still around?"

"Nope. They ran while we were bombing Sydney, the chickens!"

"Good. OK, why don't you guys get some rest and put on some clean clothes. Sly and I will stay up here and keep an eye on things." Frank and Traylor nodded in appreciation. On their way to the door, Traylor gave Brandon a light punch on the arm.

"Hey Sparks, you're not as bad as I thought you would be," said Frank, and the two walked out of the room.

Sly walked over and sat in the pilot's chair. "Wow, that's high praise coming from Frank, don't you think?" said Brandon.

"I do," said Sly with a smile.

Brandon let out a little laugh. "I'm gonna try and get some sleep. Are you all right to stay up and watch the ship?"

"I am."

"I figured you would be. Wake me if anything happens." Sly nodded and spun around in the chair. Brandon moved around in the captain's chair to get comfortable and closed his eyes. He was asleep in a few short seconds.

◆   ◆   ◆

"The armada is close. The armada is close."

Brandon awoke suddenly. He looked around the room and saw the back of Sly's head peeking above the back of the pilot's chair. "The armada is close."

"What?" said Brandon.

Sly spun around in his chair. "You're awake."

"The armada is close."

"The armada is close?" said Brandon.

"What? How do you know?" said Sly.

Brandon pointed to his ear. He suddenly realized that he had not been dreaming and that the familiar whispery voice of V was talking to him. "The armada is close."

"How close?" asked Brandon.

"In a few hours, they will be within striking distance."

"Oh, no." The connection between Brandon and V was broken. "The armada is within a few hours of Earth."

"What are we gonna do?" said Sly.

"I don't know."

CHAPTER NINETEEN

RETURN OF THE ENEMY

"Brandon, Carlos would like to speak to you in the medical center."

"Thanks Sarah." Brandon made his way down to the medical center and walked inside. Reggie was sleeping in one of the beds, and let out a big snore. "Hey Carlos. What's up?"

"Hi Brandon. Unfortunately, while adding Blue Bomber to all of those bombs, Reggie had to move around a lot and he re-injured his ribs, which never fully healed to begin with. Plus, he's really, really tired from all the work. Actually, I could use a nap myself."

"You look exhausted. Is Reggie gonna be OK?"

"Sure but he's gonna need another week of bed rest."

"But we need him at the Nav/Com station."

"Sorry, but you're gonna have to find someone else. Reggie's not going anywhere."

Brandon nodded and walked over to Reggie. He shook his shoulder lightly. "Reggie … Reggie."

Reggie awoke from his sleep and slowly opened his eyes. "Hey Brandon."

"Hey buddy. How you feelin'?"

"Not too good. My side is killin' me."

"That stinks. I guess Frank is gonna have to be the one working the Nav/Com station when we fight the Ptevos."

"As much as I don't like him, Frank will do a good job. I just wish I could be up there with you."

"I wish you could too."

"Just remember, you've got to do whatever it takes to defeat them. I want to see my parents again."

"I know you do. Everyone does. Get some sleep."

"Good luck," said Reggie, lifting his hand into the air. Brandon grabbed it and shook it.

"Thanks. We're gonna need it."

◆　　　◆　　　◆

The elevator reached deck 1 and Brandon walked out into the hallway. "Charlie, can you hear me?"

"Hey Brandon! I can always hear you."

Brandon was happy to hear Charlie's voice. It always made him feel at ease and loved, especially since his parents weren't around. "Charlie, do you know about the armada?"

"I do Brandon. They are getting very close to Earth. What are you going to do?"

"I don't know, but I was hoping you would be with me for the long run."

"I wouldn't think of being anywhere else."

"Thanks Charlie."

Brandon walked onto the bridge to find Sly at the weapons and defense console, Frank sitting in the captain's chair and Traylor in the pilot's seat. He walked over and stood in the middle of the room. "Frank, Reggie is still feeling the effects of his injury, so you're on Nav/Com, if you want it."

Frank stood up and rubbed his hands together. "I ain't got nothin' better to do," he said and walked over to the Nav/Com station.

Brandon rolled his eyes at Frank's response and sat down in the Captain's chair. "Is everybody ready?"

"Uh, huh," said Traylor. "Is Reggie going to be OK?"

"He will be, as long as we get through this in one piece.

"We will, and I'm ready," said Sly.

"Let's go kick some Ptevos butt!" said Frank.

Brandon smiled and looked at the view screen. "Let's get going."

Frank transmitted all of the information Traylor needed to leave Earth's atmosphere. The *Hidden Sun* zoomed into space and passed through the large field of debris floating around the planet.

The ship came to a complete stop a few hundred feet past the debris field and the children watched on the view screen as the armada came into view. There were over five hundred ships, in all different sizes, some of which were at least the size of the island of Manhattan.

"That's a lot of ships," said Frank.

"They haven't even launched their small fighters yet," said Sly.

"This is impossible. What the hell are we gonna do against all these ships?" Frank stared at Brandon. He knew the boy had no plan.

"Let me think for a sec."

"A sec. That's about all the time we've got left!"

That armada's really spooked Frank, thought Brandon to himself. He ran a hand across the top of his head and tried to come up with a plan to defend against what with all the small fighters would soon be a thousand ships. He failed miserably. He went over scenario after scenario in his head, but in the end, they all lead to the Hidden Sun being destroyed. He could not figure out a plan that would work. Fortunately, he had some really great friends to help. "Remember all the missions we flew together," said Charlie in his ear.

"Yes."

"You have all the training you need. You just need to use it."

"But I can't defend against a thousand ships."

"Use everything you have available to you."

"You mean the weapons?"

"I mean everything."

"What's everything?"

Another voice popped into Brandon's head. "Follow your instincts."

"V?"

"You are Earth's only hope."

"I can't defend against a thousand ships. It would be suicide!"

"Defense comes in many forms," said V.

"He's right," said Charlie. "You can do it Brandon. I believe in you."

Brandon looked at the Ptevos ships in the distance. Charlie and V had given him the jumpstart he so desperately needed. He opened his eyes wide and stood up with gusto. "I've got it!"

"Got what?" said Traylor, her tone so pessimistic.

"A plan. Frank, send a signal to the lead ship and tell them we want to communicate with them."

"What are we gonna do? Surrender?"

"Not exactly."

"Brandon are you sure contacting them is a good idea?" said Sly.

"It's as good as any. You've all just got to trust me."

Frank pressed the appropriate buttons on his console and the view screen the Bridge of the Ptevos' lead ship filled the view screen. There were many Ptevos doing their jobs, but the one that concerned Brandon was standing in the center of the room with his back turned, taking up a majority of the screen.

"So, an Earth ship wishes to surrender? How wonderful for me," said General Zarafat in his evil, smoky voice. He slowly turned around and faced forward. When he looked up, his eyes met Brandon's and his expression went from one of frightening joy to intense anger. "You!" he snarled.

"Yes me. Hello General Zarafat. I hope I'm not interrupting."

"But you're dead! Your ship burned up in that star. I saw it myself!"

"Sorry to disappoint you. Maybe you should get your eyes checked," said Brandon. Frank and Traylor chuckled.

General Zarafat was as mad as Brandon had ever seen him. His black eyes blazed with anger. "If you're still alive then Captain Smoke is still alive. Argghh!" screamed General Zarafat.

"Keep your cool," said Charlie. On the inside, Brandon was as nervous as a person could be, but on the outside, he appeared calm with a look of supreme confidence on his face.

"I am going to destroy you Sparks, if it's the last thing I do!" General Zarafat's expression became even more menacing. "I am going to send my entire armada after you. I am going to launch every ship I have and use every weapon on your puny ship and turn it and you into dust! Do you understand me Sparks? You and your crew are all dead!"

Brandon looked around the room. The expressions of fear on Traylor and Frank's faces spoke volumes. On the other hand, Sly was as cool as cool gets. "Use your instincts," said V.

"Remember the missions," said Charlie.

Brandon looked back at the view screen and stood up straight as an arrow. "General Zarafat, on behalf of the planet Earth, I want to offer you the chance to surrender."

"Surrender?" said the General in disbelief.

"Surrender now and I will let you leave with all of your ships intact. All I ask in return is for you to tell me how to wake up the people you put to sleep."

"Surrender? Me? I have over a thousand ships to your one. Do you really think you have a chance? I'm going to enjoy killing you Sparks!"

Brandon did not flinch. "If you do not agree to surrender, and tell me how to wake up the people you put to sleep, then I will be forced to destroy you and your entire armada!" General Zarafat looked like he was ready to explode. "What will it be General?"

"You are dead!"

"You've been warned," said Brandon. He signaled to Frank to end the transmission and he did. As soon as the General blipped off the screen, Brandon collapsed into the captain's chair and the questions started to fly like lightning.

"Destroy them? How are we gonna do that? Attack them?" Traylor laughed. When Brandon nodded, she stopped.

"You're crazy Sparks. I want to blow them up as bad as you do but attacking an armada with one ship is suicide!"

"Look, it's either that or we run and everybody on Earth gets killed. All our parents and families."

"Has one ship ever attacked an armada before?" asked Traylor.

"No," said Sly.

"And that's why it'll work!" said Brandon emphatically

"What if we just sit here and fire our weapons long distance?" said Frank.

"If we sit here, we're dead. It's impossible to defend against a thousand ships. Our only chance is to attack them."

"I assume you mean the Ribbon-Cutter?" said Sly.

"Yes, the Ribbon-Cutter."

"You do remember that it is untested."

"I know."

"Hey, is somebody gonna tell me what a Ribbon-Cutter is?" asked Frank, as Traylor looked on with interest. Together, Brandon and Sly told them everything they knew about the weapon. Afterwards, everyone fell silent.

After a few moments, Frank spoke up. "So what you're saying is you want to fly this ship into the middle of that armada and fire a weapon that's never been tested and that could backfire and kill us all?" Brandon nodded. "Cool."

"Sly?"

"Like I said before, it's dangerous, but it just might work."

"Traylor?" said Brandon. Traylor stood up and swung her chair around. "What are you doing?" he asked.

"Here," she said. Brandon could see that tears had formed in her eyes. She was such a tough girl that he had never even imagined he would see her like this. It was like looking at a totally different girl. "I can't. I just can't," she said and ran out of the room.

"What's up with her?" said Frank.

"I don't know." Brandon ran out of the room after her. By the time he had gotten into the hallway, Traylor had already pressed the elevator button and was waiting for one to arrive. "Traylor, wait up!" he screamed as he ran towards her. "What's going on?"

"I can't do it," said Traylor, wiping the tears from her face.

"Of course you can."

"No, I can't. I can't fly this ship into that armada. What if I mess up? We'll all be killed!"

"You won't mess up. Don't even think like that. You're the toughest girl I've ever met, and you're a great pilot and I should know. I watch you every day."

"Thanks," said Traylor as she smiled briefly. "But I think you should fly the ship."

"Me?"

"This is the most difficult thing we've ever had to do and even though it hurts for me to say it, you're the best pilot we have, so you should fly the *Hidden Sun*."

Brandon took a moment to think as Traylor continued to wipe away the tears that were still streaming down her face. He finally had the opportunity to fulfill his dream. He could pilot the *Hidden Sun*, hopefully defeat the evil aliens and then everyone would carry him on their shoulders and chant his name in celebration. He had dreamt of this day every time he took a bath since he was a little boy. Instead he did what he thought any good captain would do. "Traylor, this isn't about who's best. This is about teamwork and we're a team. I was chosen as captain and that's the job I'm gonna do. As captain, I chose you as pilot, but if you don't want to fly this ship, that's fine. I will find someone who will."

"Brandon," said Sarah, "I don't mean to interrupt but the armada is beginning its attack on this ship."

"You'd really find someone else?"

Brandon looked her straight in the eye and said, "Yes." He didn't want to let on that he didn't have another person in mind if she said no.

Traylor thought for a moment and then looked at her friend. "OK."

"OK? You'll do it?"

"I'll do it."

"Great!" Brandon smiled and without warning, she launched herself at him. He thought she was going to punch him in the shoulder like she always did, so he tensed his muscle, but instead, she gave him a big hug. He had never been hugged by a girl before, except for his mom, but he didn't think that counted. It felt nice. Much nicer than a punch to the shoulder.

"You're a great Captain, Brandon Sparks."

"And you're a great pilot, Traylor Donovan." After one more smile, Brandon said, "let's go," and the two kids ran onto the bridge.

"Glad you could make it," said Frank sarcastically.

"Not a moment too soon," said Sly. "The Ptevos are almost in attack formation."

Traylor ran over to the pilot's seat and sat down. Brandon followed her and sat in the captain's chair. On the view screen, the Ptevos ships were moving towards the *Hidden Sun*. Hundreds of small ships were launched from within the larger ships. It looked like a tidal wave that just kept swelling larger and larger.

"Sarah, please inform everyone on board to hold on tight. This is gonna be a bumpy ride. Sly, put up the shields."

"Shields up."

"Frank, I need you to keep us updated on how far we are from the center of the armada."

"No problem."

"Traylor, are you ready?"

"Yes."

Brandon looked around the room. "Hey, chances are we're gonna take a lot of damage, so be prepared. Hopefully, we can make it out of this in one piece."

"Good luck Brandon Sparks," said V.

"Stay focused," said Charlie. "You can do it. I believe in you."

"Thanks," whispered Brandon. He took a deep breath, and looked around the room one last time. "All right, let's do it."

Brandon could feel the butterflies in his stomach. He knew that this was the only way he could save Earth and have a chance to see his family again, but he was nervous. That all changed when Traylor grabbed the controls and put her foot on the accelerator. The *Hidden Sun* jumped into action. As if a switch had been flipped in his head, Brandon became just as focused as when he had piloted the Hidden Sun away from the Ptevos with Charlie as his co-pilot.

"Sly, start firing the laser cannons to make some flying room for Traylor." Sly pushed several buttons on his console and hundreds of red beams of energy shot out of the Hidden Sun. Two small Ptevos fighters, which had very weak shields, were destroyed immediately. There was no time for celebration. The Ptevos ships fired back at the *Hidden Sun* with laser cannons of their own. Traylor turned the ship on its side and moved out of the way of most of the blasts. The ones that hit were absorbed by the shields and weakened them.

"Shields are down to ninety-six percent," said Sly.

"Start firing missiles at the larger ships." Sly furiously, and without error, pushed the buttons on his console and launched eight missiles. They flew through the darkness of space and impacted with six different Ptevos ships. Some did more damage than others but only one destroyed an entire ship.

Fifty of the small Ptevos fighters circled around the back of the Hidden Sun like a swarm of bees, and were hot on their tail.

"They've got us surrounded!" said Frank.

CHAPTER NINETEEN

"Good. That's what we want," said Brandon who figured the more ships that were around the *Hidden Sun*, the more damage the Ribbon-Cutter would do.

As the *Hidden Sun* made its way towards the center of the armada, the distance between ships became much smaller. Traylor swung the ship back and forth like a clock pendulum to avoid crashing into other ships. To make things more perilous, what at first had been a drizzle of laser fire, had now become a full on shower. No matter which way she turned, the *Hidden Sun* was pelted with laser blasts and it was taking a heavy toll on the shields.

"We're down to sixty-five percent."

"Already?" said Brandon.

"Those fighters are coming up behind us quick," said Frank."

"Brandon, they've just launched missiles at us."

Without hesitation, Brandon knew what to do. "Launch the Sun Flares." As long as those missiles don't hit us, we'll be all right, he thought.

Sly pushed a series of buttons and out of the rear of the Hidden Sun shot two small, yellow, coffee can shaped flares. The Ptevos missiles were closing in fast when the flares exploded into golden streams of fire. Traylor noticed that because of the low position of the *Hidden Sun*, the missiles might fly below the flares. With perfect timing, she lifted the nose of the *Hidden Sun* and as the ship rose, so did the missiles. They screeched through the darkness and exploded upon impact with the fire streams the Sun Flares had produced.

"Yeah!" screamed Traylor with joy.

"It worked!" said Sly.

"Good, keep clearing room for Traylor to maneuver."

"Should we fire the Carnage Missiles?" asked Sly.

"Yes," said Brandon as Ptevos laser blasts were bombarding the *Hidden Sun*.

"Shields are down to thirty percent. Firing Carnage Missiles."

Four blood red missiles shot out of the front of the *Hidden Sun* towards a group of Ptevos ships that were blocking their path. General Zarafat and the Ptevos fired flares of their own, which would have worked against standard missiles but were ineffective against these. When the Carnage Missiles were twenty feet from their targets they exploded and each released a large amount of white-hot shrapnel. The fiery metal passed through the flares and ripped the Ptevos ships to shreds. They exploded into two huge fireballs and Traylor turned the *Hidden Sun* on its side and flew right between them.

"Frank, how are we doing?" asked Brandon.

"We've barely made it through the outer rim of enemy ships," said Frank. "There's still a long way to go to make it to the center of the armada."

Brandon didn't think it was possible, but the amount of laser cannons fired at the *Hidden Sun* increased dramatically and so did the number of hits.

"We're down to eight percent shields!" said Sly.

"What are we gonna do?" asked Traylor.

After two quick hits from a laser cannon, the shields went down completely. "Try the Sun Shields," said Brandon.

"Is that gonna work?" asked Frank.

"It worked last time." Sly did as Brandon asked and a bright yellow coating quickly covered the entire ship. A series of laser blasts hit the hull of the ship and they all bounced off. There were so many Ptevos around that a few of the laser blasts that ricocheted off the *Hidden Sun* hit and destroyed their own ships. With the Sun Shields up, the *Hidden Sun* couldn't be damaged by laser blasts. Brandon breathed a sigh of relief.

"Brandon," said Sly over the noise. "I don't think these shields will hold up so well against missiles. If we get hit, it's going to cause a ton of damage."

"Then let's not get hit. At any sign of missiles, launch more Sun Flares. Frank, how much further until we're at the center of the armada?"

"At this speed, *at least* another five minutes." The battle raged on as Traylor spun the *Hidden Sun* to avoid another collision. Sly fired everything he had at the Ptevos and the Ptevos fired everything they had at the *Hidden Sun*.

"That's it. We're out of Carnage Missiles and Sun Flares."

"Damn!" said Brandon. "How much further Frank?"

"Three more minutes. Step on it Traylor!"

"If I fly any faster, we'll crash into another ship!"

"Incoming missiles," said Sly.

Traylor was able to move out of the way of the first three missiles but the fourth one caught the left side of the ship. There was an explosion and the ship shook violently. Frank and Brandon were both thrown to the floor. Sly was the only one who managed to stay on his feet.

When Brandon climbed back up, he felt his forehead, and saw blood. He was able to sit down in the captain's chair and brace himself before the next missile hit.

"Engine two is out!" said Frank.

"What should I do Brandon?"

"Keep going forward Traylor. We've got to get to the center!"

Another missile struck the *Hidden Sun*, this one from behind.

"Engine four is out!"

The Hidden Sun was beginning to slow down when another missile hit dead on. "We've got hull breaches," said Sly.

"Sarah, seal all hull breaches."

"Engine one is out! We're running on one engine!" screamed Frank.

"Let's hope it holds up. How much longer until we reach the center?"

"At this speed, another five minutes. It's impossible! We'll never make it!" As if on cue, another missile hit the *Hidden Sun*. Once again, the ship shook violently.

"The Sun Shields are down!" screamed Sly.

"The commands aren't responding," said Traylor.

"That's because they just took out our last engine. We're sitting ducks!" screamed Frank. "We need to fire the weapon now!"

"We can't fire it now," said Sly. "If we do, it will only wipe out some of them. The others would just come and finish us off."

"Well they're gonna finish us off anyway! We might as well take as many with us as we can!"

Brandon closed his eyes and tried to think. "There's still hope Brandon," said Charlie. "Use your head."

"My head. My head." Brandon had an idea.

"Sly, arm the Ribbon-Cutter."

"Good. We fire the weapon now and kill as many of those nasties as we can. Right?"

"Wrong."

"What?" said Frank, shocked by Brandon's answer.

"Frank, get me General Zarafat on the screen."

"What? Why?" Brandon thought Frank was as confused as anyone had ever been in the history of the universe.

"Just do it!"

Frank pushed a few buttons on his console and General Zarafat popped on screen. He looked extremely happy. "I am very surprised at your ferocity Sparks! You're like a younger version of me."

"I don't think so General."

General Zarafat just smiled, secure in what he could only assume was his victory. "Do you wish to surrender? Not that I would accept it. Although it would be nice to have your skull ..." The General leaned in and his gray face grew larger in the view screen, "I ... I could always use another ashtray."

CHAPTER NINETEEN

Brandon watched as the Ptevos ships slowly moved towards the crippled *Hidden Sun*. The starship was now totally surrounded. Even if the engines were working, there was no opening to fly through. The Ptevos had successfully built a wall of ships around the *Hidden Sun*.

"I just wanted to offer you one last chance to surrender," said Brandon. "If you do not then you will be destroyed."

The Ptevos ships creeped closer and closer to the *Hidden Sun*. Brandon could see the veins in General Zarafat's head popping out in anger. "Your ship has no working engines! You have no shielding! You have zero missiles! You are doomed!" He took a deep breath and composed himself. "Sparks, I'm glad that things ended up this way. Now I can watch as my fleet turns your ship into a fine powder. All I have to do is give the order."

Brandon turned to Frank and mouthed the words, "Where are we?"

"What?" said Frank aloud.

"Where are we now? Are we in the center?" mouthed Brandon, and Frank got the message. He looked down at his console and pushed a few buttons.

To his amazement he said, "ye ... yes." The Ptevos had moved all of their forces in so close to surround the *Hidden Sun* that it was now exactly where they wanted it to be.

Brandon turned back towards General Zarafat. "You've been a small thorn in my side Sparks, but now that all ends. It is time for me to take control of Earth and enslave its people. I think I'll start with your family. What do you have to say about that, Sparks?"

"What do I have to say? I say you should have surrendered when you had the chance!" Hands clenched around the armrests as he braced himself in the captain's Chair, Brandon thought carefully for a moment: "Sly, fire the Ribbon-Cutter."

"What did you say?" said General Zarafat as the transmission was cut off.

Instantly, the *Hidden Sun* started to rumble, and thunder, and rumble, and thunder. Within seconds, the ship was vibrating violently.

"Please work, please work, please work," said Brandon.

At the very moment Brandon thought the ship would never stop shaking, it did. Immediately, there was a noise that sounded like a mammoth jet engine starting up. It was so loud that Brandon, Traylor, and Frank covered their ears with their hands.

Hundreds upon hundreds of beams of light shot out of the *Hidden Sun* in every direction. They each looked like long, thin, fiery pieces of ribbon one would use to decorate a Christmas present. It even looked as if the ends had been purposely snipped into triangles. These ribbons of light slowly twisted their way through empty space, creeping along like the waves in an ocean.

Seconds later, the molten beams reached the Ptevos armada. They sliced through the ships like a hot knife through butter and emerged from the other end, eager to do it all again. Huge fireballs popped up in every direction Sun as some ships exploded and others fell from their position and crashed into their fellow Ptevos. Around them the armada was being decimated and the *Hidden Sun* held its position at the center of it all. Hundreds of small shuttles launched from some of the ships and flew off in the opposite direction. Brandon, Traylor, Sly, and Frank gathered in front of the view screen and watched the fireworks in total silence.

A short time later, the entire armada was in ruins and the ribbons of light had died out. Not a single ship had survived the Ribbon-Cutter. There was so much debris around the Hidden Sun that Brandon could not see a single star in the distance. The only light came from the burning Ptevos starships.

"That was awesome!" said Frank, breaking the silence.

"Crazy. That was totally crazy!" said Traylor.

"I'm just glad the thing worked," said Sly.

Brandon, Traylor, and Frank started to laugh. Sly joined in. "Sarah, please tell everyone on board that we have defeated the Ptevos," said Brandon with a smile.

"Of course Brandon. Congratulations."

"Yes, congratulations," said Charlie.

"Thanks Charlie. Hey V, no words of wisdom? V?"

"He must have ended the connection. I'm sure you'll hear from him again."

"Yeah, I guess."

"You're all right Sparks." Frank slapped Brandon on the shoulder, which caused him to lurch forward a bit. "Sorry about that."

"Hey, don't worry about it." The two boys shook hands, and smiled at one another.

CHAPTER TWENTY

JUST THE BEGINNING ...

"It took us almost six months but the *Hidden Sun* is finally at 100 percent again," said Brandon. He was sitting in the captain's office, eating pizza with Reggie, who had a gob of cheese hanging from his chin.

"It was a good idea to put Frank in charge of the repairs. He's really good at fixing things."

"He sure is," said Brandon before taking a bite out of the crust.

"So, when are you going?" asked Reggie with a mouthful of pizza.

"Right after we finish lunch."

"Do you want me to go with you?"

"No, I'll be all right by myself."

"Are you sure?"

"Yeah, I'm sure. No one else has had a problem, so why should I?"

"No one else went by themselves!"

"Brandon," said Sarah. "The shuttle is ready for your departure."

"Thanks." Brandon finished his drink and wiped his mouth with a napkin. He dumped his trash in the garbage can next to the desk and climbed to his feet. "Don't be so worried. I'll be fine. I'll be back in a couple of hours." Reggie stood as well and followed Brandon onto the bridge. Traylor and Sly were in their regular positions. "Hey guys, I'm off."

"Are you sure you don't want me to fly you there? I flew everybody else."

"Nah, that's OK Traylor. You need a break and I can handle it myself."

"I'll go with you for protection," said Sly.

Brandon smiled and let out a little laugh. "That's OK. I'll be fine. Remember, we already defeated the Ptevos. If I need you I'll call Sarah on my watch, and if you need me for some reason, do the same."

"OK." The two boys slapped-five and Brandon did the same to Reggie on his way out the door. He made his way down to the shuttle bay, where one of the shuttle craft was sitting in the center of the room. Brandon climbed into the cockpit and the door shut behind him. He buckled himself in and started up the engines. "I'm all set, Sarah."

"Of course Brandon," she said, and the shuttle bay door slowly lowered. The shuttle lifted a few feet into the air and slowly floated outside. Brandon weaved his way through the debris field of Ptevos ships and flew into open space. He took a moment to look around at the brilliance of the stars and the blackness in-between. It made him recall the times he lied in bed late at night and stared up at the Galaxy Program running on his ceiling. When the moment was up, he accelerated the shuttle and headed in the direction of Earth.

◆   ◆   ◆

After entering Earth's atmosphere, Brandon flew the tiny shuttle to a small town in upstate New York called Geneva. There was only one hospital in town and that was where he headed. Charlie had found out from his friend who was high up in the military chain of command that this was the hospital where all the adults on the *Hidden Sun* were taken for treatment. He even told him their room numbers. All of the other kids on board the *Hidden Sun* had visited their families and now it was Brandon's turn.

Brandon brought the shuttle to a standstill outside a fifth floor window and left it hovering as he quietly jumped inside. The wooden door at the opposite end of the room was closed and the only light came from the almost full moon hanging in the sky. The room only had two beds, which were sitting a few feet from one another. In the corner by the window sat a wooden chair. Brandon walked over to the bed furthest from the window. His father lay peacefully, breathing on his own, but in the same state Brandon had last seen him. He leaned in and gave his father a hug. "Hi Dad," he whispered.

Quietly, he walked over to the wooden chair and sat down. In front of him was his mother. She looked like she was in a deep sleep, just like Mr. Sparks. Brandon took her hand in his and placed it on his cheek. He kissed her palm and closed his eyes. He sat like this for a few seconds, trying to hold back the tears.

Without warning there was a bang at the door. A very loud bang. Then there was another. This one splintered the wood and the door flew open. Six men dressed all in black, wearing masks, bulletproof vests and night-vision goggles, with large black rifles in their hands stormed into the room. They all pointed their guns at Brandon.

"Don't move!" screamed one.

"Hands where we can see 'em!" Brandon did not move.

"Easy boys, easy," said a familiar voice from just outside the door. In walked General Swift.

"Oh no," said Brandon under his breath.

The six men stepped aside to make a path for the General but did not take their fingers off the triggers or their aim off Brandon. "Hello Sparks," snarled the General with a nasty smile on his face. The end of a lit cigar stub glowed orange, temporarily illuminating the right side of his face.

"Hello General," said Brandon. He began to see what Traylor was talking about, the similarities between the general standing before him and the one with the giant horn. At this moment, he did not know which one was worse. He gently placed his mother's hand back on the mattress and sat up straight.

"I knew that one day you would come here. I didn't expect you to be foolish enough to come so soon, but once my men saw your friends coming to see their parents at night, I knew it was only a matter of time before you showed up." General Swift ripped the four silver stars off Brandon's chest.

"Hey!" Brandon tried to get the stars back but thought twice as one of the armed men poked him hard in the chest with the barrel of his rifle. He decided it would be best if he just sat back in his chair.

"What do you want with me General?"

Before General Swift could answer, two men in black suits entered the room. "What's going on here," said one of them.

"Who are you?" said General Swift.

"Jones. Secret Service." Jones pulled an I.D. card out of his pocket and showed it to the General."

"Secret Service? That means …"

"That's right George," came a voice from just outside the door. A tall man wearing a gray suit and blue tie walked into the room. He had dirty blonde hair with a tinge of gray and bright blue eyes.

Mr … Mr. President," stammered the General. He pulled the cigar from his pursed lips and held it at his side.

"Everyone, point your guns down," said the President. "He's just a young boy. I don't think he poses a danger to you or me."

"He's not just a young boy Mr. President. He's a "Class A" menace!" General Swift sneered at Brandon, and then turned his attention to his superior. "What are you doing here sir, if I may be so bold?"

"I should ask you the same question."

"I'm here to arrest this fugitive for stealing a military starship and for damaging the Gotham Tower, among other things."

"I see," said the President. "What do you have to say for yourself young Sparks?"

Brandon had never thought about the consequences of taking the Hidden Sun from General Swift. "Everything I did was for good. I didn't mean to steal anything or hurt the Gotham Tower. All I wanted was to help. I tried to tell General Swift how to defeat the Ptevos but he wouldn't listen."

"General, this boy had information concerning the Ptevos and you did not listen to him?"

"He's just a stupid kid sir. What does he know from anything? I was trying to run a war. I'm commanding hundreds of thousands of troops. I can't listen to every kid who's got some hair-brained idea!"

"He told me you had never served a day of your life in the military," began Brandon, "and that you didn't know what you were talking about."

"I never!" said General Swift. His face turned red with anger and embarrassment. "Sir, this child has broken over a thousand international laws and ..."

"General Swift, you do realize that this boy is responsible for saving our world from certain destruction?"

"Yes sir, but he still broke ..."

"General, I want to meet with you first thing tomorrow morning. You are dismissed."

"But sir, I ..."

"Dismissed!" shouted the President.

The General took a deep breath, popped the cigar back in his mouth, and adjusted his tie. "Yes sir. Come on men." He walked towards the door, following the six military men.

"General?" said the President. General Swift turned around and the President pointed to his hand. He walked over and handed him the four silver stars. "Thank you. General, you know, you really shouldn't be smoking in a hospital."

The General stared into the President's eyes for a moment. "I'll take that under advisement," he said and stormed out of the room.

The President turned to his two Secret Service men. "I'll be a few minutes, guys. Would you mind waiting outside?"

"Are you sure sir?" said Jones.

"Yes. The only thing that could hurt me in here is George Swift's second hand smoke. A bit of privacy would be welcomed."

"Of course, Mr. President," said Jones. The two men left the room and closed the damaged door as best they could. The President pulled up a chair and sat across from Brandon. Only his mother separated the two.

There was silence.

"These are your parents?"

"Yes sir," said Brandon glumly. The President nodded.

There was more silence.

"That is a very nice watch you've got there," said the President, trying to break the ice. "May I ask where you got it?"

Brandon looked down at the old, beat up watch, which had saved his life on numerous occasions. He rubbed his hand over the face to clean it. "A good friend gave it to me."

"Ah, a good friend indeed," said the President.

Brandon looked up at him and he could see something in the President's eyes. It was almost as if the man had seen the watch before. "Why are you here, sir?"

"I am here for two reasons. The first is to see you, Brandon Sparks. I was tipped off about General Swift's raid of this hospital. I wanted to thank you personally for saving Earth. You did a marvelous job and the people of this world are grateful. You're a true hero."

"Thanks," said Brandon in a very sad voice. "But I don't feel very much like a hero."

"You don't? Why not?"

"Well, when we fired the Ribbon-Cutter, it ripped through General Zarafat's ship and I watched it explode. I didn't think about it at the time. I was so happy we won, but now I'll never find out how to wake up my parents. I'm glad I saved a bunch of people but it doesn't feel good when you can't do that for the people that mean the most to you."

"I see," said the President. "Well, that's the other reason I'm here." Brandon looked up. "I have it on pretty solid intelligence that General Zarafat survived the Ribbon-Cutter and escaped on a small shuttle in the direction of the Ptevos home-world, Draculous. I'm here to wish you and your crew the best of luck."

"What?" Brandon perked up. "So ... so I can continue to captain the *Hidden Sun?*"

The president stood up and walked towards the door. "It was nice meeting you Brandon Sparks."

Brandon stood up. For the first time, he was able to see the president's face in the light and he couldn't stop looking. "Hey this might sound strange, but have we met before? I know you're the President and all but your face looks very familiar."

"I don't believe we have. You've probably seen me on television, or in the papers."

"I guess." The president opened the door to leave. "Hey, wait!" said Brandon. "Can I have the silver stars back?"

The president looked at the silver stars that he had taken from General Swift, and showed them to Brandon. "I'm sorry but I cannot give these to you. They belong to Captain Smoke, and I am going to locate his family and give the stars to them."

"Oh," said Brandon and he nodded.

The president stared at Brandon to see his reaction and then smiled. He pulled out a small black felt box and held it out for Brandon to take. "I've had my men attach a large weapons container to your shuttle. I assume that after the last battle, you could use some fresh ammunition. Good luck." The President walked out of the room and Brandon was left alone with his parents. He opened the felt box and inside sat four silver stars. He took them out and looked at them. They were so shiny; he could see the reflection of the big smile on his face. He flipped them over and on the back they read:

AWARDED TO:
CAPTAIN BRANDON SPARKS
BY: PRESIDENT VICTOR J. MATTHEWS

Brandon smiled and pinned the stars to his chest. He walked between the two beds and kissed his mother and father on the forehead. After lingering for one last moment, he rushed out the window and back into the hovering shuttle.

◆   ◆   ◆

Brandon came to a very smooth landing inside the shuttle bay of the *Hidden Sun*, as did the weapons container. He made his way to the elevators and headed up to deck 1. When he arrived, he walked onto the Bridge to find it completely dark.

"SURPRISE!" yelled eighty-eight children (even Frank). The lights came on and they all threw colorful streamers into the air. The walls had been changed to a wavy, light blue and tables were set up with all sorts of food (mostly cookies and cakes). The captain's chair had been covered with a white blanket.

"What's going on?" asked Brandon with a smile.

"It's a surprise party!" said Reggie.

"For me?"

"Well, for you, and the whole crew," said Traylor. "Things have been so crazy these past six months that we never had a chance to celebrate our victory."

Brandon smiled and joined the fun. He hadn't been to a party in years and he enjoyed it. He ate tons of cake and food, and shared many laughs with the kids aboard the *Hidden Sun*. He also took this opportunity to chat with some of the kids he hadn't spent much time with. He found most of them to be very nice and promised to himself that he would spend more time with them in the future.

◆   ◆   ◆

Brandon stood at the front of the room and raised his hands in the air. After a few seconds, everyone quieted down. "I'd like to say thanks to everyone involved in planning this party. It's been a lot of fun. Is everyone having a good time?"

"YEAH!" screamed the group in appreciation.

"Well that's great! This is probably the only time I'll have to talk to all of you as a group. I just wanted to thank all of you for the work you've done on this ship. Without each and every single one of you, we never would have defeated the Ptevos." The group of kids screamed with joy again. "Many of you know that I've just come from seeing my parents. Everyone has had a chance to see his or her family and that's good. I have some news. I just found out that General Zarafat survived the battle and I've decided to go after him to find a way to wake up our parents." There was some soft grumblings among the crowd. Most of them nodded in agreement. "The most logical way of doing that is to go to Draculous, the Ptevos' home planet." The chatter among the children grew louder. Brandon had to almost shout to be heard. "If there are any of you that would like to be dropped off on Earth, I understand. We've defeated the Ptevos once, and I know we can do it again. I will give you a full day to decide. Take this time and think about it. This might just be the most important decision of your life. Thank you."

Brandon stepped down and joined the crowd. There was quite a bit of murmuring coming from all parts of the room. Sly walked over to his friend. "How'd everything go on Earth? Any problems?"

"Nothing I couldn't handle."

"Good. I just want you to know, I'm with you."

Brandon put his arm around his friend's shoulder. "Thanks Sly. I knew I could count on you.

◆　　　◆　　　◆

A few hours later, after all the cake and cookies had been polished off, the party died down. Only Brandon, Reggie, Traylor, and Sly were left on the bridge. Together they cleaned up the room and threw all of the streamers into the garbage.

"What's with the blanket on the captain's chair?" asked Brandon. He had wanted to know since the lights came on, but he had been having such a good time, he hadn't found the time to ask.

"Well, that's a surprise," said Traylor. "Why don't you pull it off?"

Brandon gave it a big tug and the chair was revealed. The word "SMOKE" that was stitched across the center of the backrest had been removed. It was replaced by the word "SPARKS" in orange, red, and silver thread, sewn to look like it was written in fire.

"Wow! This is awesome. Thanks guys." Brandon was truly excited and thankful.

"You're welcome," said Reggie.

Traylor walked over and gave him a hug. Reggie and Sly joined in. They stood like that for a full minute before breaking it up.

"I just want you all to know that this is the first time in my life I've felt like part of a family," said Sly. Everyone smiled.

♦   ♦   ♦

Brandon awoke the next morning feeling very well rested. After some breakfast, he made his way to the bridge. He was the first one there and spent some time looking at his name on the captain's chair. It made him feel good. He was thankful he had made such great friends. "Morning Sarah."

"Good morning Brandon. How are you today?"

"I'm good. I was hoping to take an English lesson. What do you say?"

"Sounds good to me."

Brandon practiced writing and finished reading *The Twins*, over the next hour. When he was done, he thanked Sarah and contacted Charlie.

"Hey buddy, I just finished flossing. How's it going?" asked the house computer.

"Good," said Brandon with a chuckle.

The two spent a solid hour talking about stuff. Nothing specific. Just stuff. Charlie made him laugh many times and Brandon returned the favor.

"Good luck on your mission."

"You'll be with me the whole way, won't you?"

"Of course I will."

"No matter what happens, or who I meet, you'll always be my best friend Charlie."

"And you'll always be mine, Brandon Sparks. Remember to be careful. You're only twelve and you've done more than enough crazy stunts."

"I'll try my best to be safe."

"Good. That's all I ask."

Brandon smiled again. "Bye Charlie."

"Bye Brandon."

◆   ◆   ◆

Brandon ate dinner in the captain's office that night. He spent the meal surfing the Galactic Internet for information on Draculous, and didn't come up with much. It wasn't a very desirable destination and Brandon could understand why. The Ptevos were not the friendliest beings in the galaxy.

Reggie walked into the room and put his hands on the backrest of one of the chairs in front of the desk. "I just want to let you know that me and Traylor are in. Wherever you go, we go."

"Thanks Reggie. That means a lot to me." Brandon dumped his plate in the garbage and walked onto the Bridge with his friend. Traylor was sitting comfortably in the pilot's seat, and Sly was performing a checkup of the weapons and defense console. Reggie walked over to the Nav/Com station and Brandon sat down in the captain's chair. "So, where do we stand?"

Traylor swung around in her chair. "It's unanimous. No one wants to go back to Earth."

"Really?"

"Yeah. I guess everybody wants to help save their parents."

"Cool," said Brandon. We can use all the help we can get!"

"Hey Brandon, is Frank mad that he's not working on the Bridge anymore?"

"Nope. I gave him a really important job that he's good at. He's now in charge of all repairs and taking care of the engines."

"That was a good decision," said Reggie. "Let's just hope nothing needs repair, especially the engines!"

The four children had a long laugh.

"In case you don't already know this, you guys are the best friends a kid could ask for." Brandon looked around the room and everybody smiled. He smiled back and then turned to the business at hand. "Is everybody ready?" His friends nodded. "Reggie, set a course for Draculous. Traylor, let's get a move on."

"Aye, aye Captain!" Traylor swung around to face the controls. The *Hidden Sun* lurched forward and weaved its way through the debris field. When it had cleared all of the metal garbage, the ship jumped to light-speed and zipped off like a sprinter between the bright, beautiful stars.

978-0-595-42396-5
0-595-42396-5

Printed in the United Kingdom
by Lightning Source UK Ltd.
126456UK00001B/153/A